THE BONES OF LOGAN ROCK

SALLY RIGBY

Storm
PUBLISHING

Ebook ISBN: 978-1-80508-918-6
Paperback ISBN: 978-1-80508-919-3

Cover design: Lisa Horton
Cover images: Shutterstock

Published by Storm Publishing.
For further information, visit:
www.stormpublishing.co

ALSO BY SALLY RIGBY

A Cornwall Murder Mystery

The Lost Girls of Penzance

The Hidden Graves of St Ives

Murder at Land's End

The Camborne Killings

Death at Porthcurno Cove

The Marazion Murders

The Victims of St Just

Cavendish & Walker Series

Deadly Games

Fatal Justice

Death Track

Lethal Secret

Last Breath

Final Verdict

Ritual Demise

Mortal Remains

Silent Graves

Kill Shot

Dark Secrets

Broken Screams

Death's Shadow

PROLOGUE
21 JUNE 1996

The wind was different that night. Not sharp and salty like usual, but almost soft. It felt strange, as if the air had secrets it wasn't quite ready to spill. She stood at the edge of the cliff path, flip-flops in hand and her toes curling into the cool dirt. She looked out at the ink-dark water.

She lit a cigarette and inhaled deeply, wincing as the menthol stung the back of her throat. It wasn't her first choice, but she didn't have enough money to buy her own, so she resorted to stealing a few from her mum's emergency pack kept on top of the kitchen cupboard.

Glancing around, she shivered. Her arms were covered in goose pimples, though it was warm outside. Something was off. She didn't know what, but couldn't shake the weird feeling that engulfed her.

The evening had started out as a bit of fun. There was nothing unusual with that. A group of them had planned days ago to celebrate the solstice down on the beach with music, cheap cider, and a firepit dug into the sand. Some of her friends were still on the beach, dancing barefoot, while others were tucked into corners of the cliff path, getting off with each other in the shadows.

She was supposed to be there too... be a part of it all.

But she'd slipped away while everyone was distracted and walked further along the headland, past the music and the shouting and the firelight. It was daring and special. And she was going to meet *him*.

They'd been seeing each other in secret for weeks now. Stolen moments when no one else was around. It was nothing serious. Not yet. But it was real enough to make her believe she mattered. He had a girlfriend, of course. The best ones always did. That's why their relationship had to be kept secret. But it was their secret.

Did she feel guilty?

No. It was what it was. And it wasn't like she was the one doing the cheating.

He liked her a lot. She could tell by the way he'd whispered to her when they were on the beach. He said they'd meet later. Just them. When no one else was watching.

Earlier in the evening she'd told her friends she planned to walk all the way to Logan Rock and touch it when the moon was directly overhead. She hadn't intended to walk that far, but when arranging to see him, she'd suggested there, so no one would worry when she disappeared.

She heard footsteps crunching behind her and turned. Her mouth went dry. There he was. A silhouette against the low moonlight. She sucked in a breath.

'You're here,' she said, trying to sound casual.

He shrugged. 'Of course. Did you doubt me?'

'No,' she said with a giggle. Not wanting to admit that she'd thought he might change his mind and stay with his girlfriend instead of meeting her. 'I hope your girlfriend didn't see you leave. What would she say if she knew you were seeing me?'

He moved in closer, his trainers scuffing along the path.

'Are you planning on telling her?' he asked irritably.

Now was her chance to push it. To make him see that being with her was a much better idea.

'No, but I can't see the problem. Dump her and then we can be together instead of creeping around in secret.' She ran her fingers playfully up his arm.

He didn't laugh. Didn't smile. Something coiled in her belly, tight and cold. She took a step back and thought about leaving, but something made her stay.

'That's not going to happen. You're just a kid,' he sneered, his lip curling.

'I'm sixteen,' she responded, standing tall as if that would make her seem older.

'Still just a kid,' he snapped.

'Who you like to screw,' she retorted, staring directly into his eyes.

'This is mad,' he muttered, glancing up at the sky. 'Come on, it's almost time.'

She frowned. 'Time for what?'

He checked his watch, then looked out at the sea. 'Three twenty-three. That's when the solstice happens. It's why you wanted to be here, right? Then we can go back to the beach. This was a mistake.'

She gave a nervous laugh. 'If you don't want to be here, then go. I'm fine on my own. I don't like you being like this.'

He swore under his breath and turned away, pacing. His shoulders were hunched, and he muttered something she didn't catch.

'Maybe I will,' he said suddenly, spinning around and glaring at her, his jaw tight.

The air around her changed. There wasn't a sound. It was like the sea was holding its breath. He stepped closer and she didn't move. She wanted to, but her feet seemed glued to the ground.

'Go then. I don't care.' Her voice cracked. She hated that.

He grabbed her wrist. Not hard. Not at first.

'Stop acting like a child. You know why we're here.' He grabbed at her T-shirt and tried to rip it off.

'Get off me or I'll scream.'

'Who do you think will hear? If you don't want it, then fuck off.

We're over. And you're going to keep your mouth shut about us, or else.'

'I'll say what I want and you can't stop me. You don't scare me, you know.' She pulled out of his grasp, smoothing down her T-shirt, her words belying how she truly felt. Because she was scared. Shit scared. He'd never been like this before.

He lunged towards her and she screamed.

Loud.

A hand clamped over her mouth and she struggled to get free, kicking him in the shins. But his arm was around her neck now, trying to keep her still.

'Shut up,' he hissed in her ear. 'You're going to let me—'

She bit his hand, tasting blood.

He swore and hit her. Not with his fist. With the flat of his palm. But her head snapped back and she skidded in the dirt until she was perilously close to the edge.

The sea was still.

The cliffs silent.

She sensed him crouching beside her, his hot breath on her face, and she tried to speak...

No words came out of her mouth.

She began to lose consciousness but not before she felt him dragging her into the gorse and stopping at a patch of ground.

What was he going to do with her?

Was she going to die?

The moon hung above, pale and distant.

But the wind still whispered. As if it had seen.

As if it would remember.

ONE
MONDAY 19 MAY

'Matt, are you busy?' Detective Inspector Lauren Pengelly asked, stepping into the team's office and striding over to where her detective sergeant was sitting hunched over a computer screen, his brow slightly furrowed in concentration.

He glanced up at her.

'Just doing a bit of paperwork, ma'am. Finishing up on the Wilson case. I'm more than happy to be distracted from this, because I'm in danger of falling asleep.' He chuckled.

Lauren perched on the edge of his desk, her arms folded. 'I've received a message from downstairs regarding an archaeological dig near Treen. It's close to Logan Rock if you haven't yet been there. The dig's director, Dr Eleanor Trewin, has reported finding some skeletal remains that appear to be lot more recent than what they were expecting and so she's called it in.'

'Interesting,' Matt said, with a nod, clearly his interest piqued. 'Let me close this document and I'll be with you.'

'Bones?' Billy, one of the detective constables, called out. 'Does that mean another murder?'

'Steady on, Billy,' Matt said, rolling his eyes. 'Let's find out more before we go jumping to conclusions.'

'My sentiments exactly,' Lauren added, moving away from Matt's desk.

'It's been sooooo boringly quiet around here recently, we could do with something to get our teeth into,' Billy replied, clearly undeterred.

A loud groan went up from the other members of the team.

'No we don't, Billy,' Clem said.

'Agreed,' Tamsin followed. 'I've more things to worry about like my interview this afternoon for the family liaison officer training.'

Lauren glanced at the officer. They'd miss her if she was successful, and there was no reason why she shouldn't be. Lauren had given her an excellent reference, fully supporting her decision to become a FLO.

'We really don't want another murder,' Matt added with a grimace. 'My mum and dad are going on holiday in three weeks, which means they won't be around to look after Dani.'

Lauren had a special relationship with Matt's young daughter, and wanted Dani to be able to spend as much time with Matt, her widowed father, as possible. 'Don't worry, we'll manage. Anyway, back to these bones. I phoned Henry and told him, so he's going to meet us at the dig with the forensic anthropologist because it's not his area of expertise. How he could get one there so quickly is anyone's guess, but he seemed certain about it. The rest of you: continue with your work, and once we get back, we'll know more.'

It was warm, as it often was in May, and as Lauren drove along the narrow lanes leading down to Treen, they passed by thick green hedgerows with primroses and celandines peeking out from beneath the brambles. The sea, which was visible from high points in the road, shone a cool turquoise blue under a quilt of shifting fluffy white clouds.

'Did you have a nice weekend?' Matt asked, breaking the peaceful silence.

Lauren gave a soft laugh, her fingers tapping the steering wheel.

'Very quiet. It was nice not to be called in. I took the dogs for a long walk on the beach, did some knitting, read a bit. Had a proper break. It was lovely.' She glanced at him with a wry smile. 'I shouldn't say this, especially bearing in mind where we're heading, but it's a welcome change when we do have a bit of downtime. Unlike Billy, I'm more than happy not to be chasing murderers all over the place.'

Matt chuckled. 'You do realise that you've now jinxed us for the next month.'

'I don't believe in jinxing, as you well know,' Lauren responded, with a grin.

They fell into a companionable silence again as the road narrowed even further. A weathered sign pointed the way to Treen, a small, picturesque village made up of granite cottages and narrow footpaths that meandered between stone walls. Beyond the village, the road opened out into a coastal plain where tents and dig equipment had been set up against the dramatic backdrop of cliffs and sea.

They parked near a series of low, white tents and muddy excavation pits that were roped off with red-and-white tape. The air had that earthy scent of disturbed soil and damp grass.

Dr Henry Carpenter, the pathologist, was already there, standing beside a woman of about his height and age. She had short grey hair neatly tucked behind her ears and wore a dark green waxed jacket and jeans. A clipboard was under one arm.

'Morning, Henry,' Lauren called as they approached.

'Detective Inspector,' Henry replied with a nod. 'Detective Sergeant.'

'You're being a bit formal, aren't you?' Matt said, with a frown.

Henry smirked. 'Not really. I just wanted Claudia to know who you were. This is my wife, Dr Claudia Harper. She's a forensic anthropologist.'

Lauren exchanged a quick glance with Matt, surprised. She'd

known Henry was married, but not to whom. But it now made sense that he was able to get someone out straight away.

'What happened to Sue?' she asked, referring to the forensic anthropologist they'd used in the past.

'I'm a locum, and only step in as and when needed,' Dr Harper said, briskly.

Lauren smiled and extended a hand. 'Well, it's very nice to meet you, Dr Harper.'

'Call me Claudia,' she said, shaking Lauren's hand with a firm grip. 'Henry briefed me a little while we drove over here. We've looked at the bones. They're still in situ. Everything's left as it was found.'

'Good.' Lauren nodded. 'Before we take a look, I want to find Dr Trewin and get a rundown on how they discovered the bones. Do you have any idea where she is?' she asked, looking directly at Henry.

Henry gestured toward a temporary wooden structure on the edge of the site. 'In the hut over there. It's their makeshift office.'

Lauren and Matt made their way towards the building, their boots crunching on the gravel and dry grass. The wind had picked up, sending salt-laced air sweeping across the site. Lauren pushed open the door and peered inside. The room smelt faintly of coffee and damp paper.

There were six people inside, all gathered around a table covered with maps and notes.

'Dr Trewin?' Lauren asked, scanning the small area.

One of them, a tall woman who looked to be in her fifties, with dark hair pulled tightly into a ponytail, glanced up. 'That's me.'

She stood, towering over the others, and offered a polite smile.

'I'm DI Pengelly. This is DS Price from Penzance CID. Can we have a word?'

'Of course,' the woman replied, striding towards them.

They stepped outside into the open air. A gust of wind lifted strands of Lauren's hair, which she pushed out of her eyes.

'Can you tell me exactly what happened this morning, please?' she asked.

'We had our usual morning briefing,' Dr Trewin explained, tucking her hands into the pockets of her coat. 'Then everyone went to their designated areas to continue excavation. About an hour in, one of the local diggers, Verity, called out, saying she'd found something. We all gathered around, as we always do when there's a potential find. It looked like a clavicle. Verity carefully dug around it, using her trowel, to see if there were more and she uncovered what appeared to be a human skull.'

'And then?'

'We stopped digging immediately. It was obvious the remains were more recent than any of the Roman or Iron Age materials we're looking for. That's when I made the call.'

Lauren noted the flicker of unease in the woman's eyes. Dr Trewin was keeping it together, but this had clearly shaken her.

'We've got a forensic pathologist and forensic anthropologist on site. They'll take custody of the remains for further examination. Until we know more, the dig needs to be paused.'

'Paused?' Trewin's eyes widened. 'For how long? We're on a very tight budget.'

Lauren gave her a look. 'You've just unearthed human remains. Potentially a modern death. We need to treat this as a potential crime scene. Sorry, I can't give you a timeline.'

Dr Trewin nodded slowly. 'Of course. I'll inform the rest of the team.'

'We'll be questioning them as part of our inquiry. For now, please keep everyone away from the dig area until we give the all-clear.'

'I understand,' Dr Trewin said, giving a tight smile as she turned back and stepped into the hut.

Lauren and Matt walked away. Something was already niggling at her. It wasn't just the presence of bones. It was their placement. The fact they were somewhere they shouldn't be, in the middle of a meticulously controlled archaeological environment. But it depended on how long they'd been there.

'Come on, let's see what Henry and Claudia have.'

Back at the dig pit, Claudia was crouched by the remains and Henry stood nearby, his arms folded, watching her work.

'Any early thoughts?' Lauren asked as they approached.

Claudia looked up. 'There are more bones. From what I can see so far, the remains were not buried particularly deep: only about forty centimetres down. That's odd in itself. Most archaeological layers would have deeper stratification. These were deliberately placed. Possibly in a shallow grave.'

'Have you come across any clothes or personal belongings?' Matt asked.

'No,' Claudia said. 'If the person had been wearing natural fibres, like cotton, they'd have decomposed when exposed to the moisture, bacteria and fungi in the soil. Any synthetic fibres could still be present, but so far nothing. It's early in the excavation though. I'll let you know if we do discover anything.'

'Can you estimate their age?' Matt asked.

'It's too early to say definitively, but clearly, they're not ancient. That's all I can say for now.'

'So now we have a possible homicide,' Matt said, looking at Lauren.

She nodded grimly.

And just like that, the quiet weekend and her peaceful walks with the dogs felt like a lifetime ago.

TWO

MONDAY 19 MAY

'I suspect they'll ask you something about how you maintain your professional distance when faced with people's trauma,' Matt heard Clem say as he walked through the door into the team's office, with Lauren close behind him. 'In other words, how do you support a family without getting too emotionally involved? It's pivotal if you're going to be successful in the post.'

The team hadn't yet noticed their return and Matt paused in the doorway, taking in the scene. Tamsin was sitting on the empty desk beside the whiteboard, her legs swinging, while Clem and Jenna had moved their chairs out from behind their computers and were facing her. Billy was sitting back in his chair, a half-eaten sandwich in his hand.

They were all so supportive of Tamsin, and it filled Matt with a sense of pride. None of them wanted to lose the officer, but they weren't going to let that interfere with their desire to give her as much help as possible.

'That's exactly what I'm worried about,' Tamsin replied, her fingers fidgeting with the bottom of her blouse. 'What if I can't hold it together?'

It was strange seeing Tamsin so nervous but, then again, Matt knew she was desperate to become a family liaison officer. It was the first time he'd seen her so committed. Not that she wasn't good at her job, because she was. They certainly had no complaints.

'You have no need to worry,' Clem said with a reassuring nod.

'It's easy to say in an interview that I'll maintain boundaries when I'm in a FLO situation, but in practice, how will I cope with someone who's just received the worst news of their life...'

'That's where you're strongest, though,' Clem pointed out, leaning forward in his chair and steepling his fingers. 'We've known you a long time and have witnessed you connecting with people without losing sight of the job.'

Matt stepped fully into the room, followed by Lauren. 'I see you're preparing for the big interview.'

Four heads turned simultaneously.

'Yes, Sarge,' Tamsin said, jumping off the desk and heading back towards her seat.

'What time's the interview?' Lauren asked.

'Three o'clock, ma'am,' Tamsin said, with a grimace.

'What kind of questions have you been practising?' Lauren continued.

'The usual stuff. Dealing with bereaved families, maintaining professional boundaries while showing empathy, coordinating between families and the investigation team,' Tamsin replied, counting off the points on her fingers.

'They'll ask you a time when you demonstrated these skills,' Lauren said, moving towards Tamsin's desk and standing there. 'Make sure you have something concrete for them.'

'I've got several examples prepared, ma'am. There was the Kendal case last month, and the elderly gentleman who'd lost his wife of fifty years and I spent some time with him.'

Matt nodded, remembering his and Tamsin's visit with the old man. She'd patiently gone through his wife's final movements, gently steering him back on topic when grief made his thoughts wander. He'd been impressed by her natural ability to balance compassion with the necessary focus on gathering information. It was a skill that couldn't be taught, not really. You either had that instinct or you didn't.

'You were brilliant with him,' Matt said.

A flush of pride coloured Tamsin's cheeks. 'Thanks, Sarge.'

'What about when things go wrong?' Matt asked, thinking through scenarios he'd encountered. 'They might throw you a curveball about a family who's uncooperative or hostile towards you.'

'I've thought about that, too.' Tamsin nodded. 'I'll talk about building trust gradually, and being transparent about the investigation process without overpromising. I'll also acknowledge their frustration or anger as valid responses to whatever situation they're facing.'

'Perfect,' Lauren commented, looking impressed.

'I've been swotting up, ma'am,' Tamsin replied with a shrug.

'Excellent. And when they ask why you want to move from being a detective constable to a family liaison officer, what will you say?' Lauren continued.

Tamsin hesitated, and Matt could see her searching for the right words. Not because she didn't know the answer, he suspected, but because it mattered so much to her.

'Because it makes a difference,' Tamsin finally said. 'I know that might sound a bit of a cliché, but I really mean it. The role's so important. Not just to the investigation, but to the families, too. Having someone who's there specifically for them, someone who can translate police-speak and be a constant point of contact through what might be the worst experience of their lives...' She paused. 'It matters.'

The room fell silent for a moment and Matt found himself nodding in agreement. He'd seen enough grieving families over the years to know how vital that role could be. In his first years on the force, before the family liaison officer position had become a thing, he'd witnessed the damage that could be done by well-meaning but untrained officers trying to support families while needing to gather evidence at the same time. Too often, both tasks had suffered. The specialist role made sense, both for the families and for the investigation.

'They'd be mad not to take you on,' Matt said with a smile. 'Because I would – in an instant.'

'Thanks, Sarge.'

Matt made a mental note to catch Tamsin before she left for the interview. The family liaison role would suit her perfectly: her natural empathy combined with her investigative instincts made her ideal for a position that required both emotional intelligence and police acumen. While he'd miss having her as a constant part of their team if she got the position, he couldn't think of anyone better suited for the job.

Lauren checked her watch. 'Right, as much as I'd like for you all to continue Tamsin's interview prep, we must get back to work. Matt and I need to update you on the human remains found at the archaeological dig in Treen.'

'Is it a case for us?' Jenna asked.

'We don't know yet,' Lauren replied, moving over to the whiteboard. 'Matt, can you fill everyone in on what we saw?'

Matt moved over to stand beside Lauren. 'Dr Trewin, who's in charge at the dig, said they found some human remains while working. They could tell they weren't very old, so called the police. The pathologist and forensic anthropologist dug up further bones and they're being taken to the morgue. Until we hear back from them, we don't know for definite, so we have to wait. Hopefully we'll hear something by the end of the week.'

'Now, let's get back to work,' Lauren said. 'Where are we with the boat theft from the marina? Jenna, you were following up with the harbour master. Did he have any CCTV footage?'

'Their system had been down that week,' Jenna explained. 'But I've been able to access some footage from the fuel station across the road which should give us a partial view of the entrance and hopefully the people who went in there.'

'Good. Let's hope we find something. I certainly don't want a spate of boat thefts to deal with on top of everything else. Clem, where are we with the witness statements from the bus crash in the river? Still no serious injuries, I hope.'

Clem began his update. Thankfully, there were no major injuries. While he was speaking, Matt pondered the team and how it would, of necessity, change in makeup if Tamsin got the job and someone else took her place. He wasn't looking forward to it, to be honest. But that wouldn't be a reason to stop Tamsin from leaving. This was something so clearly suited to her talents. She had a great career ahead of her and he couldn't wait to witness her success.

THREE

THURSDAY 22 MAY

The morning sun filtered through the dusty windows of the morgue as Lauren and Matt approached the entrance. Lauren's stomach tightened with anticipation. Henry had been cryptic on the phone earlier, only mentioning that they had something significant to tell them.

'Ready?' she asked Matt.

Matt nodded and exhaled loudly. 'As ready as I'll ever be to look at a bunch of old bones. But at least I know there'll be no blood.'

Lauren pushed open the heavy door, wincing slightly at the familiar antiseptic smell that greeted them. The morgue was quiet and their footsteps echoed against the tiled floor as they made their way into the main area.

Henry and Claudia, both clad in white overalls, were already waiting, bent over a large steel table.

'Morning, Henry. Morning, Claudia,' Lauren said, forcing brightness into her voice despite the grim setting.

She glanced sideways at Matt as they walked into the room. His face was a mask of professional detachment, but it didn't hide the subtle tension in his jaw. His fear of death-related scenes had been a hurdle throughout his whole career, though she'd been impressed at how he hadn't let it interfere with his work.

Henry straightened up, his solid frame casting a shadow across the table. The overhead lights buzzed faintly as he turned to face them. 'Good to see you both.'

'So, let's hear this significant information that you were so mysterious about,' Lauren said, her eyes drawn to the arrangement of bones on the examination table.

'This job could very well get me down, without licence to be a tad melodramatic, occasionally,' Henry responded, his eyes twinkling. He gestured towards Claudia and stepped aside to make room for Lauren and Matt. 'I'll hand over to you, my dear.'

Lauren approached the table, her breath catching in her throat as she took in the sight of a complete human skeleton, each bone carefully arranged in its correct anatomical position. The bones were a pale yellowish-brown, clearly aged, with visible signs of weathering along the surfaces.

Matt stepped forward and stopped beside Lauren, studying the remains with surprising composure. 'You managed to find them all then?' he said, peering more closely at the arrangement.

'Yes. It took quite a while, but we did find them all,' Claudia replied, adjusting her latex gloves. 'They were all situated in close proximity.'

The bones looked small to Lauren, almost too small for an adult. Were they from a child? She swallowed hard as the implication of that settled in her mind.

'Right, so let me start,' Claudia said, moving around the table to stand opposite them. Her demeanour was professional, but Lauren could see the excitement of the discovery in her eyes.

'I don't know how much you know about forensic anthropology and our work,' Claudia began.

'A little,' Lauren responded. 'From previous cases we've worked.'

'Same for me,' Matt added. 'But start from the beginning if you like, because I might have forgotten something important.'

'Yes, please. I always find it most interesting,' Lauren said genuinely, nodding in agreement. Her gaze never left the bones, trying to see the person they had once belonged to, and give them back their humanity.

Claudia appeared pleased with their interest and she gestured towards the skeleton.

'Okay, well, in order for us to predict how long the bones have been buried, and also whether they belong to a male or female, we need to examine various things, including how long they've been exposed to the environment,' she explained.

Lauren leant in closer, noticing the subtle discolorations along the ribs and spine. Small details, but each one told part of a story. A story that had ended in this person being buried and forgotten.

'Bones go through separate stages of weathering,' Claudia continued. 'They crack, they flake, and they bleach when they're exposed to the elements. But obviously, how much of this depends on where they're situated. So, if they've been buried, then they'll be less weathered than those lying around, so to speak. I mean, obviously we don't tend to find them just *lying* around. The aging of remains is complex and influenced by countless variables: soil acidity, temperature fluctuations, presence of bacteria, even insect activity.' Claudia gave a small shrug. 'If bones are buried, we have to look at the soil itself and its constituents which also change over time. So, you can see it's not a straightforward process. Any questions?'

Lauren exchanged a quick glance with Matt and they both shook their heads.

'Okay. I'll continue. Based on everything I've explained so far, it's my view that these bones go back around thirty years.'

Thirty years. To around 1996.

Their first port of call would be to investigate missing persons cases from that era.

'Can you tell the age and sex of the person?' Lauren asked.

'You've pre-empted me. I was about to get to that,' Claudia replied, nodding, her expression solemn. 'I believe that the bones belong to a person who was around sixteen years of age when they died.'

Lauren's chest tightened. Little more than a child. She fought to keep her expression neutral, but inside, a familiar anger began to simmer. Someone who never got to grow up.

'You can tell that because...?' she prompted, wanting to focus on the science to keep her emotions in check.

'The long bones are still fusing,' Claudia explained, pointing to the ends of the femurs. 'Some of them are only partially fused, and others are still open because they haven't yet finished growing.'

'Are their teeth different at that age?' Matt, who'd been quietly observing until now, asked.

'Yes,' Claudia replied with an approving nod. 'A sixteen-year-old wouldn't have their third molars fully formed. That's wisdom teeth,' she clarified. 'You can see that here.' Claudia picked up part of the jawbone carefully, turning it to show them the dental arrangement.

'Is it possible to know whether this person is male or female?' Lauren asked.

Claudia set down the jawbone and gestured to the pelvis. 'That was my next discussion point. These bones belong to a female. You can tell by the pelvis and the shape of the skull.'

A heaviness settled in Lauren's stomach. A sixteen-year-old girl. In her mind's eye, she saw a teenager with hopes and dreams, friends and family... all cut short.

'Do you have any idea about the cause of death?' Matt asked.

Lauren held her breath. Were they looking at a suspicious death? Although it could hardly be anything else if the body had been buried in such unusual circumstances.

'I can't be precise, obviously, because we're unable to carry out blood tests etc,' Claudia began cautiously. 'But there's a hole in the skull that had been caused by something.'

She picked up the skull in her gloved hands and showed them where the damage was located. Lauren's eyes narrowed as she focused on the jagged opening in the temporal region.

'Was this done intentionally?' Lauren asked.

'Impossible to tell. It could have been caused by her being hit with something. But equally, she may have fallen and banged her head.'

Lauren frowned, processing this information. 'Even if she'd fallen and banged her head, that doesn't account for why she was buried where she was found. That's certainly suspicious.'

'Exactly,' Claudia agreed, carefully placing the skull back in position.

Lauren's mind was already racing ahead, assembling the beginnings of an investigation timeline. Thirty years ago. Sixteen-year-old female. Blunt force trauma to the head. Deliberate burial.

'I think we can assume we're now looking at a suspicious death,' Lauren said, turning to Matt, her detective instincts fully engaged now.

'Yes, ma'am,' Matt agreed with a solemn nod. 'Did you discover any fibres?'

'Nothing. As I mentioned at the site, it's not unusual not to find anything if the person wore natural fibres.'

'Thanks for letting us know your findings straight away, we really appreciate it,' Lauren said, turning back to Claudia.

'I had my instructions from Henry,' Claudia said, with a smile. 'I'll write up the report and I'll send it to you by tomorrow.'

'Excellent,' Lauren said, though her mind was already elsewhere, plotting their next steps, making connections. They had a teenage girl who deserved justice, even if it was three decades later. 'Thanks, Henry. Claudia. We'd better get going. We've got a lot to do.'

As they turned to leave, Lauren cast one last glance at the skeleton.

What on earth had happened?

They left the morgue in silence and once outside, Lauren paused, taking a deep breath of fresh air to clear the morgue's sterile scent from her lungs. The morning had brightened considerably and the sun was now fully above the horizon, casting long shadows across the car park.

'What are you thinking?' Matt asked, as she unlocked her car with a beep.

'I'm thinking we need to pull all missing persons reports from the mid-nineties, focusing on teenage girls.' She slid into the seat and clicked her seatbelt in place. 'I'm also thinking that someone has got away with this for thirty years, and they probably think they're safe by now.' She started the engine and began driving towards the car park entrance. Her fingers tightened around the steering wheel. 'But they're not. Not anymore.'

'I agree,' Matt said.

'We'll start with the archives,' she said finally, breaking the thoughtful silence. 'And then see if we can trace her from dental records. If not, we might have to get a forensic artist to give her a face. I'll have to get permission from the DCI for that because it's not a cheap process.'

But she'd fight for it because there was a sixteen-year-old girl who deserved to be more than just a collection of remains on a cold metal table. She deserved a name, a story, and justice.

And Lauren was determined to give her all three.

FOUR

THURSDAY 22 MAY

Matt's footsteps echoed down the corridor as he made his way back to the office. The morning's visit to the morgue still lingered in his mind. The way the bones were laid out with such clinical precision, telling their silent story. His usual unease around death had been overshadowed by a growing sense of purpose. This wasn't just any old human remains... this was someone's teenaged daughter. He couldn't even begin to imagine how awful it was going to be for the family.

He'd left Lauren in the corridor, deep in conversation with DCI Mistry, explaining what they'd discovered at the morgue, so he could get the team started on the investigation.

'It looks like we've got a suspicious death on our hands,' Matt announced, once he'd entered the room.

'Oh my goodness, another murder?' Billy exclaimed, abandoning whatever he'd been doing and pressing his hand dramatically against his chest, feigning distress. His eyes, however, betrayed his excitement.

Matt shook his head slightly, suppressing a smile. Billy's enthusiasm was both inappropriate and infectious.

'Stop it, Billy,' Jenna said with a laugh, a coffee mug cradled in her hands. 'There's more to this job than hunting down murderers, you know.'

Billy straightened in his chair, attempting to appear more professional. 'I didn't say there wasn't, but it does make the job more interesting, you have to admit. I can't be the only one fed up with having to search for graffiti artists or children who steal from corner shops.'

'I suppose so,' Jenna responded. 'But I couldn't bear it if we only had murders to investigate. It would be way too stressful.'

Matt took off his jacket, hung it on the coat stand at the side of the room, and headed over to the whiteboard, to write up what little they knew of the deceased so far.

'How much do we know, Sarge?' Clem asked, his weathered face serious.

Matt drew in a breath and twirled the whiteboard marker in his fingers. 'The bones that were dug up belong to a teenage girl, around age sixteen.'

He glanced around the room, watching as the information registered on his team's faces. The energy shifted instantly, the excitement replaced by something heavier, more sombre.

'Dealing with murder is bad enough... but a kid... that's a whole different ballgame,' Clem said.

'I couldn't agree more,' Matt said, his tone serious. 'First things first. We need to discover who our victim is. Check records of missing teenage girls from thirty years ago, around the mid-1990s. Also, dig into old media reports from that time. There could be details in there of someone going missing. The DI suggested we get an artist's impression of the victim based on their skull, but it's expensive and time consuming. Hopefully we can use dental records to help identify the victim.'

'I'll get onto that straight away,' Tamsin said, already turning to her computer. Then, almost as an afterthought, she added, 'It'll give me something to occupy my mind whilst waiting to find out whether I've got a place on the course.'

Billy swivelled his chair back towards Tamsin. 'How long's it going to take?' he asked, genuine concern replacing his earlier theatrics. 'It's ridiculous having to wait this long.'

Tamsin's shoulders tensed. 'It's only been three days and they've got to interview all the other applicants. I wasn't the only one,' she explained, her fingers already typing searches into the database.

'How many applicants were there?' Billy continued.

'I've no idea. I didn't ask,' Tamsin replied, not looking up from her screen. 'All I know is that I was pleased with how it went and the DCI, who was on the interview panel, kept nodding at my answers, so I'm hoping it means I did well.'

'You'll get it. They'd be crazy not to take you,' Billy said. 'I would if it was up to me.'

'Me, too. And all my fingers are crossed for you,' Matt added encouragingly.

'Thanks,' Tamsin said.

Matt turned his attention back to the case, his mind already mapping out potential aspects of the investigation. Lauren would direct the strategy, but he liked to have ideas ready when she asked. The whiteboard would soon be filled with timelines, photographs, and possible connections. For now, though, they needed more information.

'We need to get all the members of the dig team in for further questioning. Jenna, can you do that, please,' Matt said.

Jenna looked up from her screen, frowning. 'Why? Surely you don't think it's one of them if the body's from thirty years ago.'

Matt shook his head. 'No, of course we don't, but it will be useful for us to know more about the dig itself. Like how long it's been going on, what else they've discovered, that sort of thing. There could be some clues regarding the body that might show up elsewhere.'

As Matt spoke, his attention was drawn to movement out the corner of his eye and he spotted the door leading from Lauren's office opening. She walked in and made her way over to where he was standing.

'Right, okay,' she began, addressing the team but standing close to Matt. 'I've informed the DCI and although this is a cold case, we need to get cracking. This is someone's daughter who'd gone missing at the age of sixteen and was never found.'

Matt nodded in agreement. 'I've instructed the team to start working on it, ma'am.'

'Good,' Lauren responded.

'I also thought we should call in the dig team to find out more about the dig itself.'

Lauren nodded. 'Good idea. Get them in tomorrow, and we'll spend the rest of today researching. Our top priority is to identify the young woman.'

As the team dispersed to their respective tasks, Matt remained standing for a moment, watching them.

He glanced at the empty space on the whiteboard where they'd eventually place a photo of the victim. Hopefully, a genuine portrait rather than a forensic reconstruction. Every case started this way, with blank spaces waiting to be filled, questions waiting to be answered. Lauren would build the timeline once they had more information.

Matt finally sat down at his desk, opening his notebook to a fresh page. At the top, he wrote *16-year-old female, mid-1990s* and underlined it twice. Then, beneath it, he added a single word: *Why?*.

Because that was always the question that haunted him most in cases involving children. Not just who and how, but why. Why this girl? Why that location? Why had she remained undiscovered for so long, in a county where most folks knew their neighbours' business?

He stared at the word for a moment longer, then closed the notebook and turned to his computer. The why would come later. For now, they needed to give her back her name.

Someone had taken this girl's future thirty years ago. The least they could do now was to uncover the truth about her past.

FIVE

FRIDAY 23 MAY

Lauren pushed open the door to one of the larger interview rooms with a confident stride. This was a routine fact-finding interview. These people weren't suspects. They simply might have useful information about the archaeological site where the bones had been discovered.

When she entered, with Matt close behind, six pairs of eyes turned towards them simultaneously. Lauren offered a professional smile, briefly taking in the group dynamics, noting who sat where and how they positioned themselves in relation to each other. She found these observations often revealed the natural hierarchy of a team.

'As some of you know, I'm Detective Inspector Pengelly, and this is Detective Sergeant Price,' she said, gesturing to Matt, who nodded politely.

Four members of the team were seated on the two sofas, two on each, and the other two sat on easy chairs. Their body language varied from openly curious to visibly uncomfortable.

Lauren and Matt took the two remaining dark grey fabric easy chairs.

'Why did you want to speak to us?' one of the men asked.

'You are?' Lauren initially responded without answering his question.

'Liam. Liam Blackburn. I'm the site supervisor... For my sins,' he added with a self-deprecating smile.

'We've asked you here so we can learn about the dig and its operations.'

'So we're not suspects?' Liam asked.

'No, not at all. Sorry if you were given that impression,' Lauren said, glancing at them all in turn, as they visibly relaxed.

'See, I said there was nothing to worry about,' Liam said, flashing a relieved grin at his colleagues.

'Please will you tell us your names and your role on the dig,' Lauren said. 'Then we'd like to know a little bit more about the dig itself. But before you do, we wanted you to know that the bones have been assessed and they belong to a teenage girl, currently identity unknown, and have been buried for approximately thirty years.'

There was a loud sharp intake of breath coming from the entire team at the same time.

'Dr Trewin, if you could start, please.'

The woman nodded, sitting up straighter. She had the weathered look of someone who spent considerable time outdoors, with sun lines around her eyes despite the English climate.

'Of course. As you know, I'm Eleanor Trewin, the director of the dig. This means that I'm overall in charge and liaise with outside agencies—'

'How long has the dig been at Treen?' Lauren asked, interrupting as she jotted down some notes in the notebook she'd been carrying.

'We've been here fifteen months,' Dr Trewin replied. 'It's a Bronze Age settlement dig.'

'What sort of things have you found, and are hoping to find?'

Dr Trewin's eyes brightened, her manner becoming more animated. Lauren recognised the enthusiasm of an expert talking about their passion.

'The typical finds of these sorts of digs are settlement structures. We've got post holes indicating houses or dwellings that people used to live in. In the trenches, we've also found some pottery fragments and several tools and ornaments. We also hope to discover some weapons such as axes, spearheads, daggers.' Her hands moved expressively as she spoke. 'We expect to find some evidence of tin processing, too, because of where we are in Cornwall. And burial sites. We may find cremation urns, barrows, or stone cists containing human remains.'

Lauren's pen stilled momentarily. Human remains. Expected but from thousands of years ago, not mere decades. 'We've also found some personal belongings,' Dr Trewin continued. 'Bracelets and necklaces of bronze. We're hoping to find some of amber, jet or bone. It's not unusual to find things associated with religious practices in these digs, but we haven't yet.' She suddenly stopped, looking apologetically at Lauren. 'Sorry, I know you wanted everyone to introduce themselves. I got carried away.'

'No, that's fine,' Lauren assured her. 'It was most informative.' She shifted her attention to the man sitting next to Dr Trewin. 'Mr Blackburn, Liam. What does your job involve?'

'Being site supervisor means I manage the daily operations and oversee the trenches where we dig. I make sure no one's digging where they shouldn't be.' Liam shrugged. 'It's actually more interesting than it sounds. I get an overview of everything found, giving me a clear picture of life in earlier times. It's fascinating... like putting together a puzzle of how people lived back then.'

'Okay, thanks,' Lauren said, looking to the next person, a younger woman with dirt still embedded under her fingernails. Someone who didn't mind getting her hands dirty.

'I'm Naomi Walters. A field archaeologist, so I've got a sort of broader knowledge about archaeology. Most of my time is spent in the field dig. Up until recently I spent my time working overseas in China and Egypt doing—'

'I don't think the inspector needs to know your background, Naomi,' Dr Trewin interrupted.

'Sorry,' Naomi said, blushing, as she looked at her boss.

Was there a problem between the two of them?

'It's fine,' Lauren assured her, noting how Liam Blackburn rested a comforting hand on his colleague's arm.

'I'm a field archaeologist, too,' the woman next to Naomi jumped in before Lauren could ask. 'I'm Verity Crowther.'

'Thank you,' Lauren said, wondering whether the eagerness was nervousness or simply Verity's personality. She turned to the next team member, a very tall man who appeared to be in his early thirties, with a serious expression on his face. 'You are?'

'Scott Goodman. I'm an environmental archaeologist, so I do things like sampling the soil, which is obviously crucial during these sorts of digs.'

'Right, okay,' Lauren said, noting his role.

Another man cleared his throat. 'We sometimes double up on roles. I'm Adam Fielding, the dig photographer, and I'm also responsible for processing, identifying, and cataloguing everything we find.'

Lauren scanned the room, her eyes moving from face to face. 'So there are six of you in total on the dig?'

'Yes, that's right,' Eleanor confirmed.

'Do you all come from around here?' Lauren asked.

'None of us do,' Eleanor replied. 'We're from various parts of the country. Some of us stay here all the time and others come down for the week and then go home at weekends.'

Lauren tapped her pen against the paper. 'Does anybody else help you on the dig?'

'Sometimes we have some students from the archaeology course at the University of Exeter, if they want to gain some field experience during their holidays,' Eleanor explained. 'Local people often help, too.'

'So basically anyone can be involved if they want?' Lauren asked.

'Yes, that's correct.'

'Who found the bones?'

'That would be me,' Verity Crowther said, raising her hand slightly. Her face had paled a bit. 'I was digging in that spot and I came across the skull and straight away stopped digging because immediately I could see it wasn't from the Bronze Age.'

'I see.' Lauren nodded, studying Verity's expression. 'So no one else was digging there with you?'

'We all have our own spot to dig in,' Verity explained. 'Obviously everyone came to see what I'd found because it was unusual.'

Lauren's eyes narrowed slightly as she formulated her next question, even though it was a stab in the dark. 'Were any of you around here thirty years ago?'

She observed their reactions carefully as they all shook their heads.

'No, not in Cornwall,' Eleanor said. 'I was at university in Exeter, Devon.'

'So was I,' Naomi Walters added quickly.

'Me too,' Adam Fielding said, smiling.

'Yeah, and me,' Liam Blackburn said.

Lauren frowned. 'So you've all known each other a long time.'

That would explain why they all looked around the same age.

'Well, yes,' Eleanor said with a small smile. 'We studied the same course at Exeter university. Although we weren't all in the same year... but we still knew each other. After university we went our separate ways.'

'When was this?' Matt asked.

'Between the years of 1993 and 1997,' Eleanor responded.

'How come you're all here together now? Was it intentional, like a reunion?' Lauren asked.

Eleanor glanced briefly at the others before answering. 'We all keep up to date with one another on a social media group for our course's alumni. When I got funding for the dig, I asked them if they were available to join. Being so close to Exeter I thought it would be fun. So yes, a sort of reunion, I suppose. It helped that I knew the quality of their work. Scott and Verity applied for the other two positions after they were advertised online.'

'Where do you live while you're here?' Lauren asked.

'We're all in various types of rented accommodation.'

'Who pays for this, because it can't be cheap?'

'We've had a grant from the Cornish Preservation Foundation,' Eleanor explained. 'That covers salaries, small stipends for helping students or volunteers, and accommodation. Some of us are in cottages on our own while others are in bed and breakfasts. Also covered is the cost for all our equipment and transport, and any laboratory analysis we might need.'

'That must have been an extremely large grant,' Lauren said, unable to hide her surprise.

'Yes. These things aren't cheap to run,' Eleanor agreed with a nod.

Lauren glanced at all of them in turn. There was nothing else they needed from them at this point.

'Thank you for coming in. That will be all for now, but we may have questions later, depending on what else we discover at the dig.'

They all stood, and as Lauren held open the door for them to leave, her mind was already processing the information they'd gathered. Thirty years was a long time, but having these archaeological experts might help with understanding the context of how the remains had been missed until now.

It was certainly a good start – and it might be worth following up with the Cornish Preservation Foundation to make sure there was nothing amiss.

SIX

FRIDAY 23 MAY

Matt waited until the archaeological team had left the police station before voicing what had been bothering him throughout the interview.

'Did you think that Dr Trewin was acting a little strange?' he asked Lauren as they turned from the entrance and walked past the reception desk towards the stairs.

Lauren glanced at him, frowning. 'What do you mean?'

Matt paused, trying to articulate the nagging feeling that had settled at the base of his skull during the interview. He'd been a detective long enough to trust these instincts, even if they were sometimes difficult to put into words.

'I got the feeling that she was uneasy about something.'

'I can't say that I noticed anything but it could be because the dig has come to a standstill and she was worried about that. They're not cheap to run and she might have been concerned about the Cornish Preservation Foundation pulling the plug. We must look into them, by the way.'

'Maybe. But I watched her carefully, and she kept fidgeting and her eyes were darting all over the place. You might not have noticed because you were focused on whoever was speaking.'

'Are you suggesting that she had something to do with the remains we found?' Lauren asked, her tone sharpening slightly.

Matt held up his hands in a placating gesture. 'I don't want to go that far. But we do know that some of them lived fairly close to the area at the time the teenage girl was buried. Exeter to Treen isn't that far, is it?'

'I think that's too much of a leap to make at the moment, but certainly we're not going to dismiss it,' Lauren said.

'Good, because she definitely seemed on edge.'

Lauren turned to him. 'To be honest, her body language didn't strike me as someone who was hiding something. But that doesn't mean we'll totally ignore her. We'll keep an open mind.'

Matt appreciated Lauren's balanced approach. It was one of the reasons they worked well together.

When they reached the office, he pushed open the door and stepped to the side to allow Lauren to enter first.

'Ma'am,' Clem called out enthusiastically.

'Yes?' Lauren answered, heading towards his desk.

'We've made progress on identifying the body. After going through all the records and media, there's only one person who fits the description and went missing around thirty years ago.'

Matt stood next to Lauren, the base of his spine tingling at the thought of a potential breakthrough.

'Go on, then,' Lauren said impatiently.

'This young girl was last seen on the summer solstice of June 1996. Which fits in with what the pathologist came up with.' Clem turned his screen to reveal a black and white image of a young girl with long dark hair and a hesitant smile.

Something about her eyes made Matt's chest tighten. There was a vulnerability there that made the thirty-year-old case suddenly feel immediate and raw.

Lauren nodded. 'I take it we have a name?'

'Yes,' Clem said, his voice softening slightly. 'Ruth Penrose. She was sixteen when she went missing. There were other people who were also reported to be missing at the time, but none of them were of the same age as the remains that were found.'

'That's excellent. Have you discovered anything else about her?'

'Nothing other than her parents still live locally. I'll text you the address,' Clem replied.

A weight settled in Matt's stomach. Informing families, even after all these years, was never easy. He'd seen firsthand how the absence of closure could suspend people in a kind of emotional limbo for decades. The Penroses had been waiting thirty years for answers.

'Okay, thanks. I want more digging into Ruth Penrose and her family,' Lauren said decisively, glancing at Matt. 'We'll visit the family now and inform them of what we know.'

'Are you sure, ma'am?' Matt asked. 'What if it turns out not to be Ruth?'

'I've considered that, but it's really the only way to move forward on this. If Ruth has been in touch since being reported missing then we know to focus our research on a different direction. Obviously, we can't say one hundred percent it's her but maybe if we can track dental records...' She turned to Clem. 'Will you please give Henry a ring and ask him to track the dental records of Ruth Penrose, as a matter of urgency. If they match, we'll have a positive identification, and that will also save having to ask for a facial reconstruction.'

'I'm onto it, ma'am,' Clem replied with purpose.

'Also, please send the photo of Ruth to our mobiles,' Lauren added.

'Yes, ma'am.'

'Billy, please contact the Cornish Preservation Foundation and ask if they've had any issues with the dig at Treen. They provided a grant for the dig to take place, so I'm sure they'll be monitoring it carefully, and I imagine Eleanor Trewin as the dig's director will have to provide regular reports on their findings.'

'Yes, ma'am,' Billy said immediately. 'Do you think the dig

could have something to do with the dead girl? But then how could it – it only started recently and she's been buried for thirty years?' he added, answering the question for himself.

'I doubt the two are linked but nothing is excluded from our investigation yet, as you well know. Matt and I will be back later and you can update us then.'

Matt's phone pinged as they got to the door. It was the photo of Ruth Penrose in her school uniform. He stared at it, feeling the weight of responsibility that came with knowing she was their victim.

He returned his phone to his pocket, making a silent promise to the smiling teenager whose life had been cut mysteriously short that summer in 1996 to discover what had happened so tragically to her.

SEVEN

FRIDAY 23 MAY

Lauren knocked on the door of the small, grey-bricked semi-detached property in an area on the outskirts of Penzance that she wasn't too familiar with. The house had a small front garden which was paved, but neglect had allowed weeds to grow between the cracks. It seemed to be the kind of place owned by either elderly people who couldn't manage anymore, or perhaps those who had given up caring.

She glanced at Matt, who stood beside her, his expression neutral but his eyes alert. He gave a small nod. They were going to have to handle this delicately, especially as they didn't yet have confirmation the remains belonged to the family's daughter.

The door opened slowly, revealing a woman who looked to be in her late sixties. Her hair hung straight to her shoulders, coloured an unnatural light blonde that didn't quite hide the grey at her roots.

'Yes?' she said, looking at them suspiciously, her fingers gripping the edge of the door as though ready to slam it shut.

Lauren held out her warrant card, keeping her voice gentle but professional. 'I'm DI Pengelly, and this is Detective Sergeant Price. Are you Mrs Penrose?'

'I am. What's the matter?' The woman's eyes flicked between Lauren and Matt, her knuckles whitening on the door.

'Can we come in, please?' Lauren asked. 'We'd like to talk to you about your daughter Ruth.'

At the mention of her daughter's name, the woman's eyes widened and she visibly paled. She swayed slightly, her other hand moving to the doorframe to steady herself. It was the reaction of someone who had been waiting for this moment for years. Dreading it and perhaps, in some corner of her heart, hoping for it too.

'Yes... okay, come in.' Mrs Penrose's voice had dropped to barely above a whisper.

'Is your husband home?' Lauren asked.

'Yes, he's in the kitchen, having a late breakfast.' Mrs Penrose stepped back to let them through. 'We don't get up early these days, not since we've retired. Come in.'

They followed her through the hallway, which was lined with a worn carpet that might once have been green but had faded to an indeterminate colour. On the wall there were framed photographs that looked as though they went back years. A young girl with dark hair appeared in several of them. It was Ruth.

Mrs Penrose led them to the kitchen, which had dated kitchen units, at least thirty years old. Despite its age, the room was clean. Just worn and tired, like its occupants.

A man with thinning grey hair sat hunched over a newspaper, a half-eaten piece of toast on a plate beside him. He looked up as they entered, his eyebrows drawing together in a frown.

'What is it, Vera?' he asked gruffly, in a strong Cornish accent.

'It's the police, Murray,' Mrs Penrose replied, her voice trembling slightly. 'They want to talk to us about Ruth.'

'Ruth?' he said, blinking several times as he sat up straighter. His eyes narrowed with the apprehension of someone who'd been nursing his wounds for three decades.

'What about her?'

Lauren stepped forward. 'Shall we go through to the lounge

and sit down? It might be easier to talk,' she suggested, knowing that what she had to say would hit them hard and she didn't want to risk any accidents on top of everything else.

'Sit at the kitchen table,' the man replied firmly, pointing to the other three chairs. His wife sat on the chair next to him, her movements cautious, as though she might break if she made any sudden move.

Lauren exchanged a quick glance with Matt. This wasn't ideal, but they'd work with it. She took the seat opposite Mr Penrose and Matt sat next to her.

'Well, what is it?' Mr Penrose demanded, folding his newspaper with deliberate movements.

Lauren took a deep breath, her hands resting flat on the kitchen table. 'I'm sorry to have to tell you this,' she said gently, watching their faces carefully. 'But we have recovered some human remains at the archaeological dig in Treen, and we believe that they might belong to Ruth. We're waiting for confirmation from the pathologist, but it's all pointing to them being her. I'm so sorry,' Lauren repeated, even though she knew it wouldn't do anything to ease the shock. She watched the couple carefully, in case either of them needed help.

Mrs Penrose made a small, strangled sound and stared blankly at the table, her fingers tracing invisible patterns on its surface. Her shoulders had slumped, as if the weight she'd been carrying for thirty years had suddenly doubled.

'Ruth?' Mr Penrose questioned, sounding like he was hearing his daughter's name for the very first time.

'We'd like to ask you some questions if you're up to it,' Lauren said. 'I really think we'd be better in the lounge,' she suggested again, wanting to move them to a more comfortable setting.

'Okay,' Mr Penrose said, gruffly, this time agreeing. 'This way.' He scraped his chair back on the kitchen floor and stood up, remaining silent as he walked out of the kitchen into the hall, and turned right into the lounge.

The room had a worn red velour sofa and two matching

armchairs that had also seen better days. The carpet was thin in places from years of foot traffic, and the wallpaper, a floral pattern that might have been fashionable in the eighties, had faded where the sun hit it. On the mantelpiece, Lauren noticed more photographs, including school pictures of two girls at various ages.

The couple sat on the sofa, close enough that their shoulders touched, while Matt and Lauren took the armchairs.

'Please could you go through exactly what happened when you reported Ruth missing, if you remember?' Lauren asked, her voice gentle but direct.

Mrs Penrose clasped her hands tightly in her lap. 'Of course I remember. It's etched on my mind. I phoned the police in the morning after realising that Ruth hadn't come home the night before. A policeman came to see us and we told him everything but after he'd gone back to the station, they telephoned us to say that they'd decided that Ruth had run away. They said that because she was sixteen, they weren't going to do anything about it. We kept telling them that she hadn't but they didn't believe us. They wouldn't listen and there was nothing we could do. It's not like we had any money to employ one of those private detective people.'

'Why were you so convinced that Ruth hadn't run away?' Lauren asked softly.

'Because she'd left some things that she would have taken with her. I know that for sure.' Mrs Penrose's voice caught slightly, and tears filled her eyes, one of them rolling down her cheek, which she brushed away with her fingers.

'What things were these exactly?' Matt asked, speaking for the first time since they'd entered the house.

'Some of her favourite photos. Her make-up, which she never went anywhere without, and her clothes,' Mrs Penrose replied, looking up at Matt with glassy eyes. 'Why would she run away and not take those things with her? It made no sense. At least, it didn't to us. But the police would have none of it.'

Lauren's jaw tightened. Clearly the original investigation had been poorly carried out.

'What can you tell us about Ruth?' Lauren asked.

Mr Penrose sighed heavily. 'Ruth wasn't an easy child,' he said, his voice gruff but tinged with sadness. 'She was always in trouble at school and couldn't wait to leave so she could get a job and start earning money.'

'What was she planning to do after leaving? Because presumably when she went missing, it was towards the end of the academic year and she'd made some plans.'

'She talked about going to London and trying to find work there,' Mrs Penrose said. 'But nothing was definite. That's another reason why I didn't think she'd run away. She had no reason not to tell us she was going.'

'Can you think of a reason why the police wouldn't accept your account?' Lauren asked, wondering whether there was more to the story than they'd heard so far.

'Well... the thing is... Ruth had run away a couple of times in the past and we'd contacted the police both times,' Mrs Penrose admitted reluctantly. 'But she came back of her own accord.' Her voice cracked with emotion. 'We've always hoped that she'd get back in touch with us. And if not us, her younger sister, Jasmine. They were close.'

A pang of sympathy hit Lauren. These people had lived in limbo for thirty years, never knowing what had happened to their daughter, oscillating between hope and despair.

'Where's Jasmine?' Lauren asked.

'She lives in Penzance,' Mr Penrose replied, 'but she's away for a couple of days.'

'We'd like to speak to her, so please could you ask her to contact us when she's back,' Lauren said.

'Yes.' Mrs Penrose nodded. 'She might be able to tell you...' Her voice trailed off, as though she wasn't sure what her younger daughter might know but was grasping at anything that might help.

Mr Penrose clasped his weathered hands between his knees. 'So you say you found her remains. What happened to her?' His voice was steady, though Lauren could tell it took tremendous effort.

'We don't know exactly, yet. But we're treating her death as suspicious.'

Mrs Penrose gasped. 'You think someone killed her?'

'She was buried, Vera,' Mr Penrose said. 'What else could it have been?'

'Oh my God,' the woman whispered.

'When can we have Ruth back?' Mr Penrose asked. 'So we can have a funeral for her. Say our final goodbyes.' There was a desperate need for closure in his words, and Lauren's throat tightened.

'At the moment, we can't do anything while the inquiry's ongoing and we need confirmation that the remains are actually Ruth's,' Lauren explained carefully. 'When everything is complete, the coroner's office will contact you and let you know when you can have Ruth.' She paused. 'We're so very sorry for having to bring this news to you, and for your loss.'

Mr Penrose's jaw tightened. 'It's been thirty years, and we've learnt to live with it. Not accept it... but live with it.'

Mrs Penrose raised her gaze to meet Lauren's, her eyes swimming with tears. 'At least now we know,' she whispered. 'Not a day goes by when I wonder if this is the day when my Ruthie comes home.'

Tears filled her eyes, and she began to quietly sob. Mr Penrose put his arm around his wife's shoulders, pulling her closer to him in a gesture of comfort that spoke of decades of shared grief.

'Before we go, do you remember the names of any of Ruth's friends or boyfriends?' Lauren asked, subtly steering the conversation towards potential suspects.

Mrs Penrose shook her head. 'She didn't bring anyone home. She said we were embarrassing. But all teenagers are like that, aren't they?' She looked at Lauren as if wanting reassurance.

'Yes, they can be difficult. What school did she go to? They might be able to help.'

'The local high school. It's the only one around here.'

Lauren cleared her throat softly, the signal to Matt that it was time to wrap things up. Mr and Mrs Penrose needed space to process what they'd just learnt.

'Thank you for your time,' Lauren said, rising from her chair. 'Once we know more, we'll contact you. We'll leave you now and see ourselves out.'

As they walked to the front door, Lauren cast a final glance back at the lounge. Mr and Mrs Penrose remained on the sofa, clinging to each other like survivors of a shipwreck.

Outside, the overcast sky matched the heaviness in Lauren's chest. She took a deep breath of the salt-tinged air, letting it clear her head.

Sliding into the driver's seat, her mind was already racing with the implications of what they'd learnt. Ruth had run away before. She had a sister who might know more. She'd left behind personal items that were important to her.

'We need to track down the sister as soon as she's back from holiday,' Lauren said, starting the engine. 'I want to look at the original missing persons report. Let's see if there's a clue in there as to why they were so quick to dismiss Ruth as a runaway. Because from where I'm standing, they have a lot to answer for. If their job had been done properly, we wouldn't be here working the case today.'

Matt nodded. 'I'll call the station and have them dig up the archived files.'

Lauren glanced in her rearview mirror at the Penrose house, watching it grow smaller behind them as she pulled away. Thirty years of not knowing, of living in that terrible purgatory between hope and grief. At least now they had answers, however painful.

But for Lauren, the questions were just beginning.

'We also need to discover who Ruth's friends were back then,' she said, her voice hardening with resolve. 'Someone knows something, even after all this time, and I'm going to find them.'

EIGHT

FRIDAY 23 MAY

'Hey, Sarge. Glad you're back,' Tamsin called out as Matt walked in and hung his jacket up on the stand.

Matt nodded in acknowledgement, running a hand through his slightly damp hair. The persistent Cornish drizzle had followed him from the car to the station, leaving tiny droplets clinging to his jacket.

'I've got something for you,' Tamsin continued, her eyes bright.

He smiled. After the emotional weight of breaking the news to Ruth's parents, they desperately needed a breakthrough. He hurried over to her.

'Okay, what is it?' he asked, leaning forward and resting his hands on her desk.

'Right,' Tamsin began, fidgeting in her chair with enthusiasm, her curly hair falling across her face. She absent-mindedly pushed it away. 'We've heard back from the pathologist, and dental records have confirmed the bones belong to Ruth Penrose.'

'That was quick,' Matt responded.

'Yes, they struck lucky,' Tamsin explained. 'An email sent out by Dr Carpenter asking local dentists if they recognised the work, and a junior dentist at the time replied straight away. She's now got her own practice. It turns out that Ruth's teeth were quite distinctive because she'd had one knocked out as a child and the lower teeth were crossed at the bottom.'

'That's excellent,' Matt said, straightening up.

The pieces were starting to come together.

'I've also contacted the school I assumed she'd have gone to, as it's the only one in the area, and the school secretary, who's been there thirty-five years, remembers her,' Tamsin continued, a note of triumph in her voice. 'I asked about her friends, and she gave me the names of two girls Ruth hung around with.'

'That's great news. Friends from that time might hold crucial information. Go on.'

'One of them, Kelly Hartley, still lives in the area,' Tamsin said. 'But the other one I haven't been able to trace yet. She might've left the area or married and changed her name.'

'That's excellent work, Tamsin. Tell me about Kelly Hartley?'

'She still goes under the same name and works at the caravan park; she lives on site.'

Energy coursed through Matt. He couldn't have asked for more from Tamsin. Now they had an identification and someone who knew Ruth, who might remember her last days, her state of mind, who she was seeing... Any of these details could provide the breakthrough they needed.

'Thanks. I'll let the DI know, and we'll head out there,' he said decisively, already planning the interview in his head. Would Kelly Hartley be forthcoming, or would three decades of silence make her reluctant to talk? 'Did you actually speak to her about finding Ruth's remains?' he wanted to clarify.

'No. I just said we're relooking into Ruth's disappearance,' Tamsin replied. 'I also said we'd probably be calling out to have a chat with her. It was okay to say that, wasn't it?'

'Yes, of course,' Matt replied, nodding. 'This could be a pivotal interview. Whether she'll remember anything remains to be seen. After thirty years her memory might be hazy.'

'Or, if she witnessed anything, her memory of it might be

crystal clear,' Clem, who'd been listening, said. 'Trauma has a way of preserving moments like that. And—'

'Watch out, Clemipedia is off again. Don't tell me you're now going to launch into a psychological analysis about trauma,' Billy said, with a smirk.

'That's enough, Billy. I don't know how you put up with him,' Matt said, turning to Clem, rolling his eyes, but with a wry smile so they knew he realised it was all done in fun.

'It's his age. One day he'll grow out of it,' Clem responded, grinning.

'True,' Matt agreed. 'Right. I'm off to have a chat with the DI.'

He walked across the office and knocked on Lauren's door, opening it without waiting for a response. She wouldn't mind – they'd only just got back so she'd hardly be immersed in a task.

In fact Lauren hadn't even sat down. She was standing by her desk, taking off her jacket.

'What is it?' she asked, her expression telling him she was still processing their earlier conversation with Ruth's parents.

'We have confirmation the remains are Ruth Penrose,' he began, watching Lauren's face as she absorbed this information. 'Tamsin's also managed to locate one of her friends who still lives in the area,' he continued, leaning against the doorframe. 'Kelly Hartley. She works at the campsite near Hayle.'

Lauren's eyebrows rose slightly. 'Ah... That's good.'

'Am I right in assuming you want to head out there now?' he asked, already knowing the answer.

'Yes,' Lauren said, picking up her jacket. 'Grab your coat. We'll go in my car.'

As Matt turned to leave the office, his thoughts returned to the Penrose couple, sitting in their faded living room with thirty years of grief hanging over them. He remembered the photos on the mantelpiece. Ruth at various ages, frozen in time, while her parents aged with the weight of not knowing where she was or who she was with. They'd need to return and give them the news.

'Do you think they'll be okay?' he asked, pausing in the doorway. 'Mr and Mrs Penrose, I mean.'

Lauren sighed, meeting his eyes. 'As okay as anyone can be after learning their daughter was murdered,' she said quietly. 'But at least now they'll know the remains do belong to her. That's something, at least, and means they won't have at the back of their minds the hope that one day she'll turn up or give them a call. Come on, let's talk to Kelly Hartley. She might be the key to understanding who Ruth Penrose was, who might have wanted to harm her.'

Matt followed Lauren out of the office.

The rain had intensified when they stepped outside, drumming against the roof of the station entrance in a steady rhythm that matched his resolve.

As Lauren pulled out of the station car park, Matt found himself thinking about time. How it had changed some things but left others untouched. Ruth Penrose would forever remain in the minds of everyone at the age she disappeared. She'd be perpetually young.

As the car sped towards the caravan site, the familiar surge of determination that came with every case coursed through Matt. This wasn't just about solving a cold case. It was about restoring Ruth Penrose to more than bones in the ground. It was about giving her back her story, her voice, and ultimately, her justice.

Thirty years was a long time, but murder left echoes that never truly faded. Someone out there knew what happened to Ruth Penrose and was probably lulled into believing that they'd got away with it. But Matt disagreed. He was determined they'd be found.

NINE

FRIDAY 23 MAY

The Seabreeze Caravan and Campsite sprawled across several acres of prime Cornish coastline, its collection of caravans, glamping pods, and camping pitches arranged in neat rows that faced towards the sea. Despite the drizzle, a few determined holidaymakers moved between caravans and the small onsite shop, wrapped in waterproof clothing and wearing wellies, as though the rain were merely an inconvenience rather than a deterrent.

'It's very quiet,' Matt observed, peering through the windscreen as Lauren pulled into the car park and turned off the engine.

'It's off-season,' Lauren replied, unclipping her seatbelt. 'They probably only have a handful of guests and some of them might even live here full time.'

The reception building sat at the entrance. It was a single-storey wooden structure with a sign that had faded until it was hardly readable, no doubt from years of coastal weather. A weathervane on the roof spun lazily in the gentle breeze coming off the sea.

'Reception first,' Lauren said, reaching over to the back seat for her bag. 'They'll know where to find Kelly.'

Inside, a middle-aged woman with streaks of grey in her dark hair looked up from a computer. The small space smelt of coffee and was faintly musty.

'Hello. Can I help you?' the woman asked, smiling.

Lauren produced her warrant card. 'DI Pengelly and DS Price from Penzance CID. We're looking for Kelly Hartley. We understand she works here.'

The woman's eyebrows rose slightly, but her smile remained fixed. 'Oh, yes. Kelly's our site manager. She told me a while ago that she was going to the maintenance shed, so I'd try her there.' The woman pointed through the window towards a green shed near a row of newer-looking caravans. 'Is everything okay?'

'Nothing to worry about. This is just a routine visit,' Matt assured her with the easy smile he often used to disarm people. 'We need to ask her a few questions about an old case we're investigating.'

'Old case' was such a clinical term for a young woman's life cut so short, and for being hidden away in the ground for three decades.

'Thank you,' Lauren said, already turning towards the door.

Outside, the rain had stopped, though dark clouds still hung low overhead, which didn't bode well for it being dry for long. They made their way across the site, passing a small playground where a solitary child in a red raincoat was spinning on a roundabout, watched by a patient parent huddled under an umbrella.

'How are we going to approach this?' Matt asked quietly as they walked.

'Casual at first, so as not to put her on edge. She might not remember much of what happened after all this time. But if she's evasive...' Lauren let the sentence hang.

'Are you expecting her to be?' Matt asked, frowning slightly.

'I never assume anything,' Lauren replied. 'But, as you know, people who were the last to see a murder victim often are vague, whether they're involved or not. Guilt works in strange ways.'

The maintenance shed stood with its door half-open, revealing shelves of tools and supplies. As they approached, Lauren heard someone moving around inside, the clatter of metal tools against a workbench.

'Kelly Hartley?' Lauren called, pausing at the doorway.

A woman in her mid to late forties emerged from behind a stack of folded sun loungers. She wore jeans, boots, and a fleece jacket with the Seabreeze logo on it. Her blonde hair was pulled back in a practical ponytail.

Her eyes narrowed with caution as she took in her visitors. 'Yes?'

'I'm Detective Inspector Pengelly, and this is Detective Sergeant Price from Penzance police. You spoke to one of my detective constables about Ruth Penrose,' Lauren said, showing her warrant card. 'We'd like to ask you a few more questions if you have a moment.'

Kelly wiped her hands on a rag, her expression cautious but not seeming overly concerned. 'Yeah, sure.'

'Do you mind if we step inside? It looks like it's going to start raining again,' Lauren suggested.

Kelly gestured for them to enter, then moved to clear a space on a workbench, sweeping aside some small tools. The shed smelt of wood and metal, and there was a faint whiff of oil in the air. It was well organised, with labelled containers and tools hanging neatly on a pegboard.

'Why are you looking into Ruth's case after all this time?' Kelly asked, leaning against the cleared workbench. Her tone was appropriately sombre, but Lauren detected something almost rehearsed about it. 'At the time I thought it weird that she'd disappeared without saying anything but then decided she might really have gone to London like she always talked about. She hated living here.'

'So you knew her well?' Lauren asked, choosing to remain standing while Matt perched on a nearby stool. She didn't answer Kelly's previous question because they'd be telling her the truth about Ruth soon enough.

'We were friends at school,' Kelly said with a small shrug. 'Not best friends because Ruth didn't do them. She was more of a loner. Which was fine and none of us minded. She was who she was. But despite that we still hung out in the same group. It was a small town. Still is, really. Everyone knew everyone.'

Lauren nodded, keeping her expression neutral. 'The reason we're now investigating this case is because some human remains were recently discovered at an archaeological dig site in Treen and they've been identified as being Ruth.'

Kelly's face paled slightly, but her expression remained controlled. 'That's... God, that's awful. Do you think she was... you know?'

'We're treating her death as suspicious,' Matt replied when Kelly didn't finish her sentence.

A heavy silence filled the shed, broken only by the distant call of seagulls and the faint patter of rain on the metal roof.

'We believe you might have been one of the last people to see her before she disappeared,' Lauren continued, watching Kelly carefully.

Kelly crossed her arms, a classic defensive posture that Lauren had seen countless times in her career. 'It was thirty years ago,' she said, not making eye contact with them. 'I don't remember anything clearly.'

'What *do* you remember?' Lauren pressed gently.

Kelly sighed, fiddling with the button on her overalls. 'Well... It was the summer solstice in June, 1996. A bunch of us decided to have a party on the beach. Nothing fancy. Just some cheap beer and cider and music from a local band. We lit small bonfires in fire pits.'

'Who's "a bunch of us"?' Matt asked.

'Just local kids,' Kelly said vaguely. 'Maybe ten of us? Mostly from school. Ruth was there, obviously. Me, Jayne Tregowan, Tyler Penhaligon, and several others whose names I don't really remember now.'

'What happened that night?'

Kelly's gaze shifted to the window, where raindrops were now streaming down the glass. 'We were just hanging out, you know? But then other people heard about it and the party seemed to take on a life of its own. I bet there were over fifty people there in the end. Everyone was in a good mood and enjoying themselves. There was no trouble or anything. But—' She paused as if thinking back to the night.

'What?' Lauren pushed.

'Thinking back, Ruth was in a weird mood. She was excited one minute, quiet the next.'

'Why do you think that was?' Lauren asked.

Kelly shrugged. 'I don't know. I suppose yes, it was weird, but not unusual. Especially those last few months before she disappeared. She was often up and down. At the time I probably figured it was just Ruth being Ruth.'

'And then?' Lauren prompted when Kelly fell silent.

'Then she told us she wanted to walk to Logan Rock and touch it at the moment of the actual solstice,' Kelly said. 'I couldn't see the point... But then a lot of what Ruth did was like that.'

'Did you see her leave?'

'No. I don't think so. But it was dark, and I'd been drinking.'

'So you don't know if she was on her own, or with someone,' Lauren clarified.

Kelly shook her head. 'No, I don't. But I do remember seeing her chatting with a guy earlier in the evening. She might have gone with him... but I didn't see them leave together.'

'Do you remember his name?'

'No. I didn't recognise him. He looked older than us and not from our school.'

'Would you recognise him again?' Matt asked.

'I doubt it. It wasn't like she introduced me to him. I only saw him from a distance, and even then, that was through drunken eyes.'

'Did you see Ruth return after going to Logan Rock?' Lauren asked, exchanging a quick glance with Matt.

'No,' Kelly said, a flicker of something crossing her face. Defensiveness? Guilt?

'Weren't you worried that she hadn't returned?' Matt interjected.

Kelly shrugged again, the gesture becoming a pattern. 'Like I said, Ruth was unpredictable. It wasn't anything for us to worry about. We assumed she'd gone home. It wasn't until a couple of days later when her parents started asking around that we realised something might be wrong.'

'And you told the police all this at the time?' Lauren asked.

'Yes, but they didn't seem that bothered,' Kelly replied, an edge creeping into her voice. 'They said she'd probably run away. She'd done it before.'

Lauren nodded slowly, mentally comparing this account with what the Penroses had told them. 'What did you think about the idea that she'd run away?'

Kelly hesitated, her fingers toying with the rag she still held. 'I thought it was strange,' she admitted. 'Ruth talked about leaving, sure, but she would have told someone. She liked the drama of it all, you know? She wouldn't have just slipped away without making a scene.'

'Yet you didn't push this with the police?' Lauren asked, careful to keep accusation out of her tone.

'I was seventeen,' Kelly said defensively. 'What did I know? They were the police. I figured they knew what they were doing.'

Lauren was quiet for a moment, studying Kelly's face. There was something in her eyes that didn't match her casual tone. A wariness, perhaps, or a well-concealed guilt.

'Were you upset that Ruth hadn't confided in you about her plans?' Lauren asked, changing tack slightly. 'Or that she never contacted you again?'

Kelly's expression flickered, almost imperceptibly. 'Not really,' she said, too quickly. 'Like I said, we weren't that close.'

Lauren noted the contradiction with her earlier statements, where she'd implied that they hung out regularly. 'But you were close enough to spend the solstice together? To be part of the same friend group?'

'It was a small town,' Kelly repeated, an edge of irritation in her voice now. 'Everyone hung out together because there was nothing else to do.'

'Kelly, it's been thirty years. Whatever happened back then, Ruth's parents deserve to know the truth. If there's anything you remember. Anything at all. Now's the time to share it,' Matt said, his voice gentle in contrast to Lauren's more direct approach.

For a moment, Lauren thought she saw Kelly's composure waver. A flash of something crossed her face before she visibly steeled herself.

'We were at the beach. Ruth left to go to Logan Rock. We never saw her again.'

Lauren decided to push a little harder. 'Was Ruth seeing someone?'

Kelly started arranging tools on the workbench, keeping her hands busy. 'She was always talking about boys, but no one serious that I can recall.'

'What about enemies?' Lauren asked. 'Was there anyone who didn't get along with her?'

Kelly gave a short, humourless laugh. 'Ruth had a way of rubbing people the wrong way sometimes. She could be... I don't know, intense? But I wouldn't say enemies, no.'

Lauren watched Kelly continue rearranging tools that were already organised, a classic displacement activity. She was hiding something. Lauren was certain of it. Whether it was directly related to Ruth's murder or simply something Kelly didn't want to revisit remained to be seen.

'How come you still live in the area?' Lauren observed casually. 'You never left Cornwall. Why not?'

Kelly's shoulders tensed slightly. 'Never saw the need. I like it here. I got this job straight out of school and worked my way up to manager.' She gestured around the shed. 'It's not glamorous, but it's a living.'

'And the others from that night?' Lauren asked. 'Jayne and Tyler? Are they still around?'

'Jayne moved away years ago, I think. London or Manchester, not sure,' Kelly said. 'Tyler still lives in Hayle and runs his dad's old fishing boat. He takes tourists out in the summer.'

Lauren nodded, making another mental note. 'We'd like to talk to him as well.'

'He won't remember any more than I do,' Kelly said quickly. 'It was a long time ago, and we were all pretty drunk.'

'Still, we'd like to hear his perspective,' Lauren insisted gently. 'Do you have his contact details?'

Kelly hesitated, then nodded reluctantly. 'I can write them down for you.'

She turned to a small desk in the corner and scribbled on a piece of paper, then handed it to Lauren. Their fingers brushed in the exchange, and Lauren noted that Kelly's hand was cold despite the relative warmth of the shed.

'Is there anything else you can tell us about Ruth?' Lauren asked. 'Anything that might help us understand what happened to her?'

Kelly seemed to consider this, her gaze distant. For a moment, Lauren thought she might be on the verge of revealing something significant. But then she shook her head, her expression closing off again.

'She was a normal teenager,' Kelly said. 'Moody, dreaming of bigger things and tired of small-town life. We all were. She just never got the chance to grow out of it.'

There was something in her tone. A mixture of sadness and something else Lauren couldn't quite identify, that gave her pause to think. But after thirty years, memories were inevitably coloured by time and subsequent experiences. Whatever Kelly wasn't saying might simply be lost to the decades between.

'Well, thanks for your time,' Lauren said, handing Kelly her card. 'If you think of anything else, please call me directly.'

Kelly took the card, glancing at it briefly before slipping it into her pocket. 'Sure. But I don't think I'll remember anything else after all this time.'

As they turned to leave, Lauren paused at the door. 'One last thing, Kelly. The night of the solstice, what beach were you at?'

'Pedn Vounder,' Kelly replied without hesitation.

Lauren nodded. 'Thank you. We'll be in touch if we have any more questions.'

Outside, the rain had intensified, splattering against the ground in a steady rhythm. Lauren and Matt hurried back towards the car, hunched against the downpour.

'What do you think?' Matt asked once they were inside the vehicle, wiping raindrops from his face.

Lauren started the engine, her mind already processing the interview. 'She's hiding something,' she said decisively. 'The question is what, and whether it's relevant to Ruth's murder.'

'Could it be she's uncomfortable talking about a friend who was killed?' Matt suggested, playing devil's advocate. 'Survivor's guilt, maybe.'

'Maybe,' Lauren conceded, pulling out of the car park. 'But her story has inconsistencies. She claimed they weren't close, yet they were together on the solstice. She says Ruth would have told someone if she was running away, but apparently didn't think it strange enough to push when the police dismissed it as exactly that.'

'And she was awfully vague about this mystery boy Ruth was talking to on the beach,' Matt added.

'Exactly,' Lauren said, turning onto the main road.

As they drove away from Seabreeze, Lauren glanced in the rearview mirror. Through the rain-streaked glass, she could make out Kelly Hartley standing in the doorway of the maintenance shed, watching them leave. There was something in her tense posture that strengthened Lauren's suspicion.

Thirty years was a long time to keep a secret. But not all secrets stayed buried forever. Some, like Ruth Penrose herself, eventually found their way to the surface.

'We need to find out more about the relationship between Kelly and Ruth,' Lauren said, her mind racing ahead. 'School records, other friends, anything that might give us insight into what Kelly's not telling us.'

'I'll get Tamsin on it,' Matt replied, already pulling out his phone.

Lauren nodded, focusing on the road ahead as the wipers battled the relentless rain. Summer solstice, 1996. A beach party. A mysterious boy. And a young woman who never came home.

The pieces were there, scattered across three decades. Now they just had to put them together.

TEN

MONDAY 26 MAY

'Pengelly,' Lauren said, answering the phone as it rang on her desk that morning.

'Ma'am.'

'Yes, John?' she asked, recognising the desk sergeant's voice.

'Thought you'd want to know a body's been found at Logan Rock. The victim's been reported as Eleanor Trewin.'

Lauren's hand tightened on the handset. 'The director from the dig?'

'Yes. She was found by someone who knew her. She must have jumped.'

'We don't want to jump to any conclusions yet,' Lauren said, suddenly realising she'd inadvertently made a pun. 'Right, leave it with me. We'll go out there shortly. Has the pathologist been contacted?'

'Yes, ma'am.'

Lauren replaced the phone, her mind already racing. Eleanor Trewin dead. Had she taken her own life? And if so, why?

She stood up from her desk, smoothing down her jacket as she mentally prepared for what might lie ahead, and headed into the main office.

'Attention please, everyone,' she called out, her voice carrying across the office. 'Dr Trewin has been found dead at Logan Rock. It's been suggested that she took her own life, but we won't make any snap judgements until we have the full facts. Matt, we're going out there now.'

Lauren paused, watching as her team looked up from their various tasks, their expressions shifting from curiosity to serious attention. Matt left his desk and collected his jacket from the coat stand, his movements quick and efficient.

'Do you want us to look into her in more depth?' Clem asked.

'Yes, please. Where are we on Jayne Tregowan and Tyler Penhaligon?'

'I spoke to Tyler,' Jenna replied. 'He told me nothing more about Ruth than we already had from Kelly. Jayne's in Canada and I couldn't get any location other than that. But I'll keep trying.'

'Thanks. We'll be back later.'

As she drove to Logan Rock, Lauren's thoughts kept returning to what little she knew about Eleanor Trewin. A dedicated archaeologist, passionate about her work and seemingly devoted to the dig site. Not the typical profile for someone who'd take their own life, but then again, people often surprised you.

When they arrived, there was already a cordon around the area and a police officer on duty.

'Good morning, Jade,' Lauren said as they made their way over to the officer and signed themselves in.

'Hello, ma'am. Sarge.'

'Has the pathologist arrived yet?'

'Yes, he literally turned up a few minutes ago. He's gone to see the body, which landed on some rock formations. It's a bit precarious and there's not much space so I'm not sure if you'll be able to get right down there, too.'

'Thanks. We'll look from above and call down. Dr Carpenter, I hope.'

'Yes, ma'am.'

'Good. Where's the person who found the body?'

'Over there, ma'am.' Jade pointed to a woman standing apart from the small crowd that had gathered.

Lauren followed Jade's gesture and spotted Verity Crowther, who appeared visibly shaken. Her arms were wrapped tightly around her middle, despite the mild morning temperature.

'Have you spoken to her?'

'Not in any detail, ma'am. All I know is that she was out on her regular morning walk and spotted the body lying on the rocks. It wasn't until she got closer that she recognised it was Dr Trewin. She's formally identified the victim for us.'

'I see. Don't let her leave because we'll be back to speak to her shortly.'

'Yes, ma'am.'

Lauren gestured to Matt, and they carefully made their way to the cliff edge and peered over.

'Good morning, Henry,' she called out.

Henry looked up, his usually jovial face creased with concentration. 'Is it? Why is it every time I get called out, I'm halfway through my breakfast? You know, it's beginning to get irritating.'

Lauren managed a small smile despite the situation. 'Sorry. We won't keep you. Is it looking like the victim took her own life?'

Henry straightened, fixing her with a stern look. 'You should know better than to ask that. I don't make assumptions of that nature without first making a full examination of the body.'

Despite everything, Lauren couldn't help but smile at the familiar exchange.

'Point taken. Do you have *anything* to tell me?'

'There's something here requiring further investigation.'

Lauren's pulse quickened. 'What might that be?'

Henry paused, as if weighing up his words carefully. 'There's some bruising around the neck that seems unlikely to have been caused by the fall or hitting rocks sticking out. But I need to get a closer look once the body's at the morgue.'

Lauren leant over slightly and held her hand up to her forehead to block out the sun, hoping to study the body more closely.

But it wasn't easy from their distance. All she could see was that Eleanor Trewin's once-vibrant face was pale and still, her eyes closed. The bruising Henry mentioned wasn't visible.

'So she might or might not have taken her own life,' Lauren confirmed.

'Yes. That's all I've got for you until getting the body on the table. As soon as I have anything you'll hear from me.'

Lauren turned to Matt, catching the doubt flickering across his face.

'You do know what this could mean, don't you?' she said quietly.

'Yes. It's entirely possible we'll be looking at a second murder. Do you think the deaths could be connected?' Matt asked, with a frown.

'Nothing so far is pointing to that,' Lauren said, sharply.

Matt's frown deepened. 'But if they are—'

'They're not until we have evidence.' Lauren's jaw tightened. 'We don't have the resources to be chasing shadows.'

'And if we're wrong? If we miss something because we didn't want to see it?' Matt pushed.

'Then we deal with it. But right now, we have two separate cases and no resources for even those.' Lauren turned to the cliff's edge. 'Have you any idea how long the body's been lying there, Henry?'

'Hmmm. At a rough guess, at least twelve hours,' the pathologist replied.

'So we're saying this happened on Sunday night, at around ten or eleven?'

'Quite possibly, judging by the state of the body. But, at the risk of repeating myself several times, you'll have more details once we've got her back at the morgue and I've done the postmortem.'

Lauren could just about make out the usually affable Henry rolling his eyes. They'd better leave him to get on.

'Thanks, Henry. Come on, Matt, let's find out what Verity Crowther knows.'

They left the cliff edge and headed over to Verity, who was standing alone, looking like a deer caught in headlights. Her face was pale, and she was wringing her hands nervously.

'Hello,' Verity whispered when they got close.

'Good morning, Verity. We're very sorry for your loss,' Lauren said, softly. 'You noticed Eleanor on the rocks, didn't you?'

'Yes,' Verity replied, her voice shaky. 'I can't believe Eleanor would jump. I know she was upset about the dig being closed for a while and that she was worried about losing our funding, but she didn't seem depressed or unhappy.'

Lauren studied Verity's face, looking for any signs of deception or knowledge she might be holding back. The woman appeared genuinely distressed, and her eyes were red-rimmed as if she'd been crying.

'Do you know if Eleanor was worried about anything else going on in her life?' Lauren asked.

Verity glanced down at her hands before speaking. 'You know, it's hard to say because Eleanor always kept herself to herself. But honestly, I just... I can't believe she'd do such a thing.'

'Well, the pathologist's down there now, and we'll find out a little bit more once he's completed his investigation. You can leave now, but before you do, did you notice whether there was anyone else hanging around when you spotted Eleanor?'

'No there wasn't. I always go for an early walk along the coastline in the morning because it's so peaceful. It helps clear my head, especially now we're not working. I happened to glance down at the rocks and saw something but couldn't work out what it was. I moved closer to the cliff edge to get a better look and saw it was a body. Then I looked again and saw it was Eleanor, which is when I phoned the police.'

'Have you let the other dig members know?'

'No. I waited here like the police asked me to. Do you want me to tell them?'

'Yes, please. We'll need to question you all again, so please ask them to stay in the area.'

'Was asking her to inform the others wise?' Matt asked, as Verity moved away.

Lauren gazed out at the sea, the morning light dancing on the waves. 'I think so because we won't speak to them until we have something conclusive on the bruising. We don't want them finding out from the media, because it's bound to leak – as most things do here.'

Lauren took one last look at the scene, committing every detail to memory. The rocky outcrop, the churning sea below, the place where Eleanor Trewin had taken her final breath, whether by her own hand or someone else's.

'Matt,' she said as they reached the car, 'phone the office and ask them to start background checks on everyone associated with the dig. Financial records, personal relationships, professional disputes. The works. Whatever the cause of death turns out to be, we'll need this information.'

Matt stared at Lauren gripping the steering wheel on their drive back to the station from Logan Rock, her eyes wide and focused on the road ahead. It was obvious by the tightness of her jaw that the case wasn't sitting right with her.

'You're thinking if Eleanor Trewin didn't take her own life, then why was she murdered,' he said.

It wasn't really a question because he knew his boss well, and he'd been deliberating on the exact same thing.

'Yes,' Lauren replied, her voice tight. 'The more I think about it the more I believe that she didn't throw herself off that cliff. If she wanted to end her life there would have been far less painful methods.'

Matt nodded. 'So we're looking at murder. The questions now are why and who?'

'We need a detailed look into her life. Hopefully the team will have something when we get back. What was going on both professionally and personally? Was anyone threatened by her for any reason? Who was able to get this close enough to her to do this?'

'They'll have something for us by now, for sure,' Matt observed, undoing his seatbelt as they drove into the station car park and came to a halt.

They entered through the front entrance and headed for the main office, which was buzzing with activity. It was almost tangible. The team had clearly been working hard while they were gone.

'Right, what have we got?' Lauren called out as they entered, immediately commanding the room's attention.

Clem looked up first. 'I've got some background info on Eleanor Trewin. She divorced three years ago and it was pretty messy from what I can gather. She kept the house in Exeter, but the husband got a decent settlement.'

'Any kids?' Lauren asked, heading closer to Clem's desk.

'One daughter, Betsy,' Jenna chimed in, replacing the phone she'd been holding on the handset. 'She's married and lives in Australia. I've been trying to reach her, but it's the middle of the night there. I've left a message on her mobile to contact me.'

Lauren's expression tightened slightly. Informing the family was always the worst part of the job, especially when they were on the other side of the world.

'What do we know about Eleanor's living situation?' Lauren asked.

Tamsin looked up from her computer. 'She's renting a cottage here in town for the duration of the dig, that's being paid for as part of her salary. She doesn't pay it directly from her own account. It comes from the dig funds. She's been there fifteen months so far. Her own property in Exeter is currently being let out.' She tapped the screen. 'According to this map, the cottage is about a ten-minute drive from the dig site.'

'I've spoken to the landlord and he's leaving the keys for you,' Billy added. 'They'll be around the back under a flowerpot.'

'Very secure,' Matt said, shaking his head. He still couldn't get used to how casual people were around here. So different from Lenchester.

'It'll be fine,' Clem said with a reassuring nod.

'He said to lock up and take the keys with you,' Billy added. 'I explained it might be a crime scene and we'll need permanent access.'

'Good thinking,' Matt said. 'Any joy on Eleanor's phone records?' he added, knowing they could be crucial.

'I'm working on it,' Jenna replied. 'But it's tricky without her mobile. Having said that, I'm hoping for something by this afternoon. Same with bank statements and credit card activity.'

'Matt, let's head over to the cottage now,' Lauren said. 'While we're out, the rest of you keep digging.' She paused, then added, 'Someone needs to stay late to catch the daughter when Australia wakes up. I want her informed properly, and not find out from social media, or friends and relatives contacting her.'

'I'll handle that,' Jenna volunteered. 'Especially as I left my name on the message. I'll keep trying until I reach her.'

The drive to the cottage was short. It was in an older part of town, set back from the main road behind a small garden that hadn't seen much attention lately. It was built of local stone, probably from the early 1800s, and had small windows and a low wooden door painted in a dark green.

They went around the back and found the keys under a flowerpot, as instructed.

Matt pulled on his gloves as Lauren unlocked the door. The smell hit him immediately. It wasn't unpleasant, but definitely lived in. Cooking, coffee, and something faintly floral. The front door opened directly into a cosy living room, furnished with mismatched but comfortable-looking furniture.

'Right,' Lauren said. 'You take upstairs; I'll start down here. We're looking for anything that might tell us who wanted Eleanor dead. Letters, emails, signs of conflict, anything unusual.'

Matt nodded and made his way up the narrow staircase, the wooden steps creaking under his weight. Upstairs, there were two bedrooms and a bathroom. The smaller bedroom had been converted into a study, and had a desk positioned under the window.

He started with the desk, methodically going through drawers. Eleanor Trewin was well organised. Each drawer had dividers, and labelled, colour-coded files. Everything in there was related to the dig and comprised site maps, artefact catalogues and correspondence with museums and funding bodies.

But something struck him as odd. There was a charging cable on the desk and a printer still plugged in. Also there was a note reminding her to upload photos and email a report to the university and the funding body. Yet there was no laptop in sight.

'Can you see her laptop down there?' he called out, after stepping out of the bedroom and standing at the top of the stairs.

'Ummm, I don't think so. Wait while I check the kitchen,' Lauren replied. 'No, it's definitely not here,' she said after a short while.

'Well, it's missing then, judging by what's up here. Unless it's in her car, which we'll need to check. I assume it's hers that's parked in the drive.'

'Hang on, I'll come upstairs.'

Her footsteps echoed on the stairs as he continued scanning.

'Look,' he said when Lauren appeared in the doorway. 'Cables, notes, printer. A whole desk setup for working. But no laptop. It's got to be relevant.'

'I agree,' Lauren said.

'Did you find her phone, by any chance?' Matt asked.

'No. I found a drawer with bills in it and nothing much else. But I expect she might have had her phone on her. We have to assume that someone stole her laptop. Someone who didn't want us to see what was on them.'

'Let's check the car; did you see any keys?'

'There are some on a hook near the front door. Let's check.'

They went downstairs and took the car keys and headed outside. Once the car was opened, they searched inside.

'Definitely no laptop,' Matt said with a sigh. 'Has it been

stolen? Did her murderer come to the house and they went for a walk together? Or was she killed here and then her body was taken to Logan Rock and thrown over?'

'That's assuming that she was murdered. We still need to hear back from Henry,' Lauren cautioned.

'True,' Matt said with a nod. But he was still convinced that Eleanor's laptop had been deliberately taken. Hopefully by tomorrow they'd have Henry's report.

TWELVE

TUESDAY 27 MAY

Matt pushed open the door to the morgue with a heavy sigh and Lauren followed silently behind him.

The fluorescent lights buzzed overhead, casting everything in that characteristic sickly green-white glow that made even the living look half-dead.

'Are you okay?' Lauren asked in a low voice.

'Same as always when I come into here,' Matt said with a forced grin. 'But I'll survive.'

Henry had summoned them to the morgue first thing that morning so he could brief them on his findings, before submitting the official report.

As they entered, Matt spotted Henry sitting at his desk, hunched over a computer, his fingers dancing rapidly across the keyboard.

'Morning, Henry,' Matt called out, keeping his tone light despite the gravity of the situation.

Henry glanced up, his half-moon glasses sliding slightly down his nose, and smiled. His grey hair was dishevelled, suggesting he'd been working for hours already.

'Excellent. You're here,' Henry said, standing up and stretching his back. 'I was proofreading my report, before forwarding it to the coroner, but knew you wanted to know everything straight away.'

'Thanks, Henry, we appreciate it,' Lauren said, stepping forward.

The pathologist nodded, grabbed his white lab coat from the coat stand and pulled it on. Henry had been doing this job for much longer than Matt had been a detective, and they had total confidence in his findings.

Henry led them into the main part of the morgue and Matt tensed as they approached the stainless-steel table in the middle of the room where Eleanor's body lay uncovered, revealing the Y-shaped incision on her chest, from the post-mortem examination.

'Right,' Henry began, his voice shifting into professional mode. 'As I suspected, the victim was dead before she actually fell from the cliff.'

A chill ran down Matt's spine. It confirmed their suspicion that Eleanor's death wasn't an accident. He exchanged a quick glance with Lauren, whose expression had darkened at the news.

'What evidence do you have for this?' Lauren asked, her voice steady despite the grim confirmation.

Henry moved around to the head of the table. 'Can you see the regular patterned bruising on the neck?'

Matt leant in closer, his eyes narrowing as he saw the discoloration on Eleanor's neck. The pattern was unmistakable. 'Yes, I see it.'

'They're fingerprints,' Henry continued, gesturing with a gloved hand. 'I believe she was asphyxiated before being thrown over.'

Matt's jaw tightened. Asphyxiation was personal. It required proximity, strength, and determination. Whoever killed Eleanor had looked her in the eyes as they did it.

'There are other wounds on her as well,' Henry added, pointing to her head. 'But they'd have occurred as she bounced against the rocks on her way down.'

'Can you tell whether the asphyxiation was carried out close to where she fell?' Lauren asked, frowning in concentration.

Henry's eyebrows rose slightly. 'Good question, and actually, yes, I believe so.' He adjusted his glasses and pointed to the bruising on Eleanor's neck. 'In the bruising caused by the fingers, there are little speckled marks which would have been from grains of sand. These are also on the back of the neck from where she'd been lying on the ground. And she didn't appear to have been moved from the time of death, which I put at between eleven pm and one am on Sunday night.'

'So she was on the ground when strangled?' Matt confirmed. 'Are there any other restraining marks?'

'There's slight bruising on either side of her hips where whoever did this to her was restraining her with their legs.'

Matt's stomach clenched at the image this conjured. He rubbed his temples, processing the brutality of what had happened to Eleanor. Lauren shifted her weight beside him, her arms crossing defensively as she listened.

'They'd have to be strong,' Matt added. 'Although Eleanor was slightly built. But even so. Do you believe it to be a man who did this? Can you tell that from the size of the fingerprints?'

Henry hesitated, examining the bruising pattern again. His fingers hovered over the marks without touching them, and Matt noticed the slight tremor in the pathologist's usually steady hands. Even after all these years, cases like this still appeared to affect him.

'Not really. The prints weren't huge, but equally, they weren't tiny. I can't be more specific on that. Sorry. You're right that it would have involved considerable strength to not only restrain the victim using legs, but to then strangle her. With that in mind, I'd suggest the murderer is most likely to be male. But it isn't a firm conclusion and won't be in my report.'

Lauren uncrossed her arms and stepped closer to the table, her brow furrowed as she studied Eleanor's face. 'What about defensive wounds? Did she fight back?'

Henry shook his head slowly. 'Nothing under her fingernails, and no scratches on her hands or arms that would suggest she'd managed to claw at her attacker. It's possible she was taken by surprise, or...' He paused, glancing between Matt and Lauren.

'Or what?' Matt prompted, though he suspected he knew where Henry was going with this.

'Or she knew her attacker well enough that she didn't expect the assault until it was too late to defend herself.'

The words hung heavy in the air and Matt ran a hand through his hair, feeling the familiar weight of a case becoming more complex by the minute. Lauren's lips pressed into a thin line, and he could see her mind already working through the implications.

'Understood,' Matt said. 'You didn't by any chance find her phone, did you?'

'It might give us some insight into her movements before she died, who she was in contact with,' Lauren added.

'Yes, I did,' Henry replied, gesturing to the side of the room. 'It was in her pocket, soaking wet and damaged. It's in a bag over there.'

Matt walked over and picked up the sealed evidence bag containing Eleanor's mobile, turning it over in his hands. The screen was shattered and it was visibly water-damaged, likely from the sea spray coming up from the base of the cliffs. Through the cracked glass, he could make out the remnants of what looked like text message notifications, but the display was too damaged to read anything clearly.

'Thanks, Henry,' he said, pocketing the bagged phone. 'Forensics might be able to do something with it.' He turned back towards Lauren, who was staring ahead, a frown on her face.

Matt could see the wheels turning in her mind, the way she tilted her head slightly when she was piecing things together. It was a habit he'd noticed in their two and a half years of working together.

'We'd better be going. Thanks for the update, Henry,' Lauren said.

'You're welcome,' Henry said as he pulled the sheet up over the body, his movements respectful despite having performed this ritual thousands of times. There was something almost ceremonial about it, a final dignity afforded to Eleanor after the violence she'd endured.

Matt followed Lauren to the door, and once outside, he took a deep breath of the corridor air, grateful to be away from the antiseptic smell and harsh lighting of the morgue. Lauren was already several steps ahead, her pace quick and purposeful.

'What's our next move?' he asked, catching up with her.

Lauren slowed her stride and glanced at him, her expression thoughtful. 'First, we need to get that phone to forensics. Then build a timeline for Eleanor's last known movements.'

THIRTEEN

TUESDAY 27 MAY

The wipers squeaked rhythmically across the windscreen as Lauren guided her car through the narrow Cornish lanes in the direction of the station.

Matt's phone pinged, breaking the thoughtful silence that had settled between them and Lauren glanced over as he checked the message, noting how his eyes lit up with interest.

'I've had a text from Jenna,' Matt said, sitting up straighter in his seat. 'Ruth Penrose's sister has called. She's arrived home – and said that she kept Ruth's diary from all those years ago, if we'd like to call around to collect it. Shall we go now?'

A surge of anticipation coursed through Lauren. A diary could provide invaluable insights into Ruth's final days.

'I suppose we can, except that Ruth's case might have to take a back seat now we have Eleanor's death to investigate.'

'It's not too far out of our way, and the deaths could be linked, even if we have no evidence of this,' Matt pushed.

'You're right. Let's go now. Where exactly does she live?'

'It's not far from here, in Penzance. Turn left at the next junction. We're heading for Tremethick Cross.'

'I know it,' Lauren confirmed.

The landscape gradually transformed around them. Rolling

hills giving way to glimpses of the sea between gaps in the hedgerows. The rain began to ease and sunlight broke through the clouds, casting dappled patterns on the wet road ahead.

They drove the short distance in companionable silence, until reaching the small hamlet. Lauren slowed the car as they entered the cluster of cottages, looking for the address Jenna had provided. At the far end, standing slightly apart from the others, was a white-washed detached cottage perched on a rise that offered an unob-structed view of the ocean beyond.

'This is lovely,' Matt commented as Lauren pulled up outside.

Lauren took in the picturesque scene. The quaint cottage with its slate roof, the neatly tended garden with early summer flowers bobbing in the breeze, and the panoramic vista of the Atlantic stretching to the horizon.

'Yes, it is,' she agreed, a momentary pang at the beauty of it all hitting her, which seemed at odds with the unpleasant nature of their visit.

She parked the car carefully on the narrow lane and switched off the engine. As they approached the front door, Lauren took stock of the property, noting the well-maintained exterior, freshly painted window frames, and a collection of shells arranged artfully on the windowsill. It was clearly a well-cared-for home.

What would Ruth have thought of her sister's life now? Lauren wondered as Matt knocked firmly on the blue-painted door. Would she have ended up somewhere similar if she was alive?

The door opened to reveal a woman in her forties with dark hair cut into a short bob. She looked remarkably like the photographs Lauren had seen of Ruth. She had the same high cheekbones and wide-set eyes, though time had etched fine lines around them. She wore a casual outfit of jeans and a deep blue sweater that almost matched the door, and her expression was expectant but guarded.

'Are you Jasmine Penrose?' Lauren asked, instinctively taking the lead.

'Yes, that's me,' the woman replied, in a soft Cornish lilt.

Lauren reached for her warrant card, showing it to Jasmine. 'We're from Penzance CID. I'm DI Pengelly, and this is DS Price. You phoned the office. We'd like to speak to you, if that's okay.'

Jasmine's posture relaxed slightly at the confirmation of their identities. 'Yes, of course. I was expecting you.' She stepped back, opening the door wider. 'Come on in. I've just put the kettle on, if you'd like a cup of tea?'

'Yes, please,' Lauren said, appreciating the offer.

They followed Jasmine into the cottage. The hallway was lined with framed photographs of family gatherings, holidays and celebrations. Lauren glimpsed at what appeared to be older photos, wondering if any featured Ruth, but they moved too quickly for her to study them properly.

The kitchen was surprisingly modern, with its granite worktops and sleek cupboards, when compared with the traditional exterior of the cottage.

'Shall we sit in the conservatory?' Jasmine suggested, gesturing towards the space visible beyond the kitchen.

'Oh, yes, that would be lovely,' Lauren replied.

They wandered through to the conservatory, a bright, airy addition to the back of the cottage with comfortable wicker furniture and potted plants creating a garden-like atmosphere. The large windows offered a spectacular view of the rugged scenery.

Lauren chose a seat that allowed her to face both Jasmine and the view, settling into the cushioned chair as Jasmine returned to the kitchen to prepare the tea. Matt sat across from her, his expression thoughtful.

Jasmine soon returned with a tray bearing a teapot, cups, milk and sugar, and a plate of homemade biscuits. After handing out the tea and sitting down, Jasmine reached for a small book that had been placed on a side table.

'This is Ruth's diary,' she said, holding it carefully, almost reverently, in her hands. 'After she disappeared, I took it as a reminder. It was my only link to her.'

It was a small, well-worn book with a faded floral cover, its edges softened with age and handling.

'Have you read it?' Matt asked gently.

Jasmine nodded, a shadow passing across her features. 'Yes. Many times over the years.' She paused, turning the diary over in her hands before continuing. 'I guess you'll be interested in the last entry she made on the day she went missing.'

'Yes, we would, please,' Lauren responded.

The woman opened the diary, flipping through the pages with the familiarity of someone who had revisited them many times. 'Here it is. This is the last entry my sister ever made.'

Lauren leant in slightly, as Jasmine handed her the diary. The handwriting was youthful, somewhat untidy, with certain words underlined or emphasised with double exclamation marks and hearts instead of a dot over many of the lower case 'I's.

'She mentions going to a solstice gathering on the beath, which we already know about, and also she hopes to see Davy.' Lauren looked up, meeting Jasmine's eyes. 'Do you know this person?'

Jasmine shook her head, a flicker of regret crossing her face. 'I'm sorry, I don't. The only Davy I knew was our uncle. Well, we called him Uncle Davy but he was my parents' friend. He died of prostate cancer a few months before Ruth went missing.'

'Did Ruth bring home anyone called Davy?' Lauren pressed gently.

Jasmine sipped her tea before answering, her expression thoughtful. 'I don't remember Ruth bringing any boyfriends home, to be perfectly honest. Dad was very strict about things like that.' A sad smile crossed her face. 'Not that it bothered Ruth – she was free-spirited, as I'm sure you've already discovered.'

Lauren detected no judgement in Jasmine's tone, just a state-ment of fact, possibly tinged with a sister's affectionate acceptance of her sibling.

'Did anyone tell the police about this Davy?' Lauren asked, careful to keep her tone conversational rather than accusatory.

Jasmine's expression hardened slightly. 'Yes, I mentioned it, but they dismissed it. They'd already decided that Ruth had run away from home because that's what she'd done before.' She set her cup down with a little more force than necessary. 'Ruth was only young, and yeah, she'd been a bit of a handful for Mum and Dad, but because she was sixteen, she was legally allowed to leave home. And that's what the police thought.'

Lauren nodded sympathetically, understanding the frustration of having concerns dismissed. It often happened in cases of missing teenagers, especially those with a history of running away, that it wasn't investigated properly. Especially in the past, before CCTV or mobile phones.

'Did you show the diary to your mum and dad?' Matt asked.

'I told them I'd got it, and mentioned this Davy, but they didn't know anything about him.' Jasmine shrugged slightly. 'You know, he could just be someone she fancied at the time and wasn't even seeing. It's what teenage girls often do.'

Lauren studied the diary entry again, trying to read between the lines of Ruth's words. There was an excitement in the writing about this 'Davy'. Did that mean it was more than a passing crush?

Lauren carefully placed the diary on the coffee table between them. 'Is there anything else that you can tell us about Ruth? Anything that might help us understand what happened to her?'

Jasmine's eyes grew distant, looking past them to the hills beyond the windows. 'Well, she was a great older sister; and always looked out for me. Yes, I know she was always getting in trouble, but that doesn't mean she didn't care.' Her voice caught slightly on the last word, and her hands tightened into fists. Despite the decades that had passed, the wound of losing her sister was clearly still raw. 'It's awful that her bones have been... that she's been lying there in the ground for so long,' Jasmine continued after a moment, her voice steadier. 'But at least we can have some closure now.'

Closure. Lauren turned the word over in her mind. It was what families always said they wanted, but in her experience, learning that a missing loved one was dead rarely brought the peace they hoped for. Instead, it often opened new wounds, new questions about suffering and justice.

'May I ask,' Lauren began carefully. 'What was Ruth like as a person? Beyond being wayward or troublesome. Who was she to you?'

Understanding victims as people often provided insights that other types of questioning might not. Lauren was genuinely curious about the sixteen-year-old girl.

Jasmine seemed surprised by the question, and blinked rapidly as she considered it. A soft smile gradually spread across her face.

'She was... vibrant,' she said finally. 'Everything with Ruth was intense. When she was happy, the whole house seemed brighter. When she was angry, well, you'd best stay out of her way.' Jasmine laughed softly at some private memory. 'She loved music and would save up her pocket money for weeks to buy CDs which she'd play at full volume until Dad threatened to break the CD player.'

Lauren nodded encouragingly, watching as Jasmine's expression grew more animated.

'She was clever, too. Although you wouldn't know it from her school reports. The teachers always said she wasn't applying herself, but the truth was, she wasn't interested in what they were teaching. She could tell you everything about the planets and stars, though. She taught herself astronomy from library books and would drag me outside on clear nights to look at constellations.'

An intelligent teenager, who wouldn't conform. Hardly unusual, but it painted a different picture than the 'troublemaker' narrative that had dominated the original investigation.

'What about friends?' Lauren asked. 'Who did she spend time with?'

Jasmine's brow furrowed in concentration. 'There was a girl... Kelly, I think. They were close for a while. And a boy called Tyler.' She sighed. 'I'm sorry, it was so long ago, and I was younger. I didn't pay that much attention to who she was hanging around with.'

'That's perfectly understandable,' Lauren reassured her. 'We've already been in contact with them. Do you know anything about the solstice gathering on the beach mentioned in the diary?'

'Not that particular beach gathering. But people around here do meet up on the solstice to watch the sunrise and sunset. It's a thing. I know Ruth went the year before she went missing.'

'Did they always meet at the beach?' Lauren asked, making a mental note for them to check the previous year to see if anyone remembered Ruth being there.

'I don't think so. Often, they'd stand by the cliffs and watch. I've never been myself. I couldn't face it, not after it being the date that Ruth went missing.'

'I totally understand,' Lauren said with a nod. 'I hope you don't mind me asking, but we're now investigating the death of Eleanor Trewin, the director of the dig where Ruth was found. We don't have any evidence linking her death to Ruth's but I wondered whether Ruth had any connection to archaeology or any interest in historical sites.'

Jasmine's eyes widened slightly, surprise evident in her expression. 'Eleanor Trewin? I saw her on the news talking about finding Ruth's remains. I don't remember Ruth being interested in history. She preferred the present to the past. Although she did like stories about old places. The legends and myths. Our grandma used to tell us tales about stone circles and ancient people.'

'Would it be possible for us to take the diary with us?' Lauren asked. 'It could be important evidence, and we promise to take good care of it.'

'Ummm...' Jasmine hesitated, picking up the diary from the table, her fingers lingering on the worn cover. Lauren understood her reluctance. The diary was a tangible connection to the sister she'd lost.

'We'll return it to you as soon as we've finished with it,' Lauren offered gently. 'I promise.'

After a moment, Jasmine nodded. 'Yes, that would be fine. Of course. If it's going to help you find out what happened to Ruth.' She handed the diary to Lauren.

'Thank you. This could be very helpful in understanding the events of Ruth's last night.'

Jasmine nodded, her gaze drifting back to the outside view. 'It's strange, you know. All these years I've wondered, and now suddenly there are answers, but they only lead to more questions.' She turned back to face them, her expression resolute. 'If there's anything else I can do to help, please let me know. I want to understand what happened to my sister.'

Lauren placed the diary carefully in an evidence bag. 'We'll do everything we can to find those answers, Jasmine. I promise you that.'

As they prepared to leave, Jasmine led them back through the cottage. In the hallway, Lauren paused by one of the framed photographs she'd noticed earlier. A teenage girl with wild, dark hair and a defiant smile. Her arm was slung around a younger Jasmine.

'Is this Ruth?' she asked, though she already knew the answer.

Jasmine smiled sadly. 'Yes, that was about six months before she disappeared. Our last family holiday in Devon.'

Lauren studied the image, committing it to memory. Not just as evidence, but as a reminder of who Ruth Penrose had been. A vibrant teenager with her whole life ahead of her. Not just bones discovered in a shallow grave decades later.

'Thank you for your time and the tea,' Lauren said as they reached the front door. 'We'll be in touch if we need anything further. And, of course, we'll let you know of any developments in the case.'

'I appreciate that,' Jasmine replied, standing in the doorway as they stepped outside.

Walking back to the car, Lauren's thoughts were on the diary. Inside were the last written words of a girl who had disappeared decades ago, words that might now help solve not one but two murders.

'Do you now want to investigate Ruth's death at the same time as Eleanor's?' Matt asked as they settled back into the car.

Lauren started the engine. 'We'll try, but only if it doesn't interfere in Eleanor's, as that's our priority. I'd certainly like to identify this Davy character.'

She pulled away from the cottage, catching a final glimpse of Jasmine still standing in the doorway, a solitary figure framed against the white walls of her home.

'The original investigation was clearly inadequate,' Lauren continued, her tone hardening slightly. 'They wrote Ruth off as a runaway because it was convenient. Because she'd done it before. If they'd taken the diary's existence seriously, they might have tried to find this Davy.'

Matt nodded in agreement. 'Classic case of confirmation bias. They decided what happened and only paid attention to evidence that supported their theory.'

'Well, we won't make the same mistake,' Lauren said firmly, accelerating as they rejoined the main road. 'Ruth Penrose deserves better than that.'

FOURTEEN
TUESDAY 27 MAY

The early afternoon sun streamed through the windows, casting bright patches across the worn floor as Matt and Lauren arrived back at the station.

'Attention, everyone,' Lauren called out as they walked through the door into the office. 'Henry's confirmed that Eleanor Trewin was murdered before she was thrown from the cliff, and we now have Ruth's diary, which mentions someone named Davy. Jasmine, Ruth's sister, seemed genuinely eager to help. After all these years, she still wants answers. As do we all. But I realise we can't do everything. Eleanor's death takes priority, but where possible I want to investigate Ruth alongside it.'

'I can only speak for myself, but I don't mind putting in extra hours so we can run both cases. Ruth's family deserve it,' Clem said.

'Me, too,' added Billy.

'Likewise,' Jenna said.

'And me,' Tamsin echoed.

'It's good of you all, and we'll see how it goes,' Lauren replied, pride coursing through her at the commitment of her team.

'Could the deaths be linked, ma'am?' Clem asked.

'We have no evidence for this, but that doesn't mean we won't be mindful of the possibility. Now, I'd like feedback on what you've all found.'

'I'll go first,' Jenna said. 'We've looked into the backgrounds of everyone on the dig, and, so far, nothing untoward has come up. No criminal records. No financial issues, nothing. Sorry.' Jenna pulled a face.

'No need to apologise. It is what it is. We must start eliminating people. But before we call the team in for an interview, remind me about all of them.'

'Will do. Eleanor Trewin, as we know, was the dig director,' Jenna said. 'Then there's Liam Blackburn, the site supervisor. Naomi Walters, a field archaeologist specialising in Bronze Age artefacts. Verity Crowther's another field archaeologist. Adam Fielding's the archaeological illustrator and photographer and also a field archaeologist, and finally Scott Goodman is an environmental archaeologist. So each one has their own speciality.'

'Don't forget that Eleanor, Liam, Naomi, and Adam were at university together, so there could be history there,' Matt said.

'Yes,' Jenna acknowledged. 'Eleanor, Liam, and Naomi were in the same year. Adam was a year behind them.'

'We all know that with long-standing relationships, there's a potential for old conflicts and resentments to raise their heads,' Lauren said. 'It's certainly something to consider. Has anyone looked into their university days for anything untoward happening?'

'Me, ma'am,' Tamsin said. 'But so far, nothing stands out. They were all decent students and received good grades. Eleanor won a prize for academic excellence while she was there. I haven't come across any issues on the course. That doesn't mean there weren't any, but if there were, they were private and not on file.'

'What do we know about Verity Crowther and Scott Goodman?' Matt asked.

'Verity joined the dig about ten months ago. She previously worked at sites in Yorkshire. Scott's the newest member. He's only been with them about four months, coming from a dig in Wales.'

'Okay, so on the work front it all looks okay. Billy, the Cornish Preservation Foundation?' Lauren asked.

'I spoke to the manager who liaises with Eleanor on the dig, and he had no complaints. He's worked with Eleanor in the past and she's one of the better dig directors. Reports are sent in on time, and budgets kept to. He was shocked by the report of her death and offered any help should we need it.'

'So again, it points to work not being the potential motive. But we can't dismiss anything yet. What about personal relationships within the team?' Lauren asked, folding her arms and leaning against the edge of the whiteboard. 'Are there any romantic entanglements we should know about?'

'I don't know for sure, but photos I've found online posted recently, but showing when they were at uni, make it look as if Liam and Naomi were once in a relationship,' Tamsin said.

'We'll ask them about it,' Lauren said, with a sharp nod. 'We also need to find out if there are any other relationships. Past or present.'

'I wouldn't be surprised if there are some,' Clem said. 'These digs can be pretty isolating. People living and working in close quarters for weeks or months. They're also a perfect breeding ground for tension, even if on the surface everything seems okay.'

'For sure,' Lauren agreed. 'Has anything else come to light?'

'Yes, ma'am,' Billy said. 'I checked out the solstice gathering in 1996 and found a local newspaper report. It mostly confirms what we already knew. There was a gathering on the beach on the night of 20 June 1996. Mainly teenagers and university students, according to the reports. No major incidents reported, although there was a mention of noise complaints from nearby residents. I've printed off a copy.'

He handed it to Matt, who scanned the headline: *Summer Solstice Celebration Draws Crowd to Beach.*

'Did they name names?' Lauren asked.

'No,' Billy replied. 'But I did discover that a local band called Stone Shadows was playing that night. I'm trying to track down the members. It might be worth talking to them and seeing if they remember anything from the evening because presumably, they wouldn't be as wasted as the others if they were to continue playing for the whole evening.'

'Good work.' Matt nodded approvingly. 'Any photos from the event?'

'Just one grainy image,' Billy said, producing another printout. 'Not great quality, but you can see there was a decent-sized crowd.'

Matt studied the black and white image. It showed a group of perhaps fifty people gathered around a makeshift firepit on the beach. The quality was too poor to make out individual faces clearly, but it gave a sense of the atmosphere. Young people celebrating, some standing in groups drinking and some dancing to the band that was just visible at the edge of the frame.

A sudden exclamation drew their attention. Tamsin was staring at her computer screen, a broad smile spreading across her face.

'What is it, Tamsin?' Matt called out.

She looked up, beaming. 'I got onto the training programme. I'm going to be a FLO. Oh my goodness. I can't believe it.'

'That's fantastic,' Jenna exclaimed, congratulating her colleague.

Lauren and Matt followed, along with the rest of the team. Everyone seemed genuinely pleased for Tamsin.

'Well done, Tamsin. When does the training start?' Lauren asked.

'That's the thing,' Tamsin said, her smile faltering slightly. 'It's sooner than expected. Eight weeks from now.'

Billy looked up from his desk. 'That's quick. Who's going to replace you here? We're already stretched thin.'

'The position will be advertised,' Lauren said.

'I'm going to call Ellie, to see if she wants to apply,' Billy said, his cheeks going red.

Matt caught Lauren's eye, sharing a brief smile. Would Ellie be interested? If she was, how would Lauren take it? She hadn't objected to Billy and Ellie's relationship when they knew Ellie was only with them on secondment. This could be different.

'Sorry to bring you back on task,' Lauren said, her tone shifting to business. 'We want the remaining five dig team members in for an interview. But this time separately. I'd like to schedule them all for later today if we can.'

'We'll divvy up the calls to the dig team members,' Matt suggested. 'I'll give you all some suggested time slots so we don't overlap.'

'I'll take Liam and Naomi,' Clem offered.

'I can contact Verity and Scott,' Tamsin volunteered, the excitement in her voice indicating that she was still riding the high of her good news.

'That leaves Adam for me,' Matt concluded. 'Let's aim for this afternoon, starting at three, a thirty-minute slot for each of them.'

Clem looked up from his computer. 'I'll make sure the interview rooms are clear for the afternoon.'

'Let me know when they've arrived,' Lauren said, heading towards her office.

Matt returned to his desk and picked up his phone. He called the number in the file. After four rings, a male voice answered.

'Adam Fielding speaking.'

'This is Detective Sergeant Price from Penzance CID,' Matt began, keeping his tone professional. 'I'm calling about the investigation into Dr Trewin's death.'

There was a brief pause before Adam replied. 'Yes, of course. Have you... found something?'

Matt noted the hesitation. The slight catch in the man's voice. Grief? Anxiety? Something else entirely?

'We're making progress with our investigation,' Matt replied carefully. 'We'd like you to come to the Penzance police station this afternoon for a formal interview. Does three o'clock work for you?'

'An interview?' Adam sounded surprised.

'This is standard procedure as we develop our understanding

of the case,' Matt reassured him. 'We're interviewing all members of the dig team.'

Another pause, longer this time. 'Okay. Three's fine. Do I need to bring anything?'

'Just yourself,' Matt replied. 'When you arrive, report to the front desk and they'll let us know you're here.'

'I'll be there,' Adam agreed, sounding more controlled.

Matt ended the call and made a note in the system. He glanced at the other team members. Tamsin, who was still on a call, gave him a thumbs-up when she caught his eye.

'Liam and Naomi both confirmed for today,' Clem called over. 'Liam at three-thirty, Naomi at four.'

'Adam's coming at three,' Matt replied.

Tamsin hung up her phone. 'Scott's confirmed for four-thirty, and Verity for five.'

'Excellent.' Matt nodded. 'I'll update the DI.'

Matt headed to Lauren's office, stopping at the whiteboard on the way to study the photos, including the dig site where Eleanor had spent her final days.

'Poor Eleanor,' he muttered under his breath. 'What did you discover, or do, that got you killed?'

There was another section dedicated to Ruth Penrose. A school photograph of a teenage girl with wild dark hair and defiant eyes. A map marking where her remains had been found.

Two deaths. Decades apart. Surely they couldn't be connected.

FIFTEEN

TUESDAY 27 MAY

Lauren ushered Adam Fielding into the interview room, observing the hesitant way he walked. His wire-rimmed glasses caught the light as he looked around the sparse room and grimaced, the gravity of the situation appearing to hit him. Lauren had seen that look many times before.

'Please, take a seat,' Lauren said, gesturing to the dark green plastic chair across the table from them. 'Thank you for coming in, Adam. We're going to be recording this interview.' She nodded towards Matt, who started the recording equipment.

'Okay,' Adam replied, nervously adjusting his glasses. He placed his hands flat on the table, then seemed to reconsider and folded them precisely in his lap.

'Adam, we need to tell you something important about Eleanor's death,' Lauren said, keeping her eyes focused on him, so she could scrutinise his reaction. 'The postmortem has revealed that she was murdered. She didn't jump from those cliffs, as it first appeared. Someone strangled her and then threw her body over after she was dead.'

The colour drained from Adam's face and his mouth opened and closed twice before any sound emerged. 'Murdered?' he whispered. 'But... who would want to hurt Eleanor? She was...' He stopped abruptly, his jaw tightening. 'She was the most dedicated person I knew. She lived for her work.'

'I'm sorry for your loss,' Lauren said gently. 'We'd like to ask you some questions about Eleanor. What was she like to work with?'

Adam seemed to gather himself, though his hands remained clasped tightly in his lap. 'I assume you'll be verifying my answers with the rest of the team?'

'We will be speaking to all of them,' Lauren clarified.

'Eleanor was brilliant at her work. But...' He paused, as if searching for the right words. 'She didn't really let people get close. Everything was about the dig. The artefacts. The research. I don't think I ever heard her talk about anything else. There was never any chitchat.' His voice was oddly detached, as if discussing someone he'd barely known, rather than his murdered colleague whom he'd known for decades.

'Can you think of anyone who might have held a grudge against her?' Lauren asked.

Adam's eyes narrowed slightly behind his glasses. 'No. Why would they?'

'That's what we want to find out. Previous employees, maybe. Someone she'd upset along the way, intentional or otherwise.'

No,' Adam said, banging his hand on the table, but not in an aggressive manner. More to emphasise his point. Then he pulled his hand back, examining his fingers as if surprised by his own reaction. 'Definitely not.'

'What about outside of the dig? Are you aware of any financial or personal problems that Eleanor had?' Lauren continued.

'Not that she told me about. I'm sorry, but really Eleanor was hardworking and straight. I couldn't imagine anyone less likely to be murdered.' He shook his head and let out a long sigh. 'Though I suppose that's what everyone says in these situations, isn't it?'

'What was Eleanor like at university?'

Adam's posture shifted almost imperceptibly. 'She was one of the top students in her year. But she was also fun and not so serious as she ended up being.'

'What do you think caused this change in her personality?' Lauren asked, with a frown.

'I'm not a psychologist, so can hardly be expected to answer that question. All I will say is that although she took the work seriously, before she got married, she had time for fun. I was in the year below her but we all still hung out together in the student bar and at parties.'

'Did you know her husband?' Matt asked.

'No, I never met him. He's a professor at one of the London universities. I'm not sure of his discipline, though.' Adam's voice was carefully neutral, but a small muscle twitched in his jaw.

'That can't have been easy with her job,' Lauren said. 'If he was in London and she was in Exeter and also working on digs all over the place.'

She watched Adam's fingers briefly drum against his leg before he stilled them.

'It wasn't. I wouldn't be surprised if that's why they split up. But I don't know for sure; it's not something she told me.'

'Did Eleanor ever talk about the relationship with her husband?'

'No. Like I said before, she kept those things to herself.' Adam's response came a fraction too quick.

'Since Eleanor split from her husband, do you know whether she dated anyone?' Lauren asked, something about the man's demeanour giving rise to a hunch.

A flush crept up Adam's neck. 'Ummm.'

Ah ha. She knew it. Lauren exchanged a glance with Matt. They were onto something.

'Did *you* have a relationship with her?' Matt asked.

'Look... I'm married. Do you promise to keep secret what I tell you?' Adam's fingers grabbed the edge of the table.

'I can't promise anything if it relates to our enquiries,' Lauren replied, her voice flat. 'All I can say is we won't disclose anything that proves to be irrelevant. Although, from your answer I'm assuming that you did have a relationship with Eleanor.'

'Yes, but not for long,' Adam admitted, straightening in his chair as if preparing a defence he'd rehearsed.

'What ended it?'

'I did. I mean, it ended because...' Adam sighed heavily. 'Look, I don't want to sound mean, but dating Eleanor was like dating the excavation itself. Even when we were together, she was thinking about Bronze Age pottery or soil samples or budgets. It felt like I was constantly competing with work for her attention – and losing.'

'Are you sure she didn't discuss her husband and family with you?' Lauren asked. If they'd been seeing each other away from work then surely that would have come up at some time... even briefly.

'I told you, she never mentioned them,' Adam said, his gaze shifting slightly to the right. 'I know it seems weird but it's true. I can't tell you stuff that I don't know.' There was something defensive in the way he emphasised the last sentence, as if protecting himself from an accusation not yet made.

'Where were you on Sunday night between the hours of eleven and one in the morning?'

'In bed. Why?'

'Can anyone vouch for you?'

'No. I'd been home for the weekend and drove back. I arrived at my lodgings at around 10.30 pm and went straight to bed. Surely you don't think I had anything to do with Eleanor's death.'

'We're asking everyone, to eliminate them from our enquiries,' Matt answered.

Lauren pulled out a photograph from the folder she had in front of her. She'd brought it with her as an afterthought, remembering that there was the remote possibility that the cases could be linked. 'When you were at university in Exeter, do you remember the summer solstice celebration on 20 June 1996? There was a gathering on Pedn Vounder beach here in Cornwall.' She showed him the grainy photo of the party.

His expression shifted to surprise and he nodded slowly. 'Yes, I do remember that night. A big group of us from uni travelled there on the train. Why do you want to know?'

'Did Eleanor go?' Lauren continued, forcing her voice to remain calm, despite her pulse accelerating.

Up until now, she hadn't really believed it possible that the deaths could be linked, even though Matt and Clem suggested it. But this could be the break they needed, in both cases.

'Umm. Yes, I think she was there. Why?' he asked again.

Lauren slid Ruth Penrose's school photograph across the table. 'This is Ruth Penrose, whose bones were found at the dig. She disappeared that same night.'

Adam studied the image carefully, his brow furrowed in concentration. He took longer than necessary to answer. 'No. I'm sorry. Do you think this has something to do with Eleanor's death?'

'We don't know. But it's an avenue we're investigating. Do you remember a Davy or David who was at the party on the beach that night?'

Adam's shoulders tensed. 'I couldn't possibly remember everyone from a party nearly thirty years ago, especially as we'd been drinking.' He paused. 'But if you have a photo, I might be able to help. I've always had a good memory for faces.'

Was he deflecting? It was impossible to tell, but there was something about the clinical, almost academic, way he spoke that wasn't sitting right with Lauren.

'Unfortunately we don't. If that changes, we'll be sure to speak to you. Thanks for your time; that's all for now,' Lauren said, ushering him out of the office and escorting him to the entrance where she stood with Matt watching as he headed to a green VW Golf and drove off.

Lauren checked her watch. They had ten minutes until their next interview.

'Come on, let's go for a quick walk; I could do with some fresh air,' she said, heading out of the station and striding across the car park to the street. 'You know, I think there's more to Adam Fielding than meets the eye. Did you notice the subtle defensiveness in his responses?'

'Yes, I did. I also wondered whether he was telling the truth about his affair with Eleanor being over. It would certainly put him in the frame if they'd still being seeing each other when she died. Maybe she'd threatened to tell his wife. It wouldn't be the first time we have come across a situation like that,' Matt added, matching her strides.

'That's a good point. I hadn't considered that. I'm also thinking you're right that the two deaths are linked. It's too much of a coincidence for four members of the dig team to have been at the place where Ruth Penrose was last seen.'

'I—' Matt came to a halt as his phone rang. 'Price. Okay, thanks.' He ended the call and turned to Lauren. 'Liam Blackburn's arrived. He's being taken to interview room one.'

They turned and headed back to the station.

'Good afternoon, Liam,' Lauren said, as she pushed the door open. 'Thanks for coming in to see us.'

'No problem. I assume this is about Eleanor. I've been able to think of nothing else since Verity told me.' His voice cracked and he sniffed. 'Sorry. It's really hit me hard. I don't understand why she'd do something like that. I get that you can't always tell when someone's depressed... but not Eleanor. No way.'

'You're right about that,' Lauren said, keeping her voice soft. 'According to the pathologist's report, Eleanor didn't take her own life. She was murdered.'

'Murdered?' Liam's voice was rough with disbelief. 'Eleanor murdered?' He ran both hands through his hair, leaving it standing at odd angles. 'Why? It doesn't make sense.'

'Did Eleanor have any enemies that you know of?' Matt asked.

Liam shook his head emphatically. 'No. Eleanor was a loner. She kept everyone at arm's length.'

'Did you know that she dated Adam Fielding for a while?' Lauren asked, deciding that it was important enough to reveal.

'Liam's eyes widened. 'But Adam's married to Sonia. Are you

sure?' He sucked in a breath. 'You must think me very naive thinking that my colleagues wouldn't have an affair... It's just... I can't imagine him and Eleanor...'

'According to Adam it was only for a short time,' Lauren confirmed.

'Well, that doesn't make it right. Although, I thought she didn't have time for anything except her work. What do I know?'

'I'd like to show you a photo of the young girl whose remains were found at the dig,' Lauren said, pulling it out of the folder and sliding it over to him.

'Ruth... I don't recall her last name.' Liam studied it with the careful attention of someone accustomed to examining details but ultimately shook his head. 'Pretty girl. But sorry, I don't recognise her.'

'Do you remember the Pedn Vounder beach party during the summer solstice in 1996 when you were at Exeter university?'

A warm smile creased Liam's weathered features. 'Bloody hell, that takes me back. Yeah, I was there. Half the archaeology department turned up, I think. Eleanor was there, too. She was different then. More... normal, I suppose.'

'Normal how?' Lauren asked.

'Well, she was laughing a lot and telling jokes. Dancing around the bonfire with the rest of us. We were all drunk, including her. She didn't do much of that when she was older. More's the pity.'

'Do you remember a Davy or David being there?'

Liam shrugged. 'I don't recall anyone of that name with us from the university. They were the only people I knew there.' He glanced back down at Ruth's photo. 'Such a shame for someone so young to die. Do you have any idea what happened to her yet?'

'We're working on it,' Lauren said, neutrally. 'We're asking everyone for their movements on Sunday night from eleven until one in the morning?'

'Let me see,' Liam said, with a frown. 'Sunday. Well, I watched the match on telly, which finished at seven. Then I went to the pub to get something to eat and stayed there until around ten and then walked home. They can confirm that at the pub because I was chatting with the man behind the bar. Once I got home, I read in the chair for an hour and then went to bed. On my own. Does that help? I mean, it's not totally in the hours you asked but close enough.' He shrugged.

'That's fine, thanks,' Lauren said. 'Thanks for coming in. If you do think of anything that might help our inquiry into Eleanor's death, please contact us.' She handed him one of her cards and let him go.

In the intervening time before the next dig member came in, Lauren and Matt sat in the empty interview room.

'It's like pushing treacle uphill,' Matt said with a frustrated sigh. 'We need a proper clue. Something we can work with. Not to mention both Adam and Liam don't have cast-iron alibis for Eleanor's murder.'

'No investigation is easy, Matt. You should know that. At least now we're building up a picture of our victim and have also linked our two cases. We've still got three more people to go; something might turn up.'

SIXTEEN

TUESDAY 27 MAY

Naomi Walters arrived precisely on time. She was small with delicate features and her grey hair was short in a pixie style.

The news of Eleanor's death being categorised as murder appeared to hit her like a physical blow. She actually swayed in her chair, and one hand flew to her throat.

'No,' she breathed. 'No. That's not possible. Eleanor wouldn't hurt a fly. Who would...?' She couldn't finish the sentence.

Her reaction was almost over the top.

'Tell us about your relationship with Eleanor,' Lauren prompted gently, not wanting to give away her suspicion about the woman's response.

Naomi sucked in a breath. 'We weren't close. Not really. I mean, we've known each other for over thirty years but Eleanor didn't really do friendship. That doesn't mean we didn't get on because we did. But she was completely absorbed in her work. Sometimes I'd invite her for a drink after a long day on the dig, or suggest we grab dinner in the pub, but she always had reports to write or some other work-related tasks to attend to.'

'That must have been frustrating,' Matt observed.

'It would have been if not for others on the dig. It's not easy living away from home for months at a time. The rest of us would gather around someone's table in the evenings, sharing a bottle of wine, talking about anything except Bronze Age settlements. But Eleanor would always be in her cottage, working until all hours.'

The pattern was becoming undeniable. Eleanor Trewin had been a woman who lived entirely for her profession, cutting herself off from human connection in pursuit of academic excellence.

'You mentioned the other day about working overseas. Why did you return?' Lauren asked.

'Yes, I've spent much of my career working in Egypt and China but when I found out about the Treen dig and Eleanor approached me I couldn't resist. It was sort of like a trip down memory lane to work with the others again.' Naomi glanced away as if remembering time gone by.

'Did it work out as you'd hoped?' Lauren asked, scrutinising the woman's features for any tells that might indicate things weren't as she was making out.

Naomi cleared her throat. 'Of course things weren't as they were all those years ago. We've all grown up since then... but... yes... overall it's been good. Apart from now with what's happened to Eleanor.'

'Do you remember the solstice celebrations in 1996? You were there with the others, weren't you?'

Naomi's eyes widened in surprise. 'How did you know that? Yes, I was there. God, that feels like a lifetime ago.' A shadow of a smile crossed her features. 'Eleanor was there too. Having fun, like the rest of us.'

Lauren took out the photo of Ruth and handed it to Naomi. 'Do you recognise this girl from the beach party?'

'No, I don't. Should I?'

'This is Ruth Penrose, whose remains were found on the dig.'

'Oh, she's beautiful. So young. Such a waste.' Naomi shook her head slowly.

'She was last seen at the beach party. Is there anything about that night that stood out as being off?'

Naomi was quiet for a few seconds, as if she was reliving the evening. 'Sorry. Nothing. All I remember is it was a magical time. All of us young and stupid and thinking we knew everything about the ancient world.' Naomi's expression grew wistful. 'There was music, a band playing. And dancing. A fire. But I don't recall seeing Ruth there.'

'We're trying to trace a Davy or David from the party. Do you remember him?' Lauren asked.

Naomi frowned in concentration. 'There were loads of people there, and it was so long ago. I vaguely remember the name, I think. But can't tell you anything specific about him. I'm not being much help, am I?'

'Can you tell us what you were doing on Sunday night between the hours of eleven and one in the morning?'

'Yes. I was doing some online training on using software for modern landscape archaeology and heritage protection. I registered at the start so the training provider can verify it.'

'At night?' Lauren asked, not believing that anyone would offer a course during that time.

'The training was run from Australia,' Naomi said. 'I'll text you their details.'

'Ah. That makes more sense,' Lauren conceded. 'That's it for now. You're free to go, but please don't leave the area without first checking with us.'

The fourth interview was with Scott Goodman, the youngest member of the team and the newest addition to Eleanor's dig. His shock at learning of the murder was genuine but tinged with something else – a kind of awe at finding himself part of something so dramatic.

'I can't believe it,' he said, shaking his head repeatedly. 'I mean, Eleanor was intense... but murdered? Wow.'

'Intense how?' Lauren pursued.

'Just... completely focused on her work. I don't think she ever took a proper break. Even during lunch, she'd be reading journals or making notes. The rest of us would be joking around, and she'd be sitting there with her head buried in some research paper.'

Scott's description of Eleanor matched the others' perfectly. She was a woman isolated by her own dedication. Someone who had chosen professional achievement over personal connection.

'I tried to ask her about her life outside work once,' Scott continued. 'You know, just making conversation. But she looked at me like I'd asked something inappropriate. It was like having a personal life was somehow unprofessional.'

When shown Ruth's photograph, Scott studied it carefully but shook his head. 'Sorry, no. But then, I wasn't even born when she went missing, was I?'

Lauren smiled despite herself. 'No, you weren't.'

After ascertaining where Scott was at the time of Eleanor's murder, he was excused and Lauren and Matt prepared themselves for their final interview of the day with Verity Crowther.

The woman was in her forties, with messy, short grey hair. Her reaction to the murder revelation was different from the others. She didn't cry or gasp or make any other dramatic response. Instead, she simply closed her eyes for a while, her shoulders sagging as if a weight had settled on them.

'Poor Eleanor,' she said finally. 'She was so careful about everything. Security protocols, safety procedures, protecting the site. But she couldn't save herself.'

'What was she like to work with?' Matt asked.

'Professional. Always professional, as I'm sure the others have told you.' Verity's voice carried a note of sadness. 'I've worked with her since the start of the dig, and I don't think I knew a single thing about her personal life. She never mentioned her family, friends, hobbies, nothing. If you ever tried to steer the conversation away from work, she'd find an excuse to shut it down.'

'Did that concern you?'

Verity considered the question carefully. 'I just thought it was her way. Some people are more private than others. But looking back...' She paused. 'It wasn't healthy. She lived like work was the only thing that mattered. It was almost as if she was afraid to let anything else in.'

When Lauren showed her Ruth's photograph, Verity shook her head immediately. 'No, I'm sorry. I don't recognise her.'

Since Verity hadn't gone to university with the others and hadn't worked with any of the team in the past, there was no point asking about the 1996 solstice celebrations.

Once the interview was concluded and Verity left the station. Lauren and Matt headed back to her office. She sank down in her chair, feeling the weight of the afternoon settling on her shoulders.

'Well, we're no nearer learning why Eleanor was murdered,' Matt mused.

Lauren nodded. 'But at least now we know that Eleanor Trewin was a woman who'd cut herself off from the world. No close relationships, no personal life to speak of, completely absorbed in her work.'

'Which makes her an unlikely target for murder,' Matt observed. 'If she had no personal connections, no romantic entanglements, no enemies...'

'Then why was she killed?' Lauren finished. 'And why so soon after Ruth Penrose was found? Except, everything we've learnt about Eleanor points to her being highly principled. It could be she discovered something and the killer was frightened she'd disclose it?'

'Maybe,' Matt acknowledged. 'We need to think about the alibis of the dig members. Both Liam and Adam's alibis can't be verified.'

'Nor can Naomi's,' Lauren added. 'Just because she registered for the training and the records show it, doesn't mean that she didn't leave her house. No one would know she wasn't sitting there listening to the lecture.'

'Good point.'

They sat in contemplative silence. Five people had worked closely with Eleanor, but none of them could offer any insight into who might have wanted her dead. None of them recognised Ruth

Penrose or remembered anything significant about someone named Davy or David from the solstice celebration thirty years ago.

But something didn't quite fit. Eleanor's university friends all remembered her being different all those years ago. More relaxed. More alive. More human. What had happened between then and now to turn her into the isolated workaholic they'd all described?

'Matt,' Lauren said slowly. 'What if we're looking at this backwards?'

'How do you mean?'

'Everyone said Eleanor was different that night in 1996. More open, more social. What if something happened at that solstice celebration that changed her? What if she had something to do with Ruth Penrose's disappearance and it affected her more than anyone realised?'

Matt's eyes sharpened with interest. 'You think Eleanor knew Ruth?'

'I think it's possible. Just because the others didn't remember Ruth, doesn't mean that Eleanor didn't encounter her. Maybe Ruth approached Eleanor specifically. Maybe they talked. Maybe something happened that we don't yet know about.'

'That's a great theory. If only we can progress it,' Matt said with a resigned shrug.

Lauren stood and walked over to the window, looking out at the early evening light. 'Think about it. Eleanor goes to this beach party and she's relaxed and happy. A young girl disappears that same night, and Eleanor gradually transforms into someone who avoids all personal connections, who buries herself in work, and who lives like she's afraid to get close to anyone.'

'Guilt,' Matt said quietly. 'You think Eleanor felt guilty about something that happened to Ruth?'

'Or fear,' Lauren countered. 'What if Eleanor saw something that night? What if she knew who took Ruth, and she spent the next thirty years looking over her shoulder?'

Matt joined her at the window, staring out at the gathering

dusk. 'And eventually, whoever killed Ruth realised that Eleanor was a loose end that needed tying up.'

The theory felt right to Lauren. They were fitting the pieces together in a way that made psychological sense. Eleanor's transformation from the vibrant young woman her colleagues remembered to the isolated workaholic she'd become.

'Except, why would she want to dig so close to where Ruth was buried? And did she invite the particular members of the team to work with her because she knew it was one of them?'

'That doesn't make sense. If she was scared about someone then surely she wouldn't want them close to her?'

'True. I'm just brainstorming… We'll get the team to dig deeper into that night to find out exactly what happened at that solstice celebration. We need to know who else was there and what Eleanor might have seen or heard.'

'And we need to find Davy,' Matt added. 'Because if he was involved in Ruth's disappearance, and if Eleanor knew about it…'

'Then we've found our killer,' Lauren finished. 'I want to pop back to see Ruth's sister again. Now we know more about the team, there are a few questions I'd like to ask her. Are you okay for time?'

'Of course,' Matt replied. 'It's not like she lives miles away, and my mum knows my hours are going to be long while we're working on a murder case. It's better we speak to her now, so tomorrow we can focus our time on Davy and the solstice.'

SEVENTEEN
TUESDAY 27 MAY

Lauren and Matt drove in separate cars to Jasmine Penrose's house so Matt could head straight home afterwards. Lauren felt guilty about keeping him out late, but she knew he wanted to be part of it. Rightly so, it was part of the job. But she'd grown to like his family very much and, especially after Dani's kidnapping and then his dad becoming sick, she had realised that time with his family was precious.

She parked first, waiting for Matt to pull up behind her, then they walked up the garden path to the door of Jasmine's lovely cottage. The evening light was fading, casting long shadows across the well-tended flower beds that flanked the entrance.

When Jasmine opened the door, she appeared genuinely surprised to see them again.

'Hello, Jasmine. Sorry to come back again. I hope you don't mind. We have a few more questions that we'd like answered as soon as possible.'

'No, of course not. Come on through.' Jasmine stepped aside, gesturing for them to come into the hallway.

They followed her into the lounge. This room was more formal than the conservatory, the furniture carefully arranged, family photographs lining the mantelpiece.

'How can I help you?' Jasmine asked, settling into an armchair and smoothing her skirt nervously.

'We've been interviewing Eleanor Trewin's colleagues on the archaeological dig, and it turns out four of them, including her, were at the solstice party the night Ruth disappeared. They were studying at the University of Exeter at the time.'

'Oh, I see.' Jasmine's eyebrows rose slightly, her hands tightly clasped together in her lap. 'And you think this is relevant?'

'Well, it's certainly not something we're going to ignore,' Lauren responded, gently. 'We don't deal in coincidences.'

'But you weren't there that night, were you?' Matt confirmed.

'No. I didn't go.' Jasmine shook her head emphatically. 'My parents didn't let me go out much in the evening. I was only fourteen at the time and didn't even ask to go because I knew what their response would be. Although, to be honest, I didn't want to go. I wasn't as outgoing as my sister. Ruth got away with doing all sorts of things and I think that's why my parents were so strict with me. They couldn't have coped with two like Ruth on their hands.' She gave a wry laugh.

Lauren nodded understandingly. 'I'd like to show you some photos of these people. They're recent, but you might recognise them, if you'd seen them with Ruth at some time.'

Lauren didn't hold out much hope of Jasmine being able to help, if she hadn't gone out much, but it was still worth trying. She reached into her jacket pocket, pulled out her phone, and went into the photo app. 'First of all...' She held out Adam Fielding's photo, watching Jasmine's face carefully for any flicker of recognition.

Jasmine's brow furrowed as she studied the image, tilting her head slightly. Then she shook her head. 'No, definitely not. I've never seen him before.'

'What about this person?' Lauren held out her phone, displaying the photo of Naomi Walters.

Jasmine squinted at the screen. 'I'm sorry, she doesn't seem familiar either.'

'That's fine,' Lauren said, finally showing her Liam's photograph. Again, Jasmine shook her head, more decisively this time.

'No. Though I'd imagine, as young people they'd be very different...' She paused, considering. 'But if they were at university then they'd be a good bit older than Ruth and me. I'm not surprised I didn't come across them, at the solstice or otherwise.'

'That's fair enough,' Lauren said, slipping the phone back into her pocket. 'We just wanted to check before we do any further research. None of them recognised Ruth either.'

'Was there anything else?' Jasmine asked, her fingers fidgeting with the hem of her cardigan.

'Nothing's come up yet,' Lauren replied. 'But have you thought of anything since we spoke earlier?'

Jasmine's gaze drifted to the window. When she looked back, there was something different in her expression. A hesitation that hadn't been there before.

'Well, yes and no. Obviously, I don't recognise any of these people, but thinking back to Ruth and... and her disappearing...' She trailed off, then took a breath before continuing. 'I do remember a couple of times Ruth telling me that she'd decided to turn over a new leaf at school and work hard so she could go to university and get a good job. She seemed to be serious, but I thought it was just another one of her mad ideas because she had no interest in school up to that point, and it would have been virtually impossible for her to catch up with the work. Not that she couldn't have done it. Like I told you, she was very clever when she wanted to be.'

'What made you believe this was relevant to her situation?' Lauren asked.

'Because it shows she had no intention of running away, I suppose,' Jasmine said quickly, then paused. 'I hadn't thought about it until now.'

'Did she say which university she'd like to go to?' Matt asked, leaning forward in his chair.

'She mentioned Manchester because it was a good one,' Jasmine said, sounding more animated as the memory solidified.

'What about Exeter?' Lauren asked, wondering if there was a link.

'She said she wanted to go north, to get as far away from here as possible.'

'Did you mention this to the police?' Lauren asked.

Jasmine shook her head. 'No. My head was all over the place when she disappeared.'

'Can you remember how close it was to when she disappeared that Ruth spoke about going to university?' Lauren asked.

'A few weeks, maybe. Or a bit less. Sorry, I can't remember.'

The room fell into a comfortable silence, broken only by the ticking of the grandfather clock in the corner. Lauren studied Jasmine's face, noting the way her eyes had grown distant, as if she were sifting through memories she'd long buried.

'Now you've had time to process, can I ask you to think carefully about the weeks before Ruth disappeared?' Lauren asked gently. 'Was there anything different about her behaviour, or things that she said?'

Jasmine rubbed her temples, the gesture making her look older than her years. 'She was... secretive, I suppose. More so than usual. Ruth was always good at keeping things from our parents, but usually she told me everything. Those last few weeks, though, she seemed to be keeping things from me, too.'

'Can you elaborate more?'

'I'd ask where she was going and who she was seeing, but she'd be dismissive and not say. She'd leave the house without telling me she was going, and when she came back, she'd be... I don't know, different somehow. Excited, maybe? Like she had a secret she was bursting to tell but couldn't. Looking back, I wish I'd pushed her on it. But I didn't.'

The weight of those words hung in the air as Lauren and Matt exchanged another meaningful look. This could be the first real lead they'd had in understanding Ruth's mindset before she vanished.

'Thank you, Jasmine,' Lauren said softly. 'This has been very helpful. If anything else comes to mind, please don't hesitate to call us.'

As they prepared to leave, Jasmine walked them to the door, her steps slower now, as if the conversation had drained her.

'I hope you discover what happened to Ruth,' she said quietly, her hand resting on the door frame. 'I've spent so many years wondering where she was. Whether she'd been living the life she'd always dreamt of. Except now I know she wasn't.'

Lauren and Matt left the house and before getting into their cars, they stood still, waiting for Jasmine to close the door of her house.

'I'm so angry at the way the police investigation was carried out when Ruth disappeared,' Lauren said, letting out a frustrated sigh. 'If they'd taken seriously the family's worries, then her body might have been found sooner. Okay, it wouldn't have prevented her death, but they might have found the killer and it's entirely possible that Eleanor Trewin would still be alive.'

EIGHTEEN

WEDNESDAY 28 MAY

Matt sat at his desk, his fingers drumming against the wooden surface as he reviewed his notes from the previous day. They had the windows open and he could hear the distant cry of gulls wheeling over Penzance harbour, their calls mixing with the rumble of early morning traffic.

'Good morning, everyone.'

Lauren's voice cut through the noise like a blade. Matt glanced up from his desk, immediately noting the determined set of her shoulders and the way her eyes sparkled with the intensity. He jumped up and went over to where she'd positioned herself by the whiteboard.

'Right,' Lauren began, uncapping a marker with a decisive click. 'We know that three members of the dig, plus Eleanor, were at the solstice gathering the night Ruth died.'

She wrote the names in bold letters across the white surface, the marker squeaking slightly, and drew lines to link them together. She turned to face the team. 'I'm convinced that this isn't a coincidence. There's got to be something, and we need to find it. So our first stop today is a return visit to Ruth's friend Kelly Hartley.'

A familiar flutter of anticipation coursed through Matt. Often, re-visits yielded the most valuable information, when witnesses had had time to process their initial shock and remember details that might have seemed insignificant before.

'Jenna.' Lauren pointed to the detective constable who was staring directly at her. 'I want you to contact Tyler Penhaligon again. Send him photos of the dig workers who went to the solstice, including Eleanor, and find out if he recognises anyone. Explain that they're much older now. And don't forget to ask whether he knew anyone called Davy.'

'Ma'am,' Clem interjected, half-raising his hand like an eager schoolboy. The gesture was so characteristic of the officer that Matt suppressed a smile. 'I recently read about some software that can show you what somebody looked like when they were younger, based on their current appearance. I'd been meaning to talk to you about it sometime. Would you like me to look further into it?'

'Yes, please, that's a good idea, Clem,' Lauren said, crossing her arms and leaning back slightly. 'You get onto that now. I don't have time to spare, so we're still going to see Kelly and I'll show her the photos we already have. If you do manage to find and use the software – although I imagine there's a cost involved, which means we'd have to go through the usual channels – then text it to me.'

'Will do, ma'am. I think there might be a seven-day free trial so we could use that,' Clem said, swivelling his chair towards his computer screen.

'Well, that would be brilliant if it's possible. Billy, where are you on finding the band that was playing that night? It was the Stone Shadows, wasn't it?'

Billy straightened in his chair, consulting his notes with a quick flip of pages. 'Yes, ma'am. I've located one of them and he lives in St Ives. Would you like me to go out there and have a chat with him?'

'Good idea. Take Tamsin with you.' Lauren paused, tapping the marker against her palm. 'While you're there, show him the photos. If Clem can manage to show them when they were younger, that would be even better.'

'Shall I wait for Clem to do that, ma'am?'

'Give it an hour, and if not, take the photos we do have.' Lauren capped the marker and set it down on the ledge beneath the whiteboard. 'Right, come on, Matt. Let's head off.'

'Ma'am, before you go,' Tamsin called out.

'Yes?'

'I've heard back from forensics. Eleanor's mobile couldn't be rescued. But we do know from the carrier that it was last used the day of her death. She sent a joint message to the dig team telling them to sit tight and that hopefully the dig would reopen soon.'

'Thanks, Tamsin. Nothing that helps with her murder, unfortunately.' Lauren sighed. 'Let's go, Matt.'

Matt followed Lauren towards the door, grabbing his jacket from the coat stand on the way and shrugging it on. 'My car or yours, ma'am?'

'We'll take mine,' Lauren replied.

Matt knew that she preferred to drive when they were immersed in a case. Concentrating on driving seemed to take her mind off it, leaving time for ideas to percolate without her active thought processes getting in the way. That was how she'd explained it to him, although it wasn't something that worked for him. He preferred being a passenger because it allowed him time to weigh up everything.

The drive to the campsite took them along the coast road, where granite cliffs dropped dramatically into the churning Atlantic. Matt studied the landscape with fresh eyes, wondering how many secrets the ancient stones had witnessed. The gorse was coming into bloom, giving splashes of brilliant yellow against the grey-green moorland, and he could taste the salt air even through the closed windows of Lauren's car.

They found Kelly Hartley emerging from one of the caravans, a faded blue static home that had clearly seen better days. She was wrestling with a bag of rubbish, her movements sharp with the kind of irritation that suggested she was having a difficult morning.

'Kelly,' Lauren called out.

The woman turned around and looked at them, her expression cycling through confusion, recognition, and finally resignation.

'What is it?' Kelly asked, abandoning the rubbish bag and walking over to them.

'We've got a few more questions for you regarding the night of the solstice,' Lauren explained. 'We're trying to track down various people who were there.'

Kelly nodded, but her eyes were wary. Follow-up visits were always delicate. It often made people feel scrutinised, as if their initial statements hadn't been believed.

'These images are how the people look now,' Lauren continued, pulling out her phone. 'But there's still a chance you might recognise them.'

She showed Kelly the photos one by one, keeping each one in front of her for at least ten seconds.

Kelly stared hard at each image, her brow furrowed in concentration.

'She looks a little bit familiar,' Kelly said finally, pointing to Naomi's photo. 'Something about the eyes. But I can't remember talking to her specifically.'

'We now have Ruth's diary and in her last journal entry she mentioned looking forward to seeing someone called Davy that night. Did she mention his name to you?'

Kelly paused for a moment, and Matt could almost see the memories shifting and realigning in her mind. The sea breeze caught her hair, pulling strands free from the ponytail.

'You know, I reckon she did. Thinking back, the name Davy did come up. I remember saying to her, "Is this the boy you keep saying you won't tell me about?" And she just giggled, so I never did get an answer to that question. But it must have been. I'm sorry not to tell you before but it had totally gone out of my head.'

'There's no need to apologise. We're talking about thirty years ago,' Lauren said, reassuring the woman. 'To clarify, you didn't ever meet Davy, or see a photo of him?'

'Well, no. It's not like now when you can take photos with your phone,' Kelly reminded them.

'Do you think when Ruth disappeared, she was going to meet Davy?' Lauren asked.

'Maybe. If she said in her diary that she was going to see him…' Kelly looked thoughtful, her gaze drifting toward the hills that surrounded the campsite.

'Thanks for your help. If anything else does spring to mind, give me a call.' Lauren smiled.

They left the campsite, and Matt sighed. He hoped that Clem could come up with some younger photos, because without them it was proving impossible to discover whether the students were involved in Ruth's murder.

NINETEEN
WEDNESDAY 28 MAY

'Matt, wait.'

He turned to see Lauren charging towards him across the car park, her hair flying in all directions thanks to the coastal wind that had been picking up all afternoon. He'd been about to get into his car and drive home, but instead he ran over to join her.

'What is it?' he asked, slightly out of breath from his sprint across the uneven ground.

'We've got another body at the dig. It was discovered by one of the forensics team, who'd popped back to take some more photos of the scene.'

'Crap,' he said, the implications hitting him immediately. Another body meant another murder and another family to devastate. 'Do we know the identity of the victim?'

'No. I'm going over there now. Do you want to come with me, or do you need to get home?'

Matt hesitated for a moment, thinking of Dani waiting at home for him. Although his daughter was well used to his irregular hours, he still felt guilty when he wasn't around for bedtime. 'I'll come. But let's go in separate cars so I can leave if this runs on too long.'

He hated to say that because really, he should be available at all hours. But Lauren was aware of his situation as a sole parent and respected his need to prioritise his family sometimes.

'Good thinking,' Lauren said as she turned and headed for her car.

Matt returned to his car and pulled out his phone to call his mum. After a couple of rings, she answered.

'Hello.'

He could hear the telly in the background. It was probably one of her early evening quiz shows.

'Mum, it's me. I'm going to be late; can you put my dinner in the oven, please? Something's come up at work.' He tried to keep his voice level, not wanting to worry her, but knowing she'd pick up on the tension anyway. She always did.

'Oh no, what is it? You sound stressed, love.'

'Sorry, I can't tell you. You know how it is. I don't know what time I'll be back. So if you can put Dani to bed please and explain to her.'

'She won't mind,' his mum said gently. 'I'll carry on reading her *Charlotte's Web*. She's already been talking about what happens next.'

'Thanks, Mum. I'll see you all later.'

He ended the call and focused on where he had to go.

The journey to Treen took him along the coastal road. The evening mist was beginning to roll in from the Atlantic and the temperature had dropped noticeably since the afternoon. The weather was classic Cornwall, shifting from sunshine to storm in the space of minutes. Would he ever get used to it?

As he drove down the hill leading to the dig site, he could see the police lights already blazing in the gathering dusk. Once he'd arrived and parked, he stepped out of the car, pulling his jacket tighter, the wind immediately finding every gap in his clothing. He hurried down to the cordoned area, his footsteps crunching on the loose gravel, to where Lauren was waiting with Henry.

'Hello, Henry,' he said with a nod.

'Evening, young man,' Henry typically replied, picking up his bag, which was on the ground.

'We'll go down together, if that's okay with you, Henry,' Lauren said.

'That's fine, providing you keep out of my way,' Henry responded with a twinkle in his eye.

'As if we'd do anything else,' Lauren replied, smiling slightly.

They made their way to the dig site, along the stone path that led down to the main excavation area. Matt was grateful for the portable lighting, even though it cast everything in harsh, unnatural shadows.

In the distance he made out a body lying on the ground. As they got closer, he immediately realised who the victim was and his stomach sank.

'Adam Fielding.'

'Yes,' Lauren confirmed, her expression grim.

They walked to within two metres of the body, which lay next to one of the smaller excavation trenches, and stopped.

'You two wait here while I take a look,' Henry instructed, pulling on his latex gloves with a snap and taking out a camera from his bag.

From where they were standing, Matt spotted a trowel next to the body. That wasn't unusual, given the location, but this one was different. There was dark congealed blood on the blade and handle. Matt swallowed hard, determined not to be fazed by what he could see, but feeling the familiar churning in his stomach that accompanied every violent crime scene.

'This wasn't an accident,' Lauren called out, wrapping her arms around herself.

The chill in the air seemed to be seeping up from the ground itself.

'No,' Henry agreed, standing up slowly and brushing dirt from his knees. 'It appears not.'

'So we have another murder,' Lauren commented, her voice quiet but carrying clearly in the still evening air.

'Well, obviously I can't give a definitive answer until I've had a chance to examine the body properly,' Henry replied, his professional caution warring with what was obvious to all of them. 'But it certainly looks like this man was stabbed with that trowel, and it was left by the side of the body. There appears no attempt to hide the body or dispose of the weapon.'

'Are we being sent a message? Matt asked, his chest tightening as he processed the implications.

'If we are, we don't know by whom, and what the message is meant to be,' Lauren replied.

The three of them stood in uncomfortable silence for a moment, the weight of another senseless death settling over them like the gathering mist.

'Okay, we'll leave you to it, Henry,' Lauren said finally, turning away from the scene. 'We need to get back to the office and begin investigating this man to find out who might have wanted him dead.'

'No problem,' Henry replied, already pulling additional equipment from his bag. 'I'll get in touch and let you know once I know more. It's going to be a long night.'

They left the site, walking back up the treacherous path in single file, the wind picking up as they moved away from the sheltered excavation area. Drops of rain began splattering on Matt's face as they reached the car park, promising a proper Cornish downpour before the night was through.

'Right, I'm going back to the office,' Lauren called out as she reached her car, already pulling her keys from her pocket. 'I'll see you in the morning.'

'I'm coming with you,' Matt replied, raising his voice over the increasing wind. 'We need to find out where Fielding lives, and obviously we've got to inform his family. That's going to be the worst part of all this.'

'Okay, if you're sure. I'll see you back there.'

'I'll also ring round the team to see if any of them can come back tonight.'

Once inside his car and away from the rain, he tried Tamsin's number, knowing that she was the most likely to be available and willing to come in.

The phone rang twice before she answered. 'Hey, Sarge,' she said, her voice bright and alert.

'Where are you, Tamsin? We need you back at the office if you can make it.'

'I'm still here. I had some work to catch up on. Well... not really work. I'm doing some studying. It's easier to work here because there are fewer distractions. I want to make sure I know everything inside and out before my course starts. What do you need me for?'

'There's been another murder at the dig. Adam Fielding.'

'Oh no.' Tamsin's voice dropped.

'I'm afraid so. We need to know more about him, especially family details so they can be informed.'

'Leave it with me, Sarge.'

Matt ended the call and then phoned his mum. His dinner would be ruined now, even if it was kept in the oven. He'd make himself a sandwich once he got home.

For the rest of the journey he concentrated on driving through the increasingly heavy rain, his mind already racing through the implications of this latest murder.

TWENTY

WEDNESDAY 28 MAY

Tamsin glanced up from her computer screen as Matt and Lauren entered the office, and straightened in her chair, her fingers still poised over the keyboard where she'd been typing.

'Have you found anything yet?' Matt asked, his voice carrying a note of urgency as he headed over to her desk. He rolled his shoulders, trying to ease the tension that had settled there after their long day.

'Quite a bit, actually,' Tamsin replied, her face brightening as she consulted the top page of the notebook beside her computer screen. She tapped her pen against the paper, a habit of hers Matt had noticed when she was pleased with her work. 'Adam Fielding, aged fifty-two, originally from Bath. Born there, grew up there. He went to university in Exeter and studied for a degree in archaeology and ancient history.'

Lauren joined them and leant against the edge of Tamsin's desk, her expression thoughtful. 'Yes, we already knew that, from digging into Eleanor's death. Anything else?'

Tamsin's eyes lit up as she flipped through her notes, clearly proud of her detective work. 'He's been married to Sonia Fielding for eighteen years, and they have two teenage children. Emmeline, who's sixteen and is currently taking her GCSEs, and George, who's fourteen and apparently very keen on football.' She paused, glancing between Matt and Lauren as if to gauge their reactions. 'Sonia works part-time as a teaching assistant. I found quite a lot about the family through the usual social media channels.'

Matt nodded appreciatively, a smile playing at the corners of his mouth. 'That's excellent work, Tamsin,' he said, the admiration in his voice genuine. 'We know that Eleanor Trewin recruited him especially for this dig. Did you find any red flags regarding him working there? Was there anything on social media that he'd posted? Any complaints, arguments, or professional disagreements?'

Tamsin shook her head, her expression becoming more serious. 'His posts have all been positive. Lots of photos of interesting finds, some landscape shots of the coastline. He seemed genuinely enthusiastic about the work.' She clicked through several browser tabs on her screen, showing them some examples of what she'd found. 'When he's down here he stays in a bedsit in a converted Victorian house in Treen, owned by a Mrs Hoskins. She lives in the house, too. The dig covers the cost of his accommodation as part of his contract.'

Lauren straightened up. 'We need to contact the woman. Do you have her details?'

'Yes, ma'am. Would you like me to call?' Tamsin offered, her hand already reaching for the phone.

Matt held up a hand, shaking his head. 'Let me do it. Please text me the number.'

'Will do, Sarge,' Tamsin replied, grabbing her phone from the desk to send the information.

'Thanks. By the way, did Clem have any luck with the photo software?'

'No. There wasn't a free trial available.'

'Damn,' Matt said with a sigh.

'I'm going to see the DCI to update him on this latest murder,' Lauren said, turning to leave.

'Ma'am,' Matt called after her. 'We need to question the

remaining dig members. Shall we do this tonight or wait until tomorrow?' He glanced at his watch, noting how late it was already getting.

'I think we should wait until we've heard back from Henry. We should know something by tomorrow.' Lauren's expression was thoughtful, appearing to be weighing the benefits of immediate action against the need for more information.

'What about Fielding's family? Shall we drive to Bath and inform them personally, or ask the local force to tell them?' Matt shifted his weight from one foot to the other, not relishing the prospect of delivering devastating news to yet another grieving family.

Lauren's expression softened slightly. 'It might be a good idea to ask them to inform Sonia, and then we'll visit tomorrow morning. At least then the immediate shock will have passed and we can get on with the questioning.' She paused, her brow furrowing as if she'd suddenly realised how her words might sound. 'I didn't mean to sound callous, but you know what I mean. We need her to be in a state where she can answer our questions. It will be more useful that way.'

Matt nodded. 'Of course, I get it completely. I'll get onto the Bath police and ask them to inform her. It also means I can tell Mrs Hoskins when I phone her, if I need to. Or I might just say there's been an accident, depending on how the conversation goes. I'll play it by ear.'

'Good thinking,' Lauren replied. 'I'll leave you to make that call. Let me know how it goes.'

Matt turned back to Tamsin, who'd been quietly observing the exchange. 'Tamsin, you should get going,' he said gently, his tone paternal. 'We're going to be busy tomorrow and then for however long it takes us to solve these murders. You've done more than enough for today. We really appreciate your commitment.'

'Are you sure, Sarge? I don't mind staying and continuing with my research. I've got nothing else on this evening, and it gives me something to do. You know I love this part of the job.' She gestured at her screen, which was still filled with open tabs and research notes.

Matt smiled at her enthusiasm but remained firm. 'Very sure. Now go. You need to get some rest because we'll need you sharp tomorrow. Thanks for all your work today; it's been invaluable. I'm going to phone Mrs Hoskins now.'

'Okay, see you in the morning then,' Tamsin said, jumping up from her seat with youthful energy. She grabbed a pale blue cardigan from the back of her chair and slipped it on, gathering her personal items. 'Good luck with the call, Sarge.'

Matt waited until Tamsin had left before settling at his desk. He took a deep breath, steeling himself for what potentially could be a difficult conversation, then keyed in the number Tamsin had texted him.

'Hello?' a woman's voice answered after several rings, sounding slightly breathless, as if she'd hurried to reach the phone.

'Is that Mrs Hoskins?' Matt asked, ensuring he sounded professional but friendly.

'Yes, that's me. Who's this?' The woman's voice carried a note of wariness, the kind that came from unexpected calls in the evening.

'I'm Detective Sergeant Price, from Penzance police. I'd like to ask you a few questions about one of your guests. Adam Fielding.'

There was a sharp intake of breath on the other end of the line. 'Has something happened to him?' Mrs Hoskins asked, her voice rising slightly with concern.

Matt chose his words carefully. 'There's been an incident, which is all I can say at the moment,' he replied, deciding not to tell her everything until he had a better sense of her relationship with the victim. 'I was hoping you could tell me what Adam's like as a tenant.'

'Oh my,' Mrs Hoskins said. Matt heard her settle into a chair, the creak of old furniture audible over the phone. 'Well, I can tell you this. I wish they were all like him because it would make my life so much easier. His rent is always paid on time, never a day late. He never causes any problems, doesn't bring back guests at all hours or play loud music. And he keeps his room spotlessly clean.'

Matt made notes as she spoke, encouraged by her willingness to talk. 'What's he like as a person?' he asked, quietly drumming his fingers on the desk.

'Very nice indeed,' Mrs Hoskins said, her voice warming as she spoke about Fielding. 'Always polite and he asks how I am when we bump into each other in the hallway or in the communal kitchen. He does keep himself to himself, but in a respectful way, not standoffish. And he doesn't have any visitors. At least I haven't seen any in all the time he's been staying here.' She paused. 'What sort of incident are we talking about? Is he hurt?'

'I'm sorry, I can't say more about that just now,' Matt deflected gently. 'We know he comes from Bath. Does he go back there often?' He wasn't prepared to be drawn further into what had happened to Fielding, which was why he was still referring to the man in the present tense, as if still alive.

'Oh yes,' Mrs Hoskins said, her tone becoming more animated. 'Every weekend, without fail, he goes to Bath to be with his family. Regular as clockwork. He leaves here on Friday evening, usually around six o'clock, and comes back late Sunday evening or very early Monday morning. Sometimes I hear his car pulling up at midnight or later.'

'That must be exhausting for him,' Matt observed, genuinely sympathetic to the demands of such a commute.

'I know,' Mrs Hoskins agreed enthusiastically. 'He told me it's four hours each way, providing there are no hold-ups. And how likely is that around here, especially in the summer when the roads get absolutely chockablock with tourists.' She gave a knowing chuckle. 'But I think it shows how much he loves his family, don't you? His wife's a very lucky woman if you ask me. Not all of us have such loving husbands.' Her voice took on a slightly wistful tone, and she gave a loud sigh.

Matt sensed there was a story but didn't pursue it. 'What about during the week? Do you know his routine?'

'Yes, because he's as regular as clockwork,' Mrs Hoskins said with evident admiration. 'He gets up early, around six-thirty every morning. I know that because I can hear the shower running in the room above mine. Then he has his breakfast in the kitchen. Just toast and coffee usually. At around seven-fifteen he leaves and walks to the dig. It's not far, maybe fifteen minutes on foot. He's usually back here by six in the evening, and he rarely goes out after that. Sometimes he'll walk to the local pub for dinner, but mostly he stays in and cooks his own. After dinner he'll read or work on his laptop.' She paused. 'I know that because he sometimes sits in the lounge.'

'Have you noticed any change in Adam's behaviour recently? Anything at all that seemed different or unusual?'

'Ummm,' Mrs Hoskins said, her voice becoming thoughtful. 'Like what sort of thing?'

'Well, has he changed his routine or appeared more stressed? Maybe he seemed preoccupied or worried about something? Anything you can think of, no matter how small it might seem.'

There was a long silence, and Matt waited patiently, assuming the woman was thinking carefully about his question. He could hear the ticking of a clock in the background.

'Now I come to think about it,' Mrs Hoskins finally said, her voice slower and more considered, 'I was quite surprised the other evening when he came in and I was in the front hall sorting through the post. I smiled and said hello like I always do, but he didn't seem to hear. He just walked straight past me and up the stairs to his room. It was as if he was in some sort of a daze. That's very unusual for him. He's usually so polite and courteous.'

'Did you call after him?'

'No. I figured there was something on his mind and didn't want to interfere. I pride myself on leaving my tenants to their own devices, unless it's really important. Not like Mrs Penrite up the road. She tells you everything about her lodgers. I don't agree with that. It's disrespectful and—'

'Do you remember which evening this was?' Matt interrupted,

wanting to stop the woman from rambling because he didn't want to be caught on the phone all night and he doubted it would be useful to the investigation.

It worked because the woman was silent for a few seconds. 'Let me think... it was Monday, I believe. Yes, Monday evening. I remember because I'd collected the post and was going to check through to see if there was anything for him. But he didn't wait.'

'Was there any post for him?' Matt asked.

'No. He rarely gets anything.'

'Do you have any idea what might have caused this change in behaviour?'

'No, I didn't ask,' Mrs Hoskins replied, her voice carrying a note of defensiveness. 'I'm not nosy. I respect my tenants' privacy. But like I said, it did strike me as odd because he'll usually stop for a chat.'

Matt realised he might have inadvertently offended her. 'I didn't mean to suggest you were being nosy at all,' he said hurriedly. 'You've been very helpful, and I appreciate you taking the time to talk to me. We might need to be in touch again as our investigation progresses.'

'Investigation?' Mrs Hoskins repeated, her voice sharp with concern. 'What kind of investigation? Is Adam in some sort of trouble?'

'I'm sorry, but I can't discuss the details right now, as I previously mentioned,' Matt replied as gently as possible. 'Thank you again for your time, Mrs Hoskins. Someone will be in touch if we need further information.'

He ended the call and sat back in his chair, processing what he'd learnt. There didn't seem to be anything dramatically out of the ordinary going on with Adam Fielding. He appeared to be a model tenant and a devoted family man. Well... considering he'd had an affair, that could be questioned. But the change in his behaviour that Mrs Hoskins had noticed on Monday evening was interesting. Something had clearly happened to disturb Fielding's usual routine and demeanour. Could it have been Eleanor's murder? It made sense if that was what it was.

Matt made a few final notes and then closed his notebook. Whoever murdered Adam Fielding had a motive. The challenge now would be uncovering it, and discovering whether, as was most likely, it was connected to the other murders they were investigating.

TWENTY-ONE
THURSDAY 29 MAY

Lauren drummed her fingers on the steering wheel as she waited outside Matt's house. She didn't want to toot as it was only six in the morning and it might wake up all the neighbours. Although the journey to Bath was going to take them four hours, she'd considered it to be well worth their time. She glanced again at her watch, giving a frustrated sigh, and was about to get out of the car to knock on the door, when it opened and Matt appeared looking extremely harassed.

He hurried to the car and opened the door.

'Sorry I'm late. Dani had a nightmare and was crying. I couldn't leave her in that state. Mum's with her.'

The annoyance Lauren had been feeling quickly dissipated. 'Oh dear, poor thing. Does she have them often?'

Could it be a throwback from when she'd been kidnapped? Although that was nearly two years ago, these things could take a while to manifest and come out in so many different ways.

'No, she doesn't, thankfully,' Matt said, pulling over his seatbelt and clicking it in place. 'It was my fault, because I let her watch the cartoon version of *The Little Mermaid* before going to bed. She had a bad dream about Ursula. I won't do that again.'

'That's the trouble with so many cartoons. They're meant to be for kids but they can be quite disturbing,' Lauren said, turning on the engine and pulling out into the road. Her stomach rumbled. 'Did you have any breakfast? I'm famished.'

'No, I didn't have time.'

'In that case, we'll drive for a couple of hours, to get clear of Cornwall, and then stop at a service station for something to eat. We should then reach Sonia Fielding by around ten-thirty, which is a reasonable hour, I think.'

'I doubt she slept at all last night so I don't suppose it matters how early we arrive.'

Matt sounded strained. Was he thinking about when his wife had died? Lauren had never asked for a detailed account of the accident, and he'd never volunteered one. Some things were best left unsaid. If he'd wanted to confide, he'd have done so by now.

The early morning roads were quiet as they made their way through the winding Cornish lanes, the hedgerows still heavy with dew and the occasional rabbit darting across their path. Lauren found herself grateful for the peaceful start to what would undoubtedly be a difficult day. Questioning a bereaved family was never easy, and when children were involved, it became exponentially harder. Assuming they'd be there with their mother.

'How should we approach this?' Matt asked, staring out at the countryside as they passed through Bodmin. 'Assuming Sonia's going to want as many details as we can give her.'

'We'll tell her what we know, which isn't much yet,' Lauren replied, negotiating a particularly sharp bend. She flexed her fingers on the steering wheel. 'We need to focus on understanding Adam's state of mind recently and any problems he might have mentioned to her. Or anyone who might have had a grudge against him, for whatever reason.'

Matt shifted in his seat, turning slightly towards her. 'Are you going to mention his affair with Eleanor? It could be relevant.'

Lauren's jaw tightened. 'I'm undecided. We'll need to find out where *she* was on the evening of Eleanor's death as well as Adam's. It's not out of the question that she's our murderer.'

'She'd be hard pushed to get here and back home on both occasions, without someone being aware of it, I'd have thought,' Matt said, rubbing the back of his neck. 'But that doesn't mean she didn't do it.

Lauren glanced sideways at him before returning her focus to the road. 'It would mean her having detailed knowledge of the dig site and the strength to end the lives of both Eleanor and Adam. Although it's not out of the question.' She adjusted the rearview mirror unnecessarily. 'We'll have to play this by ear.'

They drove in silence for a while, each lost in their own thoughts. The landscape gradually changed as they left Cornwall behind, the wild moors giving way to the softer hills of Devon. Lauren's mind kept returning to the crime scene, to the deliberate way the trowel had been left beside Adam's body. There was something almost theatrical about it, as if the killer wanted to make a point. Unless she was reading too much into it and the weapon just happened to be left beside the body because the killer knew there would be no fingerprints on it.

'Tamsin did excellent work last night,' Matt said eventually, breaking the silence.

'She did. We're going to miss her when she goes.' Lauren sighed. 'We'll have to interview for someone else and hope they fit in with the rest of the team. Unless Ellie's going to apply, like Billy suggested. Will she, do you think?'

'It would be a very big step for her to take. She's been at Lenchester a long time. I can't call it. She'd be perfect for the team, that goes without question. But...' His voice trailed off, there being no need for the sentence to be finished.

'I know. But relationships can be successfully navigated in the police providing we keep an eye on things. We'll cross that bridge if and when it happens.'

By the time they reached Exeter services, Lauren's stomach was grumbling loudly enough for Matt to laugh. They pulled into the car park, which was already busy despite the early hour.

'What do you fancy?' Matt asked as they walked towards the building. 'Full English? Coffee and toast? Cereal?'

'Coffee and toast, please,' Lauren replied. 'Oh, and a croissant, too. You order and I'll find us a table.'

'Will do,' Matt replied, heading towards the long queue at the counter.

They ate quickly while seated at one of the tables near the window. Lauren noted the steady stream of traffic on the M5 and thought about all those people going about their ordinary lives, unaware that somewhere, a family was grieving the loss of a husband and father.

Lauren checked her watch. Eight-thirty. 'We should get going. I don't want to spend too long there because we have work to do at the office.'

The final two hours of the journey took them through increasingly familiar countryside as they approached Bath. Lauren had always loved this part of England, with its rolling hills and honey-coloured stone villages, and visited it often.

Bath itself was busy with morning traffic, as usual, as they navigated through the city centre towards Oldfield Park. It was a pleasant area and the Fieldings lived in a neat semi-detached property with a small front garden and a blue door. Lauren noticed a police car parked discreetly further down the street. The family liaison officer's vehicle, no doubt.

They sat in the car for a moment, neither of them seeming eager to begin what they both knew would be a difficult conversation. Lauren could see movement behind the net curtains at the front window, and realised they were probably being watched.

'Right then,' Matt said, unbuckling his seatbelt. 'Let's get this done.'

The front door had opened before they'd even reached it, revealing a woman in her early forties with short dark hair and tired eyes. She was dressed casually in jeans and a cardigan and seemed to be making an effort to appear composed despite her obvious distress.

'Mrs Fielding? I'm Detective Inspector Pengelly, and this is Detective Sergeant Price. I believe you're expecting us.'

'Yes, please come in,' Sonia said, her voice carefully controlled. 'The other police officer is in the kitchen making tea. The children are in the living room.'

As they stepped into the hallway, Lauren was struck by how normal everything looked. Coats hanging on the end of the banister. Shoes lined up beside the door. Keys on a small table. It was the detritus of an ordinary family life. It seemed impossible that such normality could coexist with the devastating news that had shattered this family's world.

A woman in her fifties, with kind eyes and a reassuring manner, appeared in the hallway. 'You must be DI Pengelly,' she said, looking at Lauren. 'I'm PC Yvonne Morrison.'

'Mrs Fielding, why don't you go into the living room, and we'll join you shortly,' Lauren said.

'I'll bring the tea through in a moment,' Yvonne added.

'How are they coping?' Lauren asked quietly once they were alone.

'As well as can be expected,' the officer replied in a low voice. 'Mrs Fielding's being strong for the children, but she's devastated. Emmeline, the sixteen-year-old, hasn't stopped crying since I arrived this morning. Jed's quiet and withdrawn. It's going to take time.'

'Have they asked questions regarding the circumstances of Adam's death?'

'Mrs Fielding has asked what happened, but I told her you'd give her more details.'

'They're aware it was a suspicious death, I take it?'

'Yes, they were informed of that yesterday.'

Lauren nodded, steeling herself for what was to come.

The living room was comfortable and lived-in, with family photos on the windowsill and magazines scattered on the glass-topped coffee table. Sonia was sitting on the sofa next to a girl, who Lauren assumed was Emmeline, clutching a box of tissues. Jed was sitting in an armchair, staring at his hands and looking much younger than his fourteen years.

'Mrs Fielding,' Lauren began, settling into the chair opposite. 'First of all, please accept our deepest condolences. I can't imagine what you're all going through.'

Sonia nodded, her composure wavering slightly. 'Thank you. We've been told that Adam was... that someone killed him. I still can't quite believe it. Who would want to hurt him? He was the kindest man you could ever meet.'

Lauren met her eyes directly. 'Although we're classing Adam's death as suspicious, that's all we know until the pathologist submits his report. We're doing everything we can to find out what happened to your husband, Mrs Fielding, but we do need your help to understand his recent state of mind and whether anything had been troubling him.'

'He'd definitely been worried about something,' Sonia said immediately. 'When he was home at the weekend, I could tell something was troubling him but he wouldn't say what it was. I asked him again on Tuesday evening when he phoned but he still wouldn't tell me. It was most unlike him. We shared everything. We always have done.'

'Did he mention the recent discovery of some human remains on the dig at Treen, from around thirty years ago?' Matt asked.

'Yes, he did tell me that. He was intrigued, but it didn't seem to bother him, other than it was frustrating because the dig had come to a standstill. Although they still had to be there, in case they could start working.'

'When you spoke to Adam on Tuesday did he mention the murder of the dig's director, Eleanor Trewin?' Lauren asked.

Sonia Fielding's hand shot to her mouth. 'No. Do you... do you think his death is connected to hers?'

The most obvious question to ask.

'We don't know yet. That's what we're looking into. Please can you tell us about Adam's routine when he travelled between here and Cornwall?' Lauren asked, gently.

'He usually left on Sunday evenings,' Sonia explained, dabbing at her eyes with a tissue. 'But sometimes he'd wait until very early on Monday morning if he wanted an extra few hours at home. The drive took him about four hours. He'd come back every Friday night, usually at around ten. He never missed a weekend home. Never.'

'Did he always follow this routine?'

'Yes, since the dig started around fifteen months ago. It's a long time to be driving back and forth every week and I knew it was exhausting for him but he said it was worth it because he loved his job so much.'

Yvonne appeared with a tray of tea, setting it down on the coffee table and quietly taking a seat near the window.

'Mrs Fielding. Sonia,' Lauren continued carefully. 'Please could you think back to when Adam wouldn't tell you what was wrong. Could you work out *anything* from what he did say?'

Sonia was quiet for a moment. 'He said that the past had come back to haunt him and when I asked him what he meant, he just shook his head and said, "It's nothing." That he was being silly.'

Lauren and Matt exchanged glances. This confirmed their suspicions about the timing.

'Are you sure he didn't say anything else? Maybe something about people from his past, or problems he might have had before?'

'Now I'm thinking about it, there was something else. Another time during the weekend, he mentioned covering for a friend,' Sonia said slowly. 'But he was very vague about it. When I pressed him for details, he got quite snappy, which wasn't like him at all. He said some things were better left in the past, and that he wished he'd never tried to help people who didn't deserve it.'

The room fell silent and Lauren's pulse quickened. Adam Fielding had clearly been dealing with something from his past, something that had been serious enough to threaten his new life.

'Is it possible that your husband had some kind of criminal record? Something from before you met, or from early in your relationship?' Matt asked.

Sonia shook her head firmly. 'No, absolutely not. Adam was the most honest person I knew. He'd never been in trouble with the police, never even had a speeding ticket. If he'd had a criminal record, I would have known about it.'

'Sometimes people keep parts of their past private,' Lauren said carefully. 'Even from the people they love most. It doesn't mean they're bad people, just that they're ashamed or trying to protect their families.'

'I suppose it's possible,' Sonia admitted reluctantly. 'But if that's the case, it must have been something minor. Adam wasn't capable of serious crime.'

In Lauren's experience, people were capable of almost anything under the right circumstances. But she kept that thought to herself.

'Have any of Adam's old friends contacted him recently?' Matt asked. 'Anyone from his past who might have needed help, or who might have held a grudge against him?'

Sonia considered this. 'There were a few people from university that he kept in touch with. But they're the ones he was on the dig with.'

Lauren made mental notes as they talked, building up a picture of a man who had seemed to live a quiet, unremarkable life until something from his past had caught up with him. The question was what, and why now?

'When did you last speak to Adam and how was he?' Matt asked.

'Tuesday evening at seven. He phoned most evenings at that time to speak to us.' Tears formed in her eyes and she blinked them away. 'He didn't seem any different from usual, did he, kids?' She glanced at her children.

'No,' Emmeline replied.

Jed shook his head.

'Sonia, please could you tell me what you were doing on Sunday between eleven at night and one in the morning?'

'I was here with the children. Adam had gone back earlier in the evening and we were watching a film until around eleven-fifteen, I think, then we went to bed. Why?'

'We're making sure to eliminate all people we speak to from our enquiries,' Lauren responded.

She wasn't going to mention the affair, if the woman had a concrete alibi for Eleanor's death. It would only add more distress to the family.

'Oh. I see,' Sonia replied.

'We'd like to look through Adam's personal belongings. His computer, and his papers etc. Is that okay with you?' Lauren asked.

Sonia nodded. 'Of course. His study's upstairs in the box room. That's where he kept all of his work things and his desktop computer. His laptop, he took with him.'

As they prepared to examine Adam's personal effects, Lauren couldn't shake the feeling that they were only just beginning to understand the complexity of the murders. There were secrets between members of the dig that had finally caught up with them.

The question now was whether they could uncover the truth before the killer struck again.

TWENTY-TWO

THURSDAY 29 MAY

Lauren's phone rang while she was driving back from Bath, following their interview with Sonia Fielding.

'Pengelly.'

'Ah, Detective Inspector, it's Henry here.' His voice came over the speaker so Matt could hear.

'I take it you've got something for us?' Lauren replied, her eyes fixed on the road ahead.

'Yes, I have my early report. Any chance you can pop in to see me so I can give you a rundown?'

Matt's pulse quickened. The sooner they had more info the better.

'We're on our way back from Bath. Hopefully we can get to you around four to four-thirty, if that works. We've already been on the road for a couple of hours,' Lauren replied, glancing over at Matt and raising a questioning eyebrow.

Matt nodded, understanding the silent question. Was he okay to go with her, or did he need to go home? Of course he wanted to go to the morgue. He was eager to hear what Henry had discovered. The visit to Sonia Fielding had been emotionally draining, watching her grapple with the news while processing that someone wanted her husband dead.

'It does. I'll see you later,' Henry said, ending the call, not bothering to chat further.

'Well, that's good,' Lauren said. 'At least we're going to have confirmed what happened to Adam Fielding.'

'True,' Matt said, shifting in his seat and turning slightly towards Lauren. 'What about the other members of the dig? They're presumably still not aware of Fielding's death unless any of them visited the dig site.'

'That's hardly likely, considering the site's closed.' Lauren negotiated a parked car. 'We'll get them in tomorrow. Message Tamsin. No, Jenna—' she corrected herself with a slight shake of her head. 'Ask her to get them all in first thing tomorrow morning. We'll tell them about Fielding then.'

'Will do,' Matt said, pulling out his phone. His thumbs moved quickly across the screen as he composed a brief message to Jenna:

> Need the archaeological team in first thing tomorrow. All of them. We'll brief them about Fielding.

Matt settled back in his seat, watching the afternoon shadows lengthen across the dashboard. The silence stretched between them, filled with the hum of the engine and the air con. He found himself staring out at the passing countryside, but his mind was elsewhere, running through what they'd have to face tomorrow. How do you tell a close-knit team that another of their colleagues has been murdered, at the same time as watching their faces for signs of guilt or genuine shock, while they're processing such devastating news?

He rubbed his temples, feeling the beginning of a headache building behind his eyes.

They reached the morgue just before five o'clock, as predicted, and as they entered, Henry was chatting with another member of his team, a younger woman in scrubs. Henry glanced up as they approached, his weathered face creasing into a brief smile.

'Glad you're here, I'm about ready to call it a day. I've been here for hours. I'll see you later,' he said to his colleague, then turned to them with a more serious expression. 'Follow me.'

Matt's stomach tightened as they headed from the office area to the main room. The familiar antiseptic smell filled his nostrils, and he found himself breathing through his mouth to avoid it. On the stainless-steel table in the centre of the room, uncovered, was the body of Adam Fielding.

Matt forced himself to look directly at the man, who appeared smaller somehow, and his skin taken on that waxy pallor that death brought.

'Right, so what have you got for us, Henry?' Lauren asked.

'Well, firstly, there doesn't appear to have been a struggle,' Henry said, moving around the table. 'There's no skin under his fingernails, and no obvious signs of a fight or altercation.'

'So most likely he knew his murderer,' Matt asked, his jaw tightening.

'It does seem that way,' Henry continued, his tone matter-of-fact. 'I want to show you exactly how the murder would have taken place. The dig tool that we found beside the body was the weapon used. The victim was stabbed in the carotid artery, rendering him dead almost instantly, within a few seconds. There would have been no way for the victim to defend himself if the killer did this at close range. The weapon was then removed from the neck and left beside the body to be discovered.'

Matt winced involuntarily. The clinical description somehow made it more brutal... more real. 'Why wouldn't they have disposed of the weapon?'

'There were no fingerprints on it, so one assumes that the killer wore gloves,' Henry said, his eyebrows raised slightly. 'No need to take it, in that case.'

'It could have been a message,' Lauren suggested, her brow furrowed in concentration.

'What message? A warning? And, if so, to whom?' Matt asked.

He continued considering this, his mind racing through the possibilities. Leaving the weapon at the scene was deliberate. It had to be. But what was the killer trying to say? That they weren't afraid of being caught? That it was personal? That there might be more to come?

'Well, I'm going to leave you to work that out for yourselves,' Henry said with a slight grimace, showing that he recognised the hard work ahead of them. 'The official report should hopefully be sent sometime tomorrow. Although we're short of admin staff, so it could take longer.'

'Was there any alcohol or drugs in his system?' Lauren asked before they left.

'His last meal was fish and chips, and there was a small amount of alcohol, probably from a beer, but that was all,' Henry replied, consulting his notes. 'So at the time, he'd have been perfectly conscious. Like I said, there was no indication of any struggle.'

Matt filed this information away with everything else they'd learnt. Fish and chips with a beer suggested he'd been at the local pub – probably the King's Head near the dig site. A single pint meant he was sober and alert. He'd have seen his killer coming, would have had time to react if he'd felt threatened.

But he hadn't. Maybe he'd arranged to meet his killer at the site.

'Time of death?' Lauren asked.

'Between ten pm and midnight on Tuesday.'

'Okay, thanks, Henry,' Lauren said.

On their way towards the exit, Matt's mind focused on the next day's interviews. Could one of those people be the killer? The thought sat heavy in his stomach like a stone.

Outside, he took a deep breath, feeling the air fill his lungs. The contrast always hit him this way... the stark difference between the world of the living and the sterile finality of death.

'So,' Lauren said as they walked towards the car, 'tomorrow we get to watch their faces when we tell them another of their colleagues is dead.'

'It's possible that one of them already knows,' Matt replied grimly. 'The question is whether we'll be able to tell which one.'

TWENTY-THREE

FRIDAY 30 MAY

'Jenna, what time did you arrange for the other members of the dig to come in this morning?' Lauren asked after hanging up her jacket in her office and coming through to see the team.

'Nine-thirty, ma'am,' Jenna replied, looking up from her computer screen. 'I spoke to them all apart from Naomi Walters, but I left a message on her phone.'

'Thanks. Feedback from the pathologist,' Lauren said, glancing around at each team member, all of whom were looking in her direction. 'It's most likely Adam Fielding knew his assailant, because there were no signs of struggle. He was killed between ten pm and midnight on Tuesday. I'm confident in our assumption that there's something linking the three murders.'

'It's got to be the solstice,' Billy said. 'It's the only time the three of them were in the same place. Eleanor and Adam must have known, or been a part of, Ruth's murder.'

'That does seem the most likely,' agreed Lauren. 'According to Adam Fielding's wife, he was concerned about something recently that related to the past. Now we need to focus on Liam Blackburn and Naomi Walters because they're the ones who were at university with the others and attended the solstice that night. We need to work fast to establish what happened because they, too, could be in danger.'

'If the killer was working their way through the group of friends systematically, then it's likely,' Jenna said.

'Unless one of them is the killer?' Clem said.

'It's a possibility,' Matt replied before Jenna could answer, his voice carrying that careful neutrality he used when he was thinking through complex scenarios. 'We need to ask them to be vigilant, in case they're in the killer's sights.'

'My money's on this Davy guy. He's picking them off one at a time,' Billy said with a knowing nod. 'Should we offer Liam and Naomi police protection?'

'It may be prudent, but I'll give it some more thought. Call me when they've arrived,' Lauren said, gesturing towards her office door. 'I've got a mountain of admin that's been sitting on my desk for way too long and the DCI has been asking for it.'

She returned to her office, closing the door behind her with perhaps more force than necessary. The paperwork spread across her desk seemed trivial compared to the weight of three murders, but she knew the importance of maintaining the administrative side of things. Budgets needed submitting and reports filing, even when people were dying. Admin stopped for no one.

She tried focusing on the numbers in front of her, but they kept dancing on the screen as she couldn't stop her mind from drifting back to the case. She agreed with Billy that this Davy person seemed key to solving it. And whatever *it* was, had clearly been festering underground for years before finally erupting into violence.

At twenty-five past nine, there was a knock on her door and Matt stepped inside. 'They're all here apart from Naomi. Do you want to wait a bit longer for her to turn up?'

'No. We'll speak to them now. She might not have checked her messages. We can always catch up with her later.'

Lauren picked up her phone and they left the office, a knot forming in her stomach as they got close to the room. Breaking the news of a death was difficult at the best of times, but when there was the slightest possibility that one of the people you were telling could be the killer, it added an extra layer of complexity.

Liam, Scott and Verity were sitting in silence, all of them appearing anxious. Lauren took a moment to observe them before sitting down. Verity was fidgeting with her phone, her leg bouncing nervously. Scott sat with his arms crossed, his jaw set in a way that suggested he was bracing himself for bad news. At first glance, Liam appeared the most composed, but his fingers were drumming silently against his thigh.

'Good morning,' Lauren said, settling into her chair and making eye contact with each of them in turn. 'Thank you for coming in. I'm afraid we have some more bad news.' Her words echoed off the walls and fear shone from their eyes. They all stiffened slightly, as if bracing themselves for impact. It was like everything was happening in slow motion, even though there were only seconds between her following up. 'On Wednesday, Adam Fielding's body was found at the dig.'

Verity gasped, her hand flying to her lips. Scott's eyes widened, and Liam's composed facade cracked, his face paling.

'Oh my God,' Verity whispered through her fingers.

'Was he murdered?' Scott asked, his voice barely above a whisper.

'We're treating his death as suspicious. He died after an archaeological dig tool was stabbed into his neck.'

'Oh my God,' Verity repeated, her voice breaking. She buried her head in her hands, her shoulders shaking.

'This is awful,' Scott said, his voice thick with emotion.

'Do you know who did it?' Liam asked, his voice steady despite the shock written across his features.

'We're currently making enquiries. We spoke to Adam's wife yesterday, and she believes he was worried about something to do with his past.'

'What do you mean, past?' Verity looked up, her eyes full of tears.

'That's what we don't know. But if we're to link the deaths of Ruth Penrose and Eleanor with Adam's, the only conclusion to draw is that it has something to do with the 1996 solstice party, which means...' Lauren paused, letting the implication of her words hang in the air.

'Which means Liam and Naomi could be next,' Scott said, finishing Lauren's sentence and looking at Liam with genuine concern.

'It's possible,' Lauren responded. 'Did Adam mention he was worried about something from the past?'

'Not to me. He was— was such a nice guy,' Liam said, his voice catching on the past tense.

Lauren observed his face carefully, looking for any sign of deception. Grief could be genuine and still coexist with guilt. She'd seen it before. There were killers who genuinely mourned their victims, even though they'd been the one to take their lives. It was the strangest dichotomy. But nothing alerted her.

'Please could you all tell us where you were between ten pm and midnight on Tuesday.'

'I went to bed at nine,' Verity said immediately.

'And can anyone confirm that?' Lauren responded.

Verity blushed. 'No. Sorry. I was all alone... As usual.'

'Scott?' Lauren asked, turning to him.

'I was in the pub until ten-thirty and then walked home. I bumped into one of the other residents in the house, a woman named Chloe, and we stopped for a chat. I was in bed by eleven-fifteen.'

'I was home all night, emailing the various bodies invested in the dig to keep them up to date with what's been happening. It wasn't an easy job because Eleanor was so well liked in the archaeology circles. Sorry, no one can vouch for me. But that's where I was,' Liam added. 'Oh... I've just thought. There should be time stamps on my emails. Does that help?'

'Yes, thank you, it does,' Lauren replied, glancing at her watch and seeing that it was already nine forty-five. 'Does anyone know where Naomi is?'

'Actually, I haven't seen her for a couple of days,' Verity replied, wiping her eyes with the back of her hand. 'I texted her yesterday but got no reply, which I thought was strange because usually she responds straight away.'

'Do you think something's happened to her?' Scott asked, his voice rising slightly with panic.

'Well, if she'd been killed, wouldn't her body be left close to the site like Eleanor and Adam?' Verity said, her voice gaining strength as she appeared to think logically through her distress.

Scott started to speak and then paused, his brow furrowed in concentration.

'What were you going to say, Scott?' Lauren prompted.

'I was thinking... and this may be totally leftfield. But what if Naomi's the killer? She might have gone on the run. Why else would she disappear for no reason?'

Lauren exchanged a glance with Matt. Scott made a good point. It was entirely possible that Naomi didn't want to be caught and, realising that the net was closing, had decided to disappear rather than face the consequences of her actions.

'No,' Liam said, shaking his head. 'That's crazy. She couldn't be.'

'Whether or not she's guilty, we need to find her, and quick. Does anyone have any idea where she could've gone? Who are her friends? What does she do in her spare time?' Lauren pushed.

'Naomi has a friend called Belinda who sometimes visits. She lives in Torquay,' Verity offered, her voice still shaky but more controlled.

'Do you have her contact details by any chance?'

'No, I'm sorry, I don't. All I know is her name and I've seen her with Naomi a couple of times in the pub.'

Lauren nodded. They needed to track down this Belinda. It wasn't much to go on, but it was a start. 'Thanks. You may all leave now, but I don't want any of you leaving the area in case we need to talk again.'

She stood up, signalling that the main part of the interview was over. The three of them moved slowly, as if the weight of the news had made everything difficult.

'I've got a family thing on at the weekend, in Bristol. May I go?' Scott asked.

'Yes. But make sure we can contact you. Before you go, Liam,' Lauren said, turning to the man. 'We'd like a quick word with you separately, if you don't mind.'

'Yes, sure,' he said, grimacing slightly.

Verity and Scott exchange worried glances before leaving the room. Their muffled voices could be heard in the corridor outside, probably discussing Adam's death, trying to process the reality that another colleague was dead, and wondering if they, too, were in the firing line.

TWENTY-FOUR
FRIDAY 30 MAY

'Thanks for staying behind,' Lauren said once they were alone with Liam in the interview room.

'Whatever it takes,' Liam responded with a slight grimace.

The atmosphere had shifted palpably once Verity and Scott had left. What had been a group interview was now something more intimate and focused.

She settled back into her chair, studying Liam's face carefully. 'We want to speak to you separately because, except for Naomi, who isn't here, you're the only one left from the original university group who went to the 1996 solstice. I know we've already asked, but please can you think of *anything* that might have led to all this? Anything at all?'

Liam stared up at the ceiling as if trying to think back thirty years. Finally he shook his head. 'I'm so sorry. There's nothing I can think of that will help you.'

'Are you sure? Because whatever went on, we believe that Adam knew. He told his wife that something from the past had come back to haunt him. Are you sure he didn't share it with you?' Liam wouldn't meet her eyes and his shoulders were hunched. Lauren was convinced he knew something. 'Liam?' she pushed.

'Ummm...' Liam answered, still avoiding her eyes.

'There's something you're not telling us, and we'll stay here until such time as you let us know what it is.' She was intentionally sharp, to force him into giving up what he knew.

'Actually,' Liam said after a while, his voice barely above a whisper, 'you're right. I'm sorry not to have told you before, but I thought it wouldn't make a difference. I was wrong.'

Lauren's eyes widened. Was this the breakthrough they'd been waiting for? She exchanged a quick glance with Matt, who had straightened in his chair, pen poised over his notebook.

'Go on,' she said with a sharp nod.

Liam cleared his throat. 'You asked us if we knew anyone called Davy and I said no. That's a lie. I'm Davy.'

'What?' Lauren spluttered. 'But your name isn't David.'

'I went out with Ruth a couple of times. It wasn't serious, but she liked to call me Davy because she said I was like her Uncle David, who'd died recently. She said we had the same eyes. I thought it was a bit weird at the time. But... you know... I should've told you but then I told myself it didn't matter. And then after a bit I didn't dare tell you in case I got in trouble.' Liam glanced down at the floor, his hands clasped together. 'I'm really sorry.'

A surge of excitement coursed through Lauren. Was this the connection they'd been looking for?

'But she was only sixteen, and you were what? Twenty-one? Twenty?' Matt asked, his voice carrying a slight edge.

'Twenty,' Liam replied, his face flushing. 'Ruth was very mature for her age, and when I met her, I didn't realise how young she was. But she was over sixteen so I wasn't doing anything illegal. It wasn't serious...'

He stopped speaking, but Lauren sensed there was more. His body language suggested he was holding something back, the way he kept glancing up at them and then looking away again.

'Carry on,' she prompted.

'At the time, I was seeing Naomi, and she found out about Ruth. We had this massive row and I promised not to see Ruth again. I didn't even have time to finish it with Ruth because she disappeared. I thought she'd gone to London because she was always talking about moving there. I didn't realise until we discovered her bones that she hadn't gone.'

Lauren tapped her chin, her mind working through the timeline. 'But if you were based in Exeter and she was here in Cornwall, how did you know that she'd just disappeared if you'd only seen her a couple of times?'

'I phoned her trying to arrange to meet once more to break it off. She wasn't there, and I can't remember who I spoke to. Maybe her sister or her mum. I asked for Ruth, and they said she'd gone and they didn't know where.'

The room fell silent, the tension almost tangible.

'Did Ruth tell you she wanted to go to university and that she was going to start working hard at school in order to do so?' Matt asked.

'Ruth, university?' Liam said with a low chuckle, and a dismissive wave of his hand. 'She enjoyed herself too much to devote time to studying.'

'Her sister told us that was her plan,' Lauren said.

'As far as I remember, it wasn't something she told me.'

'What happened between you and Naomi after she discovered you were seeing Ruth?' Lauren asked.

'We sorted it out and continued to see each other until leaving uni. Then we went our separate ways.'

'Was it a mutual breakup?' Matt said.

'Yeah. She went overseas. This is the first time we've worked together since uni and that was down to Eleanor pulling us together on—'

He paused, uncertainty flickering across his face.

'What is it?' Lauren demanded.

'You know, when we found the bones, Naomi did act weird. I've only just put two and two together.'

Lauren and Matt exchanged a glance – they'd thought Naomi's reaction had been over the top when they'd discussed Eleanor's death.

'What do you mean by *weird*?'

Liam's hands were moving restlessly now, picking at a loose thread on his sleeve and tapping on his thigh. It was as if he was struggling to come up with the right words.

'She didn't act surprised at first, but then suddenly she started acting super shocked, as if she thought that was the appropriate way to behave.'

'When we discovered the bones belonged to Ruth and we told you all, why didn't you say anything then?' Lauren asked, her voice carrying a note of frustration.

Liam blushed, the colour rising in his cheeks as he stared down at his hands. 'I didn't want to get involved. This was from a long time ago, and I just... I don't know. I'm sorry. I should have done – I could have given you more information that would have helped you identify what exactly happened to her.'

'Yes, you could have,' Lauren said firmly. 'And you *should* have. Because withholding information in a murder investigation is a serious matter.'

'I'm very sorry. Am I in trouble?'

The apology hung in the air between them. There was genuine remorse in Liam's eyes, but that was beside the point. They'd lost valuable time because of his actions.

'Do you genuinely believe that Naomi has something to do with all this?' Lauren asked, deciding not to respond to his question straight away.

Liam was silent for a long time, his internal struggle visible on his face. When he finally spoke, his voice was barely audible.

'I don't want to blame her. I mean... murder... it's... I don't know for sure, but... Maybe?'

'Do you believe she's done a runner?' Matt asked.

'Well, she's not here now, is she? Maybe she suspects I know something. Obviously, with Adam being killed... I'm the only one left.'

'Who else knew about you and Ruth?' Lauren asked.

'Nobody. I didn't tell the others that I was seeing Ruth. She was only sixteen, after all.'

'Which earlier you said was fine,' Lauren reminded him.

'That's how I justified it to myself at the time. But I suppose it wasn't one of my better decisions. Then again, I was only young myself.'

Conflict was written across Liam's face. The struggle between wanting to protect himself and wanting to help with the investigation. It was a delicate balance, and Lauren knew she had to handle this carefully.

'Why would Naomi want to murder Eleanor and Adam? Do you think they knew something?'

'The only thing they could have known was that Naomi killed Ruth. There can't be any other reason.' He paused, as the full implication of what he was saying seemed to hit him. He paled. 'Is my life in danger?'

'It's possible. You need to keep vigilant. Extra vigilant. Don't go anywhere alone.'

'Shall I stay away from the dig?'

'Yes,' Lauren said.

'Are you going to charge me with wasting police time for not telling you I'm Davy?' Liam asked, standing.

'I'll be discussing it with my boss. We'll most likely want to interview you again, so don't go anywhere.'

They escorted Liam to the station entrance. What had started as the discovery of old bones had evolved into a contemporary murder investigation with roots stretching back thirty years and the revelation about Liam and Ruth's relationship added a new dimension to everything that they thought they knew.

She watched Liam walk across the car park, noting how he kept glancing over his shoulder, his movements nervous. He was scared, and rightfully so. He'd just painted a target on his back by revealing his connection to Ruth.

After turning away from the entrance, she turned to Matt. 'If what Liam says is correct, we finally have our motive. Jealousy.

Naomi killed Ruth in a fit of jealous rage thirty years ago, and now she's killing anyone who might know about it.'

'Why wait thirty years?'

'She's been working overseas, remember. She could've accepted Eleanor's offer to join the dig in case the bones were discovered and prompted an investigation into Ruth's death.'

It made sense, in a twisted way. Naomi might have killed Ruth in a moment of passion, hidden the body, and thought she'd got away with it. But when the bones were discovered, and it became clear that Ruth's death was being investigated as a murder, she'd panicked.

'We need to find her, and get the truth,' Matt said.

'Agreed. Before she realises that Liam's confided in us.'

TWENTY-FIVE

FRIDAY 30 MAY

The weight of Liam's revelation hung between Matt and Lauren as they made their way back through the station corridors. Finally, they had a real lead, a concrete connection that could explain everything. The pieces were starting to fit together, forming a picture that was both clearer and more disturbing than Matt had anticipated.

'So Liam's Davy,' Matt said as they walked. 'And thirty years ago he was having an affair with sixteen-year-old Ruth. Naomi found out and in a fit of jealous rage killed Ruth.'

'That's what it's pointing to,' Lauren responded.

'But why Ruth and not Liam?' Matt countered.

'That's something we'll ask when she's questioned.'

'Being jealous enough to kill someone is massive,' Matt said, shaking his head.

'People have killed for a lot less.'

'True,' Matt said, in acknowledgement.

When Lauren and Matt entered the office, the team looked up as one, their faces expectant.

'Okay,' Lauren said, rubbing her hands together. 'We've had a breakthrough.'

As Lauren filled them in on Liam's confession, Clem's

eyebrows shot up when they heard about his relationship with Ruth, and Billy whistled low under his breath. Jenna just nodded grimly, as if she'd been expecting something like this all along.

'Our prime suspect in all three murders is Naomi Walters,' Lauren continued, moving to stand beside the whiteboard. 'Liam, who we now know is Davy because of a nickname given to him by Ruth, was struck by how strangely Naomi acted when Ruth's bones were discovered. Initially she was non-plussed then suddenly she acted all concerned, as if that was the correct way to behave. And now, conveniently, she's disappeared just as we're closing in on the truth.'

'What do you want us to do?' Clem asked, already pulling his keyboard closer.

'Check the CCTV again, paying particular attention to Naomi's movements,' Lauren answered immediately. 'Cover a five-mile radius of the dig site. Find out what car she drives.'

'I'll do that now, ma'am,' Tamsin said, her fingers already flying over the keys.

'As soon as we have the number, I'll contact traffic,' Billy said. 'They might have picked up something on the automatic number plate recognition system.'

'Good. Also, I want everything we can find on Naomi Walters. Bank records, phone records, employment history, social media activity. Where does she live when she's not on the dig? Who are her friends? Family? Everything. There's someone called Belinda who visited her regularly. Let's find her.'

The team was focused now, energised by having a clear direction to pursue. It was obvious in their posture, and the quick exchange of glances as Lauren gave them their tasks.

'Jenna,' Lauren continued. 'Please liaise with Exeter university. I want to know about her academic record. Whether there were any disciplinary issues, and, if possible, who she was friends with. I know it was thirty years ago but we might be able to track down Belinda this way. She could have been someone on her course.'

'I'm on it,' Jenna replied, turning her gaze from Lauren and concentrating on her computer screen.

'Matt, you and I will visit Naomi's accommodation in Treen. If she's done a runner, there might be something there that gives us a clue as to where she's gone.'

The drive to Treen took them along increasingly narrow roads, past stone walls draped with ivy and fields where sheep grazed contentedly in the morning sun.

They passed a sign welcoming them to Treen and headed down the main street.

'There,' Lauren said, pointing to a cottage. 'That's it.'

It was a typical Cornish stone cottage, probably eighteenth or nineteenth century, with thick walls and small windows. The front garden was neat but minimal with a few shrubs and a patch of lawn.

The cottage was divided into two flats, with separate front doors painted in different shades of blue. Naomi was renting the upstairs flat.

Matt glanced upwards and noticed that the curtains were closed. 'She's either still in bed, which I suspect is unlikely, or vanished,' he said as they got out of the car.

They walked up the short path to the front door and he rang the bell.

'Let's try the other flat,' Lauren suggested after no one had answered.

They walked to the other door, which was opened within seconds of Lauren ringing by a woman in her sixties, with short grey hair and kind eyes behind large dark-framed glasses. She was wearing gardening gloves with soil on the fingers, as if she'd been interrupted in the middle of potting plants.

'Can I help you?' she asked, looking slightly surprised.

Lauren showed her warrant card. 'I'm Detective Inspector

Pengelly, and this is Detective Sergeant Price. We're looking for Naomi Walters, who rents the upstairs flat?'

The woman's expression immediately shifted to one of concern. 'Oh dear, is everything alright? I'm Mrs Griffin. I own the cottage.'

'It's fine,' Matt said, in a calm voice. 'We just need to speak with Naomi but there's no answer. Have you seen her recently?'

Mrs Griffin frowned, pulling off her gardening gloves. 'Not for a few days, actually. Which is unusual because she often pops down for a chat when she gets in from work. Lovely woman, always very friendly, and so knowledgeable about old stuff.'

Matt exchanged a glance with Lauren. Another confirmation that Naomi had disappeared.

'Would it be possible for us to take a look around her flat?' Lauren asked. 'We're concerned for her welfare.'

'Oh my goodness, of course. Let me get the spare key.'

Mrs Griffin disappeared back into her flat, returning moments later with a set of keys. She led them back to the door and unlocked it for them. 'I do hope nothing's happened to her. She's been such a good tenant. Very friendly and never any trouble.'

'We'll take it from here, thanks, Mrs Griffin. We'll let you know when we've finished and you can lock up,' Lauren said.

'Okay,' Mrs Griffin said. 'Here's the key to her inner front door.'

She handed it to Lauren but remained standing outside rather than going back inside to her flat.

Matt and Lauren took the stairs two at a time. The door opened directly into a small living room, and Matt immediately knew they were too late. The flat had that empty feel to it. The drawn curtains cast everything in a dim, grey light.

'Naomi?' Lauren called out, but there was no response.

Matt moved further into the room, his eyes adjusting to the low light. The flat was simply furnished with a small sofa, a coffee table, and a television on a stand against one wall. But there were no personal items on display. No books or magazines left lying around. No jacket thrown over a chair.

'She's gone,' he muttered.

Lauren was already moving through the flat, checking the other rooms. Matt followed her into the kitchen, a compact galley with basic appliances and a small table by the window. Again, it was almost sterile in its emptiness. The fridge was humming quietly, but when Matt opened it, he found it had been cleaned out except for a few condiments and a carton of milk that was approaching its expiry date.

Next stop was the bedroom, which was barely large enough for a double bed, a small wardrobe and chest of drawers. The bed was made, but the covers looked like they hadn't been slept in recently. On the bedside table was a digital alarm clock, its red numbers glowing in the dim light, but nothing else. Lauren opened the wardrobe and Matt went to the drawers.

'Empty,' Matt called out.

'Same here,' Lauren added.

'She's packed up and gone. But when and where did she go?' Matt mused, with a shake of his head.

'Let's speak to Mrs Griffin.'

They hurried back downstairs to where the woman was hovering anxiously close to the front door.

'Mrs Griffin, do you remember the last time you saw Naomi?' Lauren asked.

'Tuesday morning,' Mrs Griffin replied without hesitation. 'But if she's left, why is her car still here?' She pointed to a white Ford Focus parked in the street.

Tuesday morning.

If Naomi was the killer and she'd been planning her escape well in advance of becoming a suspect, she must have decided to leave her car because the police would know to look out for it, and it would delay them being alert to the fact that she'd already left.

'Did she say anything to you on Tuesday?' Lauren asked.

'Just "good morning". She did seem preoccupied, now I come to think about it.'

'In what way?' Matt asked.

'I mentioned something about the weather, which is one of our favourite subjects, but she didn't really respond, just nodded. I was on my way out for the day, to meet my friend, so didn't pursue it. We spent the day in Penzance and went to the cinema in the evening. I didn't get home until gone nine at night.'

'Is Naomi's rent paid up to date?' Lauren asked.

'Oh yes. But it's paid directly by direct debit from the dig. I've never had any problems with payments.' Mrs Griffin paused, looking worried. 'They will still pay, won't they?' She coloured slightly. 'I mean… it's just that I need the money. But if something's happened to her…'

There was genuine concern in the woman's voice, but also the practical worry of someone who depended on rental income.

'We don't know at this stage,' Lauren said honestly. 'But we'll make sure you're kept informed.'

They thanked Mrs Griffin and headed over to Naomi's car. Lauren tried the door, but it was locked.

'I think Naomi knew that after killing Adam Fielding we'd start looking in her direction so she decided to run – and not take her car – rather than face the music,' Matt said, spelling out what seemed glaringly obvious.

'But is she planning on running indefinitely, or is she buying time to eliminate the last few witnesses?' Lauren added, her hands gripping the steering wheel tightly as she drove off.

Matt chilled at that thought. If Naomi was the killer, and she felt cornered, there was no telling what she might do next. And Liam was the most obvious target.

TWENTY-SIX
FRIDAY 30 MAY

Lauren pushed open the door to the main office and placed her jacket on the desk beside the whiteboard. 'Attention please, everyone. The flat's completely empty. Naomi Walters has taken all her personal belongings, apart from her car, which is still there, maybe as a decoy. What have you found in our absence?'

'We've checked the CCTV around the dig site for the past week. Her car, a white Ford Focus, shows up occasionally until Tuesday evening, then nothing,' Clem said.

'Which fits in with her leaving,' Lauren said with a nod. 'What time Tuesday evening?'

'It was spotted at seven driving past, which puts her away from the crime scene at the time Fielding was killed, unfortunately,' Clem said with a grimace.

'Her credit card was used on Monday afternoon to buy a train ticket to London. Single fare, departing from Penzance station first thing Wednesday morning,' Tamsin said. 'Do you think she planned it so she'd disappear after the murder but before the body was found because she assumed it would be a while?'

The room fell silent for a moment as everyone processed this information. Lauren could feel the pieces clicking into place in her mind, but there were still gaps. Questions that needed answering.

'So she left her car behind and took the train,' Lauren said slowly. 'That suggests either panic or planning. If it was panic, she might have just grabbed what she could carry and run. But the fact that her flat was empty suggests it was planned in detail. How did she get from Treen to Penzance station? It's what, about fifteen miles? Not walking distance, especially with luggage.'

'On it,' Clem said, already reaching for his phone. 'I'll start with the local taxi companies.'

'Try Uber as well,' Lauren added. 'And any other ride-sharing services.'

'Or she might have taken the bus somewhere. I'll check out the bus station and ask them to send CCTV footage just in case,' Clem said.

'What about her family?' Lauren asked. 'Do we have any details?'

Jenna looked up from her files. 'Working on it. The dig records show her emergency contact is her mother, who lives in Croydon. Margaret Walters, aged seventy-two.'

'Phone number?'

'Got it here,' Jenna said, holding up a slip of paper.

'I'll call her now,' Lauren said, taking the piece of paper from Jenna, and heading back to her office.

Speaking to a suspect's mother was always delicate. You had to balance the need for information with the instinct of a parent to protect their child.

The phone rang four times before a woman answered, sounding slightly breathless as if she'd hurried to the phone.

'Hello?'

'Mrs Walters? This is Detective Inspector Pengelly from Devon and Cornwall Police. I'm calling about your daughter, Naomi.'

There was a sharp intake of breath on the other end.

'Is she alright? Has something happened?'

The concern in the woman's voice was unmistakable. Lauren

made a quick decision to not reveal too much while trying to extract as much information as possible.

'We want to locate her in connection with an ongoing investigation. When did you last speak to Naomi?'

'About a week ago, I think. She's been calling regularly to check how I'm getting on after my hip operation. She's such a good girl, always worries about me.'

A pang of sympathy for the woman hit Lauren. Whatever Naomi had done, her mother clearly loved her and had no idea what else was going on.

'Is Naomi there with you now, Mrs Walters?'

'No. She's working on an archaeological project in Cornwall. Has been for months now. Why?'

'Like I said, we need to speak to her about something. It's probably nothing serious, but we do need to find her. Do you have any idea where she might go if she needs to get away for a while?'

There was another pause. 'Well, there's her friend Belinda. They were at university together and stayed close over the years. Naomi sometimes stays with her when she needs a break.'

Lauren's pulse quickened. This was the friend Verity had mentioned earlier.

'Do you have contact details for Belinda?'

'Yes, of course. Belinda Morris. She's married and lives in Torquay. Lovely girl. I'll fetch my address book.'

After returning to the phone, Mrs Walters gave Lauren the details, which she copied down carefully.

'Mrs Walters, if Naomi contacts you, it's very important that you let us know immediately. Please don't mention that we've spoken. We don't want to worry her unnecessarily.'

'Now you're frightening me,' the woman said, her voice strained. 'What's this really about? Tell me. I'm her mother. Is Naomi in some kind of trouble?'

'We just need to speak to her about an investigation we're conducting. I'm sure it will all be sorted out soon,' Lauren responded, repeating what she'd previously said, and not giving anything else away.

Lauren hated lying to the woman, but sometimes it was necessary to protect both the investigation and the innocent people caught up in it.

After ending the call, Lauren returned to the office.

'Any luck with transport?' Lauren asked Clem.

Clem shook his head, covering the mouthpiece of the phone with his hand. 'Nothing so far. None of the taxi companies have any record of picking up a fare from Treen to Penzance.'

'Keep trying. What about the buses?'

'There's a local service that runs between the villages and Penzance,' Billy said, consulting a timetable on his screen. 'But it would have been difficult with heavy luggage. The buses are small, and there's limited space for bags.'

Lauren considered this. 'I think it's more likely that someone gave her a lift. Someone we don't know about yet.'

'Unless she didn't actually take the train to London,' Matt said.

Everyone turned to look at him. 'Explain,' Lauren said.

'What if buying the ticket was another misdirection, like leaving her car? What if she wants us to think she's gone to London while going somewhere else entirely? She could have hired a car to drive somewhere and bought the ticket to put us off the scent.'

'Or she might have bought a train ticket to somewhere else, maybe paying cash,' Billy pointed out.

Lauren felt the familiar frustration of a case that seemed to offer as many questions as answers. 'We need to see the CCTV from Penzance station. If she got on the train to London, there'll be footage. Also, we can check if she caught another train.'

'I'll call them,' Jenna offered.

'No, it's fine. We'll go there and check for ourselves. That way we'll see it quicker. Jenna, I want you to contact Belinda Morris in Torquay. Find out if she's heard from Naomi recently, and whether she's planning to visit — anything that might help us track her down.'

'What if she's there?' Jenna asked.

'Then we bring her in. But carefully. Our murderer has already shown they're willing to kill to protect themselves. If it's Naomi... well, I don't need to spell it out.' Lauren paused, looking around the room at her team. 'In the meantime keep working on finding how she got away. Matt and I are going to Penzance train station. If anyone gets a solid lead on Naomi's whereabouts, call me immediately.'

TWENTY-SEVEN
FRIDAY 30 MAY

Matt glanced at his watch as they left the police station. It was four-thirty and the May sunshine was still strong, casting clear shadows as they walked to the car park.

'We'll go in separate cars,' Lauren said, fishing her keys from her pocket. 'That way we can both head home after. I'll need you in early tomorrow.'

Matt nodded. They were entering the critical phase of the investigation and the next day would likely bring developments that would require all hands on deck until they could make an arrest. He pulled out his own car keys, grateful for the chance to drive home directly rather than having to return to the station.

'See you there in five minutes,' he said, heading towards his own car.

The drive to the railway station only took a few minutes through Penzance's quiet streets and he pulled into the station car park just behind Lauren.

The railway station was a Victorian building that had seen better days but still retained a certain dignified presence. There were modern security cameras mounted at various points, and a cautious optimism built in Matt's chest. If Naomi had caught the train to London, or any other place, on Wednesday, there'd be footage of her doing so.

'I've always liked this building, even if it does appear a bit rundown,' he commented as they approached the main entrance.

'Built in the eighteen hundreds,' Lauren replied. 'They certainly knew how to build things to last back then. Not like some of the buildings we see nowadays.' She laughed. 'Listen to me sounding like an old fogey.'

The ticket office was still open and a few passengers were waiting on the platform for what Matt assumed was the evening service to London, their luggage arranged around them.

Lauren approached the customer service desk, showing her warrant card to the middle-aged man behind the counter.

'I'm Detective Inspector Pengelly, and this is Detective Sergeant Price. Please fetch the station manager.'

The man's eyebrows rose slightly, but he maintained his professional demeanour. 'I'll get Mr Hawkins for you. Just give me a moment.'

He disappeared through a door marked *Staff Only*, returning a few minutes later with a tall, thin man in his fifties wearing a dark grey suit with a crisp white shirt and red and navy striped tie.

'I'm Don Hawkins, the station manager. How can I help you?'

Lauren stepped forward. 'We're investigating a serious crime and believe one of our suspects may have travelled through here on Wednesday. We need to examine your CCTV footage from that day.'

'Of course, absolutely. Which time are you interested in?'

Matt consulted his notes. 'The London service on Wednesday morning. What time does that normally depart?'

'The main daytime London service leaves at eleven thirty-two,' Hawkins replied promptly. 'But the afternoon service at three forty-seven is more popular.'

'We'll need to see footage from both,' Lauren said. 'Our suspect's a woman, travelling alone, probably with luggage.'

'Before we do that,' Matt added. 'What other trains could this person have travelled on?'

'We're served by two train operators. GWR and Cross Country. The former operates to and from London Paddington, and also to Plymouth and Cardiff. The latter offers less services and these go to places like Birmingham, Leeds and Edinburgh.'

'Thank you, that's very useful,' Matt replied with a nod. 'I think we might need to look at general footage of the station to make sure.'

Hawkins nodded, his expression serious. 'We'll go to my office and I'll access all the camera feeds.'

They followed him through the staff area, past a small crew room where a couple of uniformed railway workers were having a break. His office was dominated by a large desk covered in papers and a bank of monitors showing feeds from various cameras around the station.

'Take a seat,' Hawkins said, gesturing to two chairs as he settled behind his desk and began manipulating the controls. 'I'll bring up the footage from Wednesday morning as that's the time you initially requested.'

'Here's a photocopy of the ticket,' Lauren said, sliding it over the desk for Hawkins.

Matt stared ahead as the screens flickered to life, showing black and white images from different angles around the station. He could see the main concourse, the platforms, the ticket barriers, and the areas around the entrance. It was such a small station it seemed impossible for anyone to hide from the cameras.

The footage began to play, showing the usual flow of passengers arriving, buying tickets, and boarding the London-bound train. Matt watched carefully, looking for a woman of average height, shoulder-length brown hair, and dressed casually in jeans and jumper, which was how he remembered her.

'Can you slow the footage down when passengers are going through the barrier, please?' Lauren asked.

'Certainly.' Hawkins adjusted the playback speed, and they

watched as each passenger was clearly visible passing through the ticket barriers. Matt scrutinised every face, every figure, but none of them were Naomi Walters.

'There,' Lauren said, pointing at the screen. 'Can you go back about thirty seconds?'

Hawkins rewound the footage, and they watched again as a woman with dark hair and a large rucksack approached the barriers. But as she turned, Matt could see it wasn't Naomi. This woman was older, with different facial features entirely.

'Not her,' he said, settling back in his chair.

They continued watching until the morning train had departed, but there was no sign of their suspect. Hawkins fast-forwarded and slowed the footage as the time approached for the afternoon service.

'Right, here we go,' Hawkins said. 'This is the afternoon London service.'

Matt's concentration intensified as passengers began arriving for the afternoon train. The camera angles gave them good coverage of the main areas, and Hawkins switched between different feeds to ensure they didn't miss anything.

'There's good coverage of the platform as well,' Hawkins explained, bringing up another feed. 'This camera shows everyone boarding the train.'

They watched in silence as passenger after passenger passed through the barriers and made their way to the platform. Matt found himself studying each woman carefully, looking for any resemblance to Naomi. But as the minutes passed and the train prepared to depart, it became increasingly clear that she wasn't among the passengers for this train either.

'She's not there,' Lauren said. 'She didn't take either train.'

'Let me check the evening service as well,' Hawkins offered. 'In case she decided to travel later.'

They watched the footage from the seven twenty-three service, but again, there was no sign of Naomi. They also checked footage for the other two trains that left the station that day but again came up blank. This confirmed Matt's suspicion that the ticket purchase had been a misdirection.

'She bought a ticket but didn't use it,' Lauren said, echoing his thoughts.

'It looks that way,' Matt replied. 'The question is, why? Was she planning to use it but changed her mind, or was it always meant to throw us off the scent?'

'If it helps,' Hawkins said, 'I can tell you that the ticket was purchased online, not at the station. The booking reference shows it was bought at ten forty-five on Monday morning.'

'She could have bought it from anywhere with internet access,' Matt said, exchanging a glance with Lauren.

'Yes.'

'So the question is, did Naomi intend to use the ticket but changed her mind... Maybe, if something had spooked her. Or did she never intend to travel?'

'We won't know that until we locate her,' Lauren replied. 'Mr Hawkins, we'd like a copy of all the footage if you could please email it to me. Here's my card.'

'I'll get that sorted for you right away,' Mr Hawkins said, taking the card and beginning the process of downloading the footage.

If Naomi hadn't taken the train to London, where had she gone?

'We need to expand the search,' Matt said to Lauren. 'Naomi must have found another way to travel.'

'She might still be in Cornwall, hiding out somewhere,' Lauren replied grimly.

A chill ran down Matt's spine. If Naomi was still in the area, free and potentially planning her next move, then Liam, and possibly the others, could be in danger.

The woman's motive wasn't clear and until such time that it was, no one was safe.

'That's it. All sent,' Hawkins said, looking up from his screen.

'Thanks for your cooperation,' Lauren said, shaking the man's hand. 'If you discover anything that might be relevant, please don't hesitate to contact us.'

'Back to the drawing board,' Matt said as they reached their cars.

'Not quite,' Lauren replied, unlocking her car. 'We know more than we did an hour ago. We know the ticket purchase was a misdirection on Naomi Walters's part, and that she's gone to considerable effort to cover her tracks. That tells us she's clever, organised, and still dangerous. I'll see you in the morning. I have a feeling tomorrow's going to be crucial.'

TWENTY-EIGHT

FRIDAY 30 MAY

'Daddy, come and play with me,' Dani said.

Matt turned around from washing up the pans after dinner. 'Let me finish this, and I'll be with you. But we can't play for long because it's nearly bedtime.'

Dani sighed and tapped her foot on the floor, just like her grandma did. Matt stifled a grin.

'Okaaaay. But hurry up.'

He was about to answer when his phone buzzed on the kitchen worktop. He glanced at the screen and smiled when he saw Ellie's name.

'Wait for me in the lounge, sweetheart, and I'll come in once I've taken this call.'

'Don't be long,' Dani responded, running out of the kitchen.

'Ellie, good to hear from you,' he said, pulling out a kitchen chair and dropping down on it, pressing the speaker button and placing his phone on the table. 'How's it going?'

It had been ages since they'd spoken, and he'd been meaning to call to catch up on how things were going in Lenchester.

'Busy as usual... but you know all about that.'

There was a slight hesitation in her voice that Matt picked up on immediately. 'And...'

'Actually, there is something I'd like to ask you. It's... well, it's quite big, really.'

Matt sat upright in the chair, giving her his full attention. 'Of course, what's on your mind?'

'It's about Cornwall. About possibly moving down there.' The words came out in a rush, as if she'd been rehearsing them. 'Tamsin told me she's got onto the family liaison officer training, and there might be an opening on your team to replace her.'

A surge of excitement coursed through Matt. Having Ellie on the team would be incredible. Her research skills were legendary in Lenchester, and everyone in Cornwall witnessed them, too, during her secondment with them.

'Wow. That would be fantastic, Ellie. You'd be brilliant here. I sense there's a "but" coming, though,' he added, having heard the uncertainty in her voice.

She laughed, but it sounded shaky. 'There are several "but"s. Moving away from everything I know and leaving my family, my friends, for a start. It's a big step. I've lived in the same area my whole life.'

'I agree, it is a big step,' Matt said, staring out of the kitchen window at the Cornish countryside beyond. 'But sometimes big steps are worth taking. Is there anything in particular that's holding you back?'

There was a long pause, and Matt could almost hear her weighing up what to say next.

'It's Billy,' she said finally.

'Ah.' Matt smiled to himself. 'Are you worried that it might be difficult if it doesn't work out between you?'

'There is that to consider.' She took a deep breath. 'Matt, can I tell you something? But you must promise to keep it to yourself.'

'Of course,' Matt immediately responded, his curiosity well and truly piqued.

'Billy's asked me to get engaged.'

Matt's jaw dropped. He hadn't been expecting that.

'Bloody hell, Ellie. That's marvellous news. When did this happen?'

'A couple of weeks ago when he visited. We went for a walk along the river, and he just asked. He said he'd been thinking about it for a while now and couldn't imagine his future without me in it.' Her voice was soft, full of emotion. 'He doesn't have a ring yet. He wanted to wait for my answer first.'

'What did you tell him?'

'That I need time to think. Which probably wasn't what he wanted to hear, but I... I need to be sure. You know, after everything that happened with Dean.'

Matt stiffened at the mention of Ellie's ex-partner who'd cheated on her, leaving her confidence in relationships at an all-time low. 'Ellie, Billy's nothing like Dean. Nothing at all.'

'I know that. Well... logically I do. Despite his outward appearance, Billy's kind, and patient, and he really makes me laugh. But it's still scary. The thought of making that commitment again.'

'You can't let Dean's appalling behaviour dictate the rest of your life. Billy loves you, Ellie. And, more importantly, he respects you. He respects your work, your intelligence, and your independence.'

'Do you really think so?'

'I know so. He talks about you all the time. The man's completely smitten, but in the best possible way.'

Ellie was quiet for a moment, and Matt could hear her sniffling slightly. 'Sorry. I'm being ridiculous, aren't I? Getting all emotional over the phone.'

'You're not being ridiculous at all. It's a big decision. The engagement and the potential move are both life changing. But in a good way. And it's not like you're going to be all alone. You have me. You have the DI and all the other members of the team. They'll always be there for you.'

'You're right, and if I say yes to Billy, then moving to Cornwall becomes an easy decision. We'll be together. We'll both be doing jobs we love, and maybe... maybe it's time for a fresh start.'

Warmth spread through Matt's chest. The idea of having Ellie down there, and seeing Billy and her together, was more appealing than he'd realised. 'It sounds like you've made up your mind.'

'I think so. But there's one more thing I'm worried about.' Her voice became more serious. 'What will the guv say? She's been so good to me. Always having my back when other departments wanted me to move over to them and trusting my judgement on important cases. It feels like I'd be letting her down.'

Matt understood her concern. DCI Whitney Walker from Lenchester had been a mentor to Ellie, and their professional relationship had grown into something much deeper. It was a real friendship built on mutual respect. It was typical of Ellie to worry about disappointing her. But Matt knew Whitney and would put money on her not wanting to stand in the way of the officer's happiness.

'Would you like me to speak to her?' he offered.

'Would you?' The relief in Ellie's voice was palpable. 'That would be amazing, Matt. If I'm going to leave, I want it to be with her blessing.'

'Consider it done. I'll call her this evening.'

'Thanks so much. You don't know how much this means to me.'

They chatted for a while about practical things. What the timeline might be and the interview process for Tamsin's job. Also, where Ellie might live if she did relocate, and how different it would be working permanently in Cornwall compared with her temporary secondment. The excitement crept into Ellie's voice as they talked, replacing the uncertainty that had been there at the beginning of the call.

'I should let you go,' Ellie said eventually. 'I know you've had a long day with the case.'

'I'll always have time for you, Ellie. Remember, life's too short to let fear make your decisions for you.'

'Thanks, Matt. You've been more help than you know.'

After ending the call, Matt sat in his chair for a few minutes, processing the conversation. Ellie and Billy potentially engaged; how that might affect the team's dynamics. But he trusted the pair of them not to let it cause any issues.

He picked up his phone again and scrolled to Whitney's number. Hopefully she wasn't too busy to talk.

'Matt Price.' Whitney's familiar voice came through the phone, with genuine pleasure. 'This is a nice surprise. How are things going down there?'

'Really well, thanks. Cornwall's been good for me. The work's interesting, the team's great, and I'm in the process of buying a house.'

'A house? That's marvellous. Tell me about it.'

Matt found himself smiling as he described the house. 'It's in great condition and ready to move in. The best part is I'll be close to Mum and Dad, so they can still take care of Dani.'

'How is that lovely daughter of yours?'

'Still bossing me around as usual,' he replied with a chuckle. 'She's going to be starting school soon.'

'Already?' Whitney's voice rose in surprise. 'I can't believe how quickly the time has gone.'

They talked for a few more minutes about work, some of the cases they'd shared back in Lenchester, mutual colleagues, and how the old team was getting on. There was a sincere warmth in Whitney's voice. She always managed to make everyone feel valued and cared for.

'Actually, Whitney,' he said eventually. 'There's something specific I want to talk to you about. It's Ellie.'

'I see.' There was a knowing tone in Whitney's voice. 'Let me guess, she's thinking of moving to Cornwall.'

Matt was momentarily speechless. 'How did you know?'

'She's been distracted recently, asking questions about Cornwall, looking up property rentals on her computer when she thinks no one's watching. And then there's Billy.'

'Have you met him yet?'

'Yes, she introduced him to us all on one of his visits. I must say he's nothing like I'd imagined. But he certainly brings her out of her shell. I'm guessing this is something to do with him?'

'Yes. It's looking serious.'

'I'm pleased for them. Ellie deserves someone who sees how special she is. Especially after the *Dean* fiasco.'

A wave of relief washed over Matt. Whitney's reaction was exactly what he'd hoped for. Supportive and understanding. 'So you won't be upset if she applies for a position down here? Because there's going to be one coming up.'

Whitney was quiet for a moment. 'Upset isn't the right word. Devastated might be more accurate.' She laughed, but it was tinged with sadness. 'Ellie's the best researcher I've ever worked with, Matt. No one can dig into a case the way she does and find connections that everyone else misses. Losing her would be like losing my right arm.'

'But?'

'But I care about her too much to stand in her way. If moving to Cornwall to be with Billy is what she wants, then that's all that matters. Her wellbeing must come first.'

Matt's throat tightened with emotion. This was exactly why DCI Whitney Walker was such a good leader. She genuinely cared about her people as individuals, not just as resources to be used.

'She's worried about disappointing you,' Matt said. 'You've been such a great mentor to her.'

'She's been a joy to work with, as you well know. But people grow and change – and eventually move on. The best thing I can do for Ellie is support her in whatever decision she makes. And also tell her there's always a place for her here if it all turns to custard, which I sincerely hope it doesn't.'

They talked for another twenty minutes, covering everything from the practical aspects of a potential transfer to Whitney's own plans. As usual, talking to Whitney left Matt feeling energised and optimistic about life.

'You know, if Ellie does make the move, it gives me even more reason to come down and visit you all. I can then see for myself why everyone seems to love Cornwall so much,' Whitney said as they were winding up the conversation.

'You'll be more than welcome. We'd love to show you around. And once I've moved you can stay in my spare room.'

'I might just take you up on that. It's been too long since I've had a proper holiday. I'm sure Tiffany and Ava would love to come with me, too,' Whitney said, referring to her daughter and grand-daughter.

'The more the merrier. Dani would love to spend time with Ava,' Matt responded.

After saying goodbye, Matt sat back in his chair, feeling satisfied with how both conversations had gone. Ellie would be relieved to know that Whitney was supportive of her potential move.

He picked up his phone to text Ellie, then thought better of it. It would be better to call and share the good news properly.

'That was quick,' Ellie said when she answered. 'Good news or bad?'

'Definitely good. Whitney wasn't surprised, and while she'll be sad to lose you, she's completely supportive of whatever decision you make.'

The sound that came through the phone was somewhere between a laugh and a sob. 'Really? She's not angry?'

'Not even close. She said you deserve to be happy, and if that means moving to Cornwall to be with Billy, then that's what counts.'

'Thank goodness. You don't know how much better that makes me feel. I was so worried about disappointing her.'

'The DCI doesn't get disappointed in people for making positive life choices. She gets disappointed in people who don't reach their full potential or who make decisions based on fear rather than hope.'

'You're right. Of course you are.' Ellie's voice was stronger now, more confident. 'I think... I think I know what I'm going to tell Billy.'

Matt smiled, looking out the window at the darkening Cornish sky. 'I think I know too.'

'Thanks, Matt. For everything. I'll speak to you soon.'

Matt said goodbye, a deep sense of contentment washing over him. Sometimes things worked out the way they were supposed to. And sometimes, if you were very lucky, you got to watch the people you cared about find their happiness.

Tomorrow would bring new challenges, but tonight, he was content to sit back and think about the future. About Ellie and Billy starting their lives together in Cornwall, and about Whitney eventually coming to visit.

It was a good life, he reflected. Different from what he'd planned, but good, nonetheless.

TWENTY-NINE

SATURDAY 31 MAY

The drive to Torquay took just over an hour in Saturday morning traffic, giving Lauren plenty of time to mull over what they might learn from Naomi Walters's friend Belinda Morris. Jenna's phone call the previous evening had been frustrating. Belinda had been unable to drive to the station because of a sprained ankle that had left her housebound, and there was no one else available to bring her in. But sometimes visiting someone in their own environment yielded better results because they were more relaxed.

'What do we know about this woman?' Matt asked as they navigated the outskirts of Torquay.

'According to Jenna, Belinda Morris works as a librarian at the local college. She's been friends with Naomi since university. Jenna said she sounded genuinely concerned and kept asking if Naomi was in trouble. She lives around this corner, according to the satnav.'

The terraced house where Belinda lived had a cheerful yellow painted door, with window boxes full of early summer flowers, hinting that the person living there took pride in their home.

Lauren pressed the bell and a few moments later, the door was opened by a woman with short, auburn hair and kind eyes behind dark-framed glasses, leaning heavily on a walking stick, her left foot wrapped in a bandage. It was clearly Belinda.

'I'm DI Pengelly and this is DS Price. You're expecting us,' Lauren said.

'Yes, please, come in. I'm on my own because my husband had to pop into the office.'

She led them into the house and then to a room overlooking the street. Bookcases lined two of the walls and photographs of Belinda and a tall man with grey hair at various locations were dotted along the shelves between the books. Belinda gestured them towards a sofa covered in a patchwork throw, whilst she settled carefully into an armchair, propping her injured foot on a cushioned stool.

'I'm sorry you've had to come all this way,' she said, adjusting her position with a wince. 'This bloody ankle has rendered me completely useless. Can I get you a tea or coffee?'

'We're fine, thank you,' Lauren replied, settling into the sofa. 'We appreciate you seeing us. As my officer mentioned on the phone, we're trying to locate Naomi Walters in connection with an ongoing investigation.'

Belinda's face creased with worry. 'She's not in trouble, is she? Since your colleague rang yesterday, I've been beside myself thinking something's happened to her. I've tried calling but it goes straight to voicemail.'

'We just need to speak with Naomi,' Matt said diplomatically. 'Can you tell us about your friendship?'

'We were at Exeter university together, initially both studying archaeology, but I switched to library sciences after my first year.' Belinda's expression softened as she spoke about their shared past. 'We clicked straight away. Naomi was always the more adventurous one, wanting to get out on digs and get her hands dirty. I preferred the research side of things.'

Lauren watched Belinda's face carefully as she spoke. There was a sincere affection there, the kind that came from decades of friendship. 'And you've stayed close over the years?'

'Oh yes, very. We ring each other at least once a week, sometimes more. She doesn't have much family. Her mum's getting on a bit, and there's no one else really. My husband always jokes that I talk to her more than I talk to him.'

'What do you know about her relationships?' Lauren asked. 'Particularly during university?'

Belinda's expression darkened slightly. 'You mean Liam Blackburn, I assume. That was a difficult time for her.'

'In what way?'

Belinda shifted in her chair, her fingers drumming against the arm. 'Naomi was completely smitten with him when they first got together. He appeared charming, laid back, considerate and fun. Not like some of the other men on the course. But he turned out to be trouble.'

'How so?'

'Behind this easy-going exterior, he was manipulative and possessive. Always wanting to know where she was and who she was with. And then there was the business with Ruth.'

Lauren's pulse quickened. 'What do you know about Ruth?'

'I know he cheated on Naomi with her. A sixteen-year-old girl, for goodness' sake. Naomi was devastated when she found out.' Belinda's voice carried the righteous anger of a loyal friend. 'She confronted him about it and they had an enormous row. He promised to stop seeing Ruth.'

'What was Naomi's reaction to the affair?'

'She was heartbroken, obviously. But also angry. She felt such a fool for trusting him.' Belinda paused, seeming to choose her words carefully. 'But if you're thinking she might have hurt Ruth, you're barking up the wrong tree. Naomi's not violent. She's never hurt anyone in her life.'

Something in Belinda's tone suggested there was more to the story. 'Did Naomi have any contact with Ruth directly?'

'She tried to warn her. Told her Liam wasn't what he seemed, and that he could be controlling and manipulative. Naomi was worried about the girl. Sixteen was so young, and Liam had a way of making you feel like you were the centre of his world... until he decided you weren't.'

'How did Ruth react to Naomi's warning?'

'From what Naomi told me, Ruth didn't want to listen. She was completely infatuated with Liam and thought Naomi was being a jealous girlfriend.' Belinda shook her head sadly. 'Young girls can be so naive.'

Matt leant forward slightly. 'You said Liam was possessive. Did that continue after the affair came to light?'

'It got worse. Much worse. He seemed to think that because Naomi had found out about Ruth, she somehow owed him forgiveness. He'd turn up when we were out together. He'd wait outside her flat and send her letters. She was genuinely scared of him by the end.'

A chill ran down Lauren's spine. 'Scared how?'

'He had this way of making threats without actually threatening, if you know what I mean. He'd say things like: "I hope nothing bad happens to you," or "You wouldn't want people to know certain things about you." Naomi never told me what he meant by that, but it frightened her.'

'Why didn't she end it?' Matt asked.

'She was too scared. I tried to persuade her but she refused to rock the boat... Her words.'

'What happened after university?'

'Luckily, Liam got a job up north somewhere. Newcastle, I think. He said it was his dream job and he couldn't say no. He didn't ask Naomi to go with him, thank goodness. She wouldn't have done, anyway. She took a job overseas, and for years we thought that was the end of it. She seemed to relax and got on with her career and began dating other men. But she never settled down with anyone.'

Lauren sucked in a breath. This was a very different picture of Naomi Walters than they'd been led to believe. 'So why did Naomi agree to work on the dig at Treen if she knew Liam would be there?'

'That's just it. She didn't know he'd be there. He wasn't on the original team. Someone dropped out at the last minute, and Liam took their place. By then, Naomi had already signed the contract and begun working there. She was stuck.'

'When did she find out he was joining the team?'

'The day he started. Naomi rang me that evening, completely panicked. She was thinking about leaving the dig, but she couldn't afford to lose the work. Jobs in archaeology aren't exactly thick on the ground.'

'How did she cope with working alongside him?' Matt asked.

'She said he hardly spoke to her, which she took as a good sign, and thought maybe he'd moved on, matured, whatever. She got on well with the other team members, especially Eleanor and Adam, who she'd known from years ago, and decided to stick it out.'

'Belinda, when did you last speak to Naomi?' Lauren asked.

'Monday evening. She rang me after work, which wasn't unusual. But she seemed agitated. Worried about something.'

'What did she say?'

Belinda hesitated, then seemed to make a decision. 'She told me she'd lied to you about Ruth.'

'Lied how?' Lauren asked, her stomach dropping.

'She told your people that she didn't know Ruth and had never met her. But that wasn't true, as you now know. She had met Ruth, when she tried to warn her off Liam.'

'Did she say why she lied?'

'Because Liam told her to. He approached her after you told them the bones belonged to Ruth and said that if she knew what was good for her, she'd pretend she didn't know Ruth. He said it would be better for everyone if certain things stayed buried.'

'Did she know what he meant by that?' Lauren asked, exhaling loudly.

'I don't think so but she was worried about what Liam might do if she didn't comply.'

The room fell silent except for the ticking of a clock on the wall. It seemed like the investigation was tilting on its axis, everything they'd assumed about Naomi suddenly cast in a different light.

'Belinda, did Naomi tell you that she was planning to leave?' Lauren asked.

'No, but she would've done because we tell each other every-thing.' Belinda's voice was firm. 'That's why I'm so worried.'

'Did she mention feeling threatened?'

'Yes. She was scared of Liam, because he'd started watching her, and following her movements around the site. Even though the dig was closed he always seemed to be where she was. Treen's such a small place, he was always able to keep an eye on her.'

Lauren exchanged a look with Matt. Everything they'd thought about this case was being turned upside down. 'Belinda, is there somewhere Naomi might go if she felt threatened, where she'd feel safe?'

Belinda sighed. 'I don't know. Her mum's in Croydon, but Naomi wouldn't want to put her in danger. There's no one she's particularly close to, apart from me. She should've come here.'

'What about other family?' Matt asked.

'There's an aunt in Scotland, but they're not close. Naomi always said I was more like family to her than her actual relatives.'

Belinda struggled to lean forwards, her face creased with anxi-ety. 'I'm really worried about her. It's not like Naomi to just vanish. She's responsible and reliable. I think something's happened to her.'

The weight of the woman's fear was almost tangible, and this added to Lauren's growing belief that they'd been chasing the wrong person.

'We're doing everything we can to find her, Belinda. Do you think Liam Blackburn could have hurt Naomi?'

Belinda didn't hesitate. 'Yes, I do. I've been worried about that man for thirty years. Naomi thought she was free of him when they left university, but men like Liam... they don't forget. They don't forgive. And they don't let go.'

THIRTY

SATURDAY 31 MAY

'We need to find her,' Matt said as they left Torquay. 'And we need to take a much closer look at Liam Blackburn.'

'Agreed. Contact the team and get them looking into him. If Liam's the one who's been killing people all along...' Lauren didn't finish the sentence. They both knew what it meant. If Liam was the killer, and if Naomi was still alive somewhere, she was running out of time.

The remaining drive to Penzance was subdued. They'd been pursuing a victim rather than a perpetrator, and while they'd been looking for Naomi as a suspect, she might have been in deadly danger.

Finally, they arrived back at the office.

'We need to reassess everything we thought we knew about this case,' Lauren said to the team. 'Our conversation with Belinda Morris has given us a very different perspective.' Lauren picked up a marker and began writing on the board. 'Liam Blackburn isn't just a witness in this case. He may well be our prime suspect.'

Lauren updated their timeline, adding new information about Liam's manipulative behaviour, his threats to Naomi, and his instruction for her to lie to the police. The pattern that emerged was disturbing. A man who used intimidation and control to get what he wanted, all the time hiding it behind a congenial veneer.

'What do we know about Blackburn's background beyond university?' Lauren asked, turning to face the team.

'I've been working on that,' Jenna called out. 'I've tracked his employment history. He's moved around quite a bit for work, over the past thirty years, at various archaeological digs across the UK.'

'We need to look deeper,' Matt said, drumming his fingers on the desk he was leaning against. 'If he's got a pattern of intimidating behaviour, there might be other incidents that didn't result in formal complaints or charges. Check with previous employers, colleagues... anyone who's worked with him.'

Tamsin was already typing rapidly. 'I'll start with the most recent projects and work backwards.'

'Good. I want everything we can get on his current living situation, finances and vehicle registration. If we're going to bring him in, I want to know exactly where to find him,' Lauren said.

'Eleanor and Adam were his university contemporaries, so I think we can assume that they knew about his relationship with Naomi – and possibly about the affair with Ruth.' Matt's shoulders tensed.

'Which is why they're now dead,' Billy added, his voice dropping.

'It's looking that way.' Lauren's fingers drummed against the side of the whiteboard. 'They could corroborate Belinda's account of his manipulative nature.'

The room fell silent as the implications sank in. If Liam was systematically eliminating anyone who could testify to his past behaviour, then Naomi was almost certainly in immediate danger.

'Ma'am,' Tamsin said, her voice tight with excitement. 'I think I've found something.'

Everyone turned to look at her. She was staring at her computer screen, scrolling.

'What is it?' Matt asked.

'There was an incident on a dig in Yorkshire three years ago.

Liam was working as a site supervisor, and there was a complaint made against him by Serena Whitmore, a junior archaeologist.'

'What kind of complaint?'

'Sexual harassment and intimidation. According to the report, he made unwanted advances towards her, and when she rejected him, he became aggressive and threatened her career, by saying that he'd make sure she never worked in archaeology again.'

Matt's pulse quickened. 'What happened to the complaint?'

'That's the interesting part. It was withdrawn before any formal investigation could take place. Serena Whitmore left the dig suddenly, citing personal reasons.'

'He intimidated her into withdrawing it,' Lauren said with certainty. 'Classic pattern. Make the threat, apply pressure and wait for the victim to back down.'

'I'm trying to track down Serena Whitmore now,' Tamsin continued, typing rapidly. 'Hopefully she'll be willing to talk to us.'

'Find her, but don't make any contact. We need to be careful. If Liam discovers we're talking to his previous victims, he'll know we're onto him and panic. He might do something desperate.'

'Jenna, what's his current address?' Lauren asked.

'He's renting a house in Mousehole on Chapel Street. I've got the landlord's details if we need them.'

'We need to bring him in for questioning. But carefully. If he's our killer, he's dangerous. Matt, we'll go together,' Lauren said.

'Shall I call for backup?' Matt asked, pulling out his phone.

'Not yet. We don't want to spook him if he's at home. We'll assess the situation when we get there.'

The drive to Mousehole took fifteen minutes through winding country roads. Matt had always found the village picturesque, a cluster of granite cottages arranged around a tiny harbour, the kind of place that featured on postcards and tourist websites. But today, knowing they were potentially confronting a killer, it felt different. More isolated... more dangerous.

'There,' Lauren said, pointing to a narrow street that led away from the harbour. 'Chapel Street's up there.'

They parked at the end of the road and walked the rest of the way, not wanting to announce their arrival with the sound of car doors slamming. The houses were typical Cornish terraces, built from local stone and squeezed tightly together.

The one Liam lived in was halfway down the street, with a small front garden that had been turned into a parking space. But the space was empty.

'No car,' Matt observed, a sinking sensation in his stomach.

They knocked on the door anyway, but there was no response. Lauren peered through the front window, cupping her hands against the glass to see inside.

'Looks empty,' Lauren said. 'No lights on, no signs of life.'

Matt tried the door handle, but it was locked. 'Let's go around the back. We might be able to get inside.'

They walked through the gate to the side of the house into the rear, which was overgrown and looked like it hadn't been mowed in forever.

'He's not taking care of the property,' Matt said, shaking his head. 'Doesn't the landlord inspect?'

'That's not our business,' Lauren said sharply. 'Sorry, I didn't mean to snap,' she immediately added. 'Come on, let's try the back door.'

It was also locked.

'We need to put out an alert,' Lauren said, taking hold of her radio as they walked. 'All units to be on the lookout for Liam Blackburn and his vehicle.'

Matt listened as she relayed the information to the control room. Within minutes, police officers across Devon and Cornwall would be watching for a blue Vauxhall Corsa with Liam Blackburn inside.

'Do you think he has Naomi with him?' Matt asked as they drove back towards Penzance.

'It's possible. If he does, let's hope she's still alive.'

Lauren's radio crackled again. 'Control to DI Pengelly.'

'Go ahead, Control,' Lauren responded.

'We've had reports of the suspect vehicle heading eastbound on the A30 near Bodmin. A traffic unit is attempting to intercept.'

Matt's heart rate spiked. The A30 was the main route out of Cornwall. If Liam Blackburn was on that road, he was leaving the county.

'Received. Please keep us updated.'

They drove back to the station in tense silence, listening to the radio chatter as units across the region coordinated their response. Matt pictured the scene playing out on the A30. Police cars moving into position, traffic officers preparing to make an intercept.

'Control to DI Pengelly. Suspect vehicle has been stopped at the Launceston services. Male driver matching description of Liam Blackburn has been detained.'

'Was he alone?' Lauren asked.

'Yes, ma'am.'

'Did you check the boot?' Matt called out, worried that Naomi's body might be in there.

'Yes. The car was empty apart from luggage.'

'Thanks,' Lauren said, as she pulled into the station car park. She turned to Matt with a grim smile. 'At least we now have him and once they've brought him in, we can discover exactly what Mr Blackburn has been up to for the past thirty years.'

'And find out what he's done with Naomi,' Matt added, praying that they weren't too late to save the woman.

THIRTY-ONE
SATURDAY 31 MAY

Lauren sat across from Liam Blackburn, studying his creased shirt, and unkempt grey hair. Very different from when she last saw him. He kept glancing at his solicitor, a thin woman in her fifties named Margaret Thornton, who sat ramrod straight beside him, her expression giving nothing away.

'Right then, Mr Blackburn,' Lauren began, after Matt had started the recording and gone through the preliminaries. 'When you were stopped on the A30, you were heading east towards Exeter. Can you tell us where you were going?'

Blackburn shifted in his seat and smiled. 'I was going to visit some friends in Exeter for a few days.'

'A few days?' Lauren's eyebrows rose slightly. 'That's interesting, because when your vehicle was searched, they found a substantial amount of luggage. A large suitcase, a holdall, and a laptop. That seems like rather a lot for a few days away, doesn't it?'

'Ummm... I was thinking of making it a longer trip. Maybe travel around a bit.' Blackburn shrugged.

Matt leant forward. 'Come on, Liam. You weren't planning a holiday. You were doing a runner, weren't you?'

'My client was simply taking a trip,' Margaret Thornton interjected smoothly. 'There's no law against carrying luggage in one's own vehicle.'

Lauren ignored the solicitor, keeping her focus on Blackburn. 'Were you planning to come back?'

'The dig was closed and I had nothing to do. I planned to come back once it re-opened.'

'Really? Because it looked to us like you'd made a very definite decision. Three murders at the dig site, and suddenly you're leaving with most of your belongings. That's quite a coincidence.'

'I wasn't running from anything. After what happened to Eleanor and Adam, I decided to get away. You told me to be vigilant and I thought that was the best thing to do.' He stared directly at Lauren and sucked in a breath.

He was certainly convincing, she'd give him that.

'It's interesting that out of the four of you at university together, two are dead and one's missing. Not to mention the discovery of Ruth Penrose's remains, who also knew you all. You've got to admit it looks very suspicious that you're leaving town.'

'I've explained why. I didn't want to end up dead, too.'

'You suggested to us that Naomi Walters was responsible for the murders. Why?'

Blackburn leant back, spreading his hands in an almost apologetic gesture. 'Because it's obvious, isn't it?' He gave a rueful half-smile, as if they were discussing something mildly embarrassing, rather than murder. 'She was unstable thirty years ago, and she's unstable now. When she found out about me and Ruth back then she went crazy. Screaming, throwing things. She completely lost control. I've already told you this.'

'No one else has described Naomi in these terms,' Lauren said, her head tilted to one side.

'They didn't see what I did,' Blackburn said with a gentle shrug, his tone almost sympathetic. 'In private, she was different. Obsessive. She couldn't handle rejection.'

'Is that why you think she killed Ruth thirty years ago?'

'Who else could it have been?' He managed a weak chuckle, shaking his head as if the whole situation was regrettably absurd.

'And now?' Lauren pressed, ignoring the question. 'What motive would she have for killing Eleanor Trewin and Adam Fielding?'

'Maybe they knew something. Maybe they saw her that night, or suspected what she'd done,' Blackburn said with another shrug.

'But nothing's changed,' Matt said. 'You've all been working together on this new dig for months. Why would Naomi suddenly decide to kill them now?'

Blackburn's easy smile faltered for a couple of seconds. 'Look, I don't know all the answers. I'm just trying to help. All I know is that she's always been... troubled. And now people are dying.'

'Tell me, why did you apply for this dig? After thirty years in archaeology, what made you want to work with the same people again? Especially Naomi,' Lauren asked.

'It's a significant site. Important work. The fact that some of the old team were involved was just... coincidence.'

'Did you know when you applied who the other team members were?'

'I knew Eleanor was leading it. She has an excellent reputation.'

'But you didn't know about the others?'

Blackburn hesitated. 'Well, I might've heard that some of the old team were involved.'

'And that didn't put you off?'

'Why should it? It was thirty years ago. I thought we'd all moved on.'

'Clearly someone hadn't,' Matt observed.

'Naomi,' Blackburn said eagerly. 'Don't you see? She couldn't let go of the past and when we all ended up working together again, it triggered something in her.'

Lauren studied him. 'You seem very eager to blame Naomi for everything.'

'Because she's the obvious suspect. She had motive then, and she's been acting strangely now.'

'Acting strangely how?'

'Jumpy. Nervous. Always watching everyone. And the way she reacted to the bones we found...'

'How did she react?'

'She went pale. Had to sit down. Said she felt sick.'

'But in an earlier interview you suggested that Naomi wasn't surprised by the bones and then suddenly decided to act so,' Matt reminded him.

'Yes. That's right,' Blackburn said. 'Then she went pale and had to sit down. It's exactly as I said.'

'Not everyone is comfortable around human remains,' Lauren reminded him.

'Except she's an archaeologist and has seen bones before,' Blackburn responded.

'Perhaps these bones were different and they reminded her of something traumatic.'

'Or perhaps she was worried we'd find evidence of what she'd done,' Blackburn countered.

Lauren tapped a single finger on the table. 'You've already told us you were at home alone when Eleanor was killed, and again when Adam died. There was no one to verify your whereabouts either time.'

'I've answered this already,' Blackburn said, frustration creeping into his voice. 'I live alone. That's not a crime.'

'It's convenient. You have no alibi for either murder.'

'Why would I need an alibi if I didn't kill them?'

'But you knew them both. You'd worked closely with them for months. And now they're both dead.'

'That's not—'

'You've worked alongside Naomi too. If she's as dangerous as you claim, why didn't you report your concerns? Why didn't you warn Eleanor and Adam?'

Blackburn's shoulders dropped. 'I regret not saying anything now. I didn't think she'd actually... I mean, it was just a feeling.'

'A feeling strong enough to make you pack up and run,' Lauren said, her voice flat.

'I wasn't running.'

'Then which friends were you visiting in Exeter?'

Blackburn opened his mouth, then closed it again. He looked at his solicitor, who whispered something in his ear.

'No comment,' he said.

Lauren made a note. 'You can't name these friends because they don't exist, do they? You were running, plain and simple.'

'My client has no obligation to—' Margaret Thornton began.

'Let's go back to thirty years ago,' Lauren said, interrupting and changing tack. 'The night Ruth Penrose died. You've admitted to being with her earlier that evening.'

'Yes, at the summer solstice party. On the beach,' Blackburn said with a nod.

'What time did you leave?'

'I can't remember.'

'Were you with Ruth?'

'No. I was with Naomi but I did see Ruth for a quick chat. I don't remember much. It was thirty years ago.'

'But you remember very clearly that Naomi was acting violent and jealous all that time ago?'

'Because it made an impression. You don't forget someone screaming at you—'

'When did this happen? This confrontation with Naomi?' Lauren interrupted.

'A few days before Ruth died. When she found out about us.'

'How did she find out?'

Blackburn hesitated. 'Someone must have told her. Or she saw us together.'

'Or Ruth told her,' Matt suggested. 'Maybe Ruth wanted to force the issue. Make you choose between the two of them.'

Something shifted in Blackburn's expression. 'Ruth wouldn't have done that.'

'She was happy being kept secret?' Matt continued.

'It wasn't like that. We just... we were being discreet.'

'Because of Naomi?'

'I guess.'

'Here's what I think, Liam. You're not afraid of Naomi. You're afraid of what she might say. What she might remember. That's why you're so eager to paint her as unstable and violent. You're discrediting her before she can tell her side of the story,' Matt said, his palms flat on the table.

'What story? She's the killer.'

'Then where is she?' Lauren asked. 'If she's a dangerous murderer, where has she gone?'

'How would I know? Hiding. Running. Just like I was trying to —' He stopped abruptly.

'Just like you were trying to run?' Lauren finished. 'Yes, that's what I thought. You're not running from Naomi. You're running from what's going to be discovered.'

Before Blackburn could respond, Matt's phone buzzed. He glanced at it, his expression carefully neutral, then showed the screen to Lauren. She read the message quickly. The search warrant had been approved for the property where Blackburn had been staying.

'Interview suspended at three-fifteen,' Lauren said, switching off the recording device. 'We'll be continuing this later, Mr Blackburn.'

'What? Why?' Blackburn looked between them, panic flashing in his eyes. 'What's going on?'

'We have some other matters to attend to,' Lauren said smoothly, gathering her files. 'We'll have you returned to your cell for now. I suggest you use the time to think very carefully about what you want to tell us when we resume.'

'You can't just leave me here.'

'Actually, we can. You're under arrest, remember?' Lauren

stood. 'If I were you, Mr Blackburn, I'd start thinking about the truth. Because whatever you're hiding, we'll discover.'

As they left the interview room, Lauren overheard Blackburn's solicitor trying to calm him. His voice, raised in protest.

'He definitely knows more than he's saying,' Matt said once they were out of earshot.

'Agreed. Did you catch that slip? He practically admitted he was running.'

'Let's hope there's something at his property that will lead us to Naomi.'

<h1 style="text-align:center">THIRTY-TWO</h1>

SATURDAY 31 MAY

Matt pulled on some disposable gloves as he followed Lauren into Liam Blackburn's rented stone-built cottage, with low ceilings and small windows. From the outside, it looked picturesque, the kind of place tourists paid hundreds of pounds a week to stay in during summer. But that was lost on them in their mission to discover where Naomi Walters, the missing archaeologist, was.

'Right,' Lauren said. 'We're looking for anything that might tell us where Naomi is. And be thorough. If Blackburn has hidden anything relevant, I want it found.'

Matt nodded, already scanning the main living room. The cottage was sparsely furnished with a tan leather sofa, a coffee table with several archaeology magazines on top, and a television on a light wooden unit in the corner. Through an archway, he could see a galley kitchen. A narrow staircase led up to what he assumed was the bedroom.

'I'll take upstairs, if you want to start in here,' Matt suggested.

'Okay,' Lauren replied, already moving towards a desk tucked into an alcove by the window.

Matt climbed the stairs, each step creaking under his weight. The staircase was so narrow his shoulders almost touched both walls, and he had to duck to avoid hitting his head on a low beam at the top. The bedroom was even smaller than the living room, dominated by a double bed with rumpled sheets. Men's clothes were draped over a chair and the bed. There was a pair of muddy boots by the door. This wasn't the careful packing of someone planning a short trip, but the mess of someone who'd grabbed what they could in a hurry.

He started with the bedside drawers. The left one contained nothing unusual: loose change, old receipts, a phone charger, some painkillers. The right drawer was more interesting. Several archaeological journals, their pages marked with Post-it notes. Matt flicked through them. There were articles about Cornish archaeology, mining history, Bronze Age settlements. Normal enough for an archaeologist, but one article caught his eye. It was about body preservation in different soil types. Liam had underlined several passages in there. Matt checked the date on the magazine and it was from a couple of years ago. Had Blackburn been researching after discovering that the dig was going to start in Treen?

The wardrobe came next. More clothes, mostly practical outdoor wear suitable for dig sites. On the top shelf, pushed to the back, Matt found a cardboard box. Inside were old photos. He recognised a younger Liam Blackburn in several. One photo in particular caught his attention. It was a group shot on a beach, with everyone smiling and holding up their drinks as if making a toast. A bonfire burnt in the background. Surely it was the summer solstice party.

He bagged the photos and continued his search, checking under the mattress, behind the furniture – to only find dust and spiders – and inside jacket pockets which, again, revealed nothing.

Matt was about to move on to the bathroom when something caught his eye. The edge of the rug beside the bed was slightly turned up, as if it had been lifted recently. He crouched down and pulled it back. The floorboard underneath looked normal enough, but when he pressed on it, it gave way slightly. There was a small gap between the board and the one next to it, just wide enough to get a fingernail into. Using his pen knife, Matt worked the board loose. It came up with a soft groan, revealing a small cavity beneath.

His pulse quickened. Hidden spaces meant secrets, and secrets were exactly what they needed right now. He shone his torch into the hole, revealing a folded piece of paper inside. Carefully, he extracted and opened it.

'Ma'am,' he called. 'Up here. I've found something.'

Within seconds, Lauren's footsteps were on the stairs, quick and purposeful. She appeared in the doorway, her face alert with interest.

'What is it?'

Matt held up his find. 'A map. Hidden under the floorboards.'

Lauren took it from him and carefully laid it on the bed. It was an old Ordnance Survey map that had yellowed with age and was thin at the creases from repeated folding. It showed the area around Penzance in detail. Someone, presumably Blackburn, had made various cross marks on it in red. There were also some notes in tiny handwriting that was hard to make out.

'Look,' Matt said, his attention immediately drawn to a red circle drawn around an area in Wherrytown. It had an arrow pointing to it and the word 'HERE' written in block capital letters.

Lauren traced the contour line around the marked area with her finger. 'What's so special about this place? It's just open ground with some paths.'

'No, it's more,' Matt responded, staring directly at the area. 'These symbols are marking mine shafts.' He pointed to the dozens of them in the circled area, some clustered together, others standing alone.

'Of course. I should have realised,' Lauren said. 'Cornwall's riddled with tin and copper mines going back centuries. Most of them have been sealed up, but...' She peered down at the map. 'The ones Blackburn has marked are disused and not sealed. Look, he's made some additional notes. What do you think the numbers beside each shaft mean?'

Matt studied the numbers. 'I'd say they're measurements of

some kind. Maybe depth? Also one shaft has been marked with a star and says fifteen feet, ledge at bottom, dry. Oh my God—'

'What?' Lauren asked, turning to him.

'This is the perfect place to hide someone,' Matt said, his stomach turning at the implications. 'Maybe I'm making a gigantic leap here... but we can't ignore it. I reckon he's got Naomi in one of these disused mines. And I bet it's the one that he's marked as dry.'

'We need to get over there, now,' Lauren said, pulling out her phone.

'Agreed. If Naomi's down there, every second counts. These old mines can be death traps. Bad air, flooding, cave-ins. She was last seen on Tuesday morning by her landlady so she could've been there for four days. And if she's in those conditions...' His words trailed off, there being no need to finish the sentence.

While Lauren phoned in to request other members of the team to meet them there, and for someone to call cave rescue, Matt studied the map more carefully. The circled area was about three miles from where they stood, in an area of rough ground between Wherrytown and the coast. According to the markings, there were several mine entrances in the area, part of what looked like an old mining complex. The map had additional notes in the margins:

Back entrance blocked
Main shaft unstable
Use eastern approach

'Clem's organising backup,' Lauren said, ending her call. 'I've told him to get Billy and Jenna to meet us there. Cave rescue are being called. We'll need search equipment. Torches, ropes and a first aid kit. I've got some stuff in the back of my car, but we'll no doubt need something more sophisticated. Come on,' Lauren said, heading for the stairs. 'If Naomi's down there, she could be injured, dehydrated, and hypothermic.'

Matt grabbed the map and followed Lauren, his mind racing as they hurried to the car. If Liam had imprisoned Naomi in an abandoned mine, it showed a level of planning that was chilling. This wasn't a crime of passion. This was calculated, cold-blooded.

'She could still be alive,' he said.

'Yes, because if he wanted her dead he wouldn't have bothered hiding her,' Lauren responded, as if reading his thoughts. 'He'd have killed her and disposed of the body around the dig, if he was keeping in line with the other murders.'

'Unless he doesn't want her body to be found.'

'Then why risk leaving a map? Even if it was hidden. I think he's planning something else. Maybe keeping her imprisoned while he establishes an alibi for himself. Or wanting her to live so he can frame her for the murders. Remember how keen he was to paint her as unstable and violent. It's all slotting into place.' Lauren pulled out of the narrow Mousehole street with a screech of tyres, narrowly missing an elderly man who'd stepped out without looking. The man jumped back, shouting something that was lost in the sound of the engine. 'The fact that he was running suggests he hasn't finished whatever he's planning,' Lauren continued, taking a corner at speed. 'Something spooked him. Made him abandon his plan and flee.'

'Maybe he thought we were getting too close,' Matt added.

'Possibly. Or maybe Naomi managed to escape somehow, and he panicked.'

But even as she said it, Matt heard the doubt in Lauren's voice. If Naomi had escaped, surely she would've contacted the police by now. Unless she was injured, lost, or... He pushed the thought away. They had to stay positive.

The drive to Wherrytown took less than ten minutes, with Lauren pushing her car to its limits on the narrow Cornish roads – although it felt much longer. As they approached the area marked on the map, the landscape changed. The pretty cottages and tourist shops gave way to rougher terrain. Spoil heaps dotted the landscape like ancient burial mounds, now covered with gorse and brambles.

'There,' Matt said, checking the map against the landscape. 'Head down that track on the left.'

Lauren turned onto what was barely more than a dirt path, the car bouncing over ruts and potholes. After about two hundred metres, the track became impassable, blocked by a fallen tree that looked like it had been there for years.

'We'll walk from here,' Lauren said, bringing the car to a halt.

Matt grabbed the emergency kit from the boot. The wind, cold and salt-laden and whipping across the open ground, hit them immediately. Dark clouds were massing to the west and the smell of rain was in the air. Matt prayed for the weather to hold because searching for someone in torrential rain wouldn't be easy.

'According to the map, the main entrance should be' – Matt used the compass on his phone and the landmarks on the map to point them in the right direction – 'that way. About two hundred metres. We're heading north-north-east.'

They set off across the uneven ground. The terrain was treacherous. There were hidden holes where the ground had subsided, and patches of bog where water had collected. Gorse bushes tore at their clothes, and more than once Matt had to detour around some impenetrable bramble bushes.

Matt scanned the ground, while walking, for any sign of recent disturbance. Footprints, tyre tracks, or anything that might confirm someone had recently been there. But the grass was long and yellowed, making it hard to identify any tracks.

Suddenly he spotted a broken branch on a gorse bush. The break appeared fresh and white against the rest of the bush.

'Look, someone's been through here.'

Lauren nodded grimly. 'Recently too, by the looks of things. Good. That means we're heading in the right direction.'

They pressed on, following what seemed to be a faint path through the vegetation. The ground began to dip, forming a shallow valley, and that's when he saw it.

'Over there,' he said.

At first, it looked like nothing more than a dark shadow in the side of the hill. But as they got closer, Matt could see it was an opening cut into the hillside. The entrance was framed with old timbers, black with age, and a rusty iron gate that should have barred entry stood open, its padlock lying on the ground nearby.

Matt ran over to the padlock and picked it up. 'This has been cut off with bolt cutters,' he said, examining it and taking in the clean cut. 'And look...' He pointed to scuffs in the dirt near the entrance. 'Someone's been in and out of here. Multiple times, I'd say, judging by the number of prints.'

Lauren shone her torch into the darkness beyond the entrance. The beam revealed a tunnel sloping downwards with old railway tracks running along the floor. It was the remains of the tram system used to bring ore to the surface. A steady flow of water was dripping from the ceiling, the sound echoing deeper into the mine.

'Come on,' Lauren said.

'We should wait for backup,' Matt said, although he knew it was pointless. Lauren had that look. The one that said she was going in regardless of what anyone said.

'We don't know how long they'll be. Text the team our exact location so they can find us. I'm not prepared to wait. Naomi could be dying in there.'

'Okay,' Matt responded with a grimace. He'd never been into a mine before, let alone one that was disused and where they could face any number of hazards.

'Remember to stay close and watch your footing. Whatever you do, don't touch any of the support beams. Some of these mines are held up with a wish and a prayer, the timber's been rotting for so long.'

'Thanks for the heads-up,' Matt said, checking his torch, and making sure the first aid kit was secure on his shoulder.

Matt followed Lauren into the darkness, the temperature dropping immediately. His breathing seemed loud in the confined space, and every drop of water from the ceiling made him flinch.

This was madness.

They should've waited for the professionals who had the right equipment and training.

Except Lauren was right. If Naomi was down here, time was paramount. Four days underground, possibly injured, and certainly terrified... It didn't bear thinking about.

They pressed deeper into the mine, their torch beams the only light in the absolute darkness. Somewhere ahead, Naomi Walters was hopefully still alive.

But in the treacherous tunnels, hope seemed like a very fragile thing indeed.

THIRTY-THREE
SATURDAY 31 MAY

The darkness in the mine pressed against Matt's eyeballs as their torch beams carved tunnels of light, revealing rough walls glistening with moisture and ancient timber supports that looked ready to collapse at any moment.

'Naomi,' Lauren called out, her voice echoing strangely in the confined space. 'Naomi Walters. This is the police.'

There was no response. All he could hear was the constant drip of water.

'Naomi,' Matt shouted, adding his words to Lauren's. But there was still no answer.

They pressed on, the tunnel branching out after another twenty or so metres. Lauren stopped and consulted the map.

'According to Blackburn's notes, the main workings should be to the left,' she said. 'That's where he marked the shaft with the ledge.'

Matt sucked in a breath. With every step they'd taken, his hopes at finding Naomi had diminished. Finding the shaft with a ledge could well be their last chance.

'If she's not there...' he said, not bothering to end his sentence.

'We can't think like that,' Lauren said as they headed into the left tunnel, which was narrower than the main entrance, forcing them to duck in places where the ceiling dipped low. 'Watch your head,' she warned, her own torch beam highlighting a particularly low section ahead.

Matt ducked, and the rough stone scraped against his back. His foot slipped on a wet stone, and he had to catch himself against the wall. The rock was cold and slimy; he shuddered, quickly pulling his hand away.

After what felt like hours but was probably only ten minutes, the tunnel opened out into a larger chamber. Their torch beams swept across the space, revealing a cave-like room carved from the living rock with old mining equipment scattered about. Several tunnels led off from it.

'It's a bloody maze down here,' Matt muttered.

'We'll search systematically,' Lauren said, her voice tense. 'You take that tunnel and I'll take this one. Don't go far, and if you find anything, shout immediately. And Matt—' She turned to look at him. 'Be careful. These places can be unstable. If you hear anything, any creaking, any sound of falling rocks, then get out fast.'

Matt nodded, not trusting his voice. The idea of splitting up in this underground labyrinth went against every instinct, but he could see the logic. They had to cover ground quickly.

He headed into his assigned tunnel, with his torch held high, and called Naomi's name every few steps. The passage was even narrower than the last, and he had to turn sideways in places to squeeze through. The walls seemed to press in on him, and he had to fight down a wave of claustrophobia.

'Naomi. Can you hear me? This is the police.'

His voice bounced back at him, distorted and strange. The tunnel twisted and turned, sometimes opening into small chambers, sometimes narrowing to the point where he had to consider whether it was safe to continue. In one of the chambers, he found more evidence that someone had been here recently. A modern plastic water bottle, empty and crushed.

He was about to call Lauren when his torch beam caught

something glinting on the floor ahead. He moved closer, careful of his footing on the uneven ground. It was a silver ring. But, unlike everything else, it was clean and free of the dust and grime covering every surface. This had been dropped recently.

Matt crouched down and studied the ring's position. It was like it had been positioned deliberately in the centre of the passage where it couldn't be missed.

'Ma'am,' he called. 'I've found something.'

He heard her responding call, then the sound of her making her way through the tunnels. While he waited, he examined the area around the ring more carefully. On the wall, scratched into the soft rock with something sharp, was an arrow, pointing deeper into the tunnel.

Lauren emerged from the darkness, her face tense and dirt smudged. 'What is it?'

Matt showed her the ring and the arrow. 'Someone left these, recently.'

'Naomi,' Lauren breathed. 'She's leaving us a trail. Smart girl. Which way?'

'Deeper in. The tunnel continues that way.'

'Then that's where we'll go.'

They pressed on, with Matt now leading, both of them calling Naomi's name. More arrows appeared at junctions, scratched into walls and marked in the dust on the floor. Whoever had made them, and Matt was increasingly certain it was Naomi, he hoped that she could be found.

Finally, Matt heard a faint sound and his muscles tensed. 'Did you hear that?'

Lauren nodded, her face alert. 'It sounded like the rustling of chains?'

They moved faster now, following the sound. The tunnel opened into another chamber, this one different from the others. It was more finished; the walls were smoother and the ceiling higher. There were rusty safety barriers that had long since ceased to serve their purpose. Warning signs, illegible with age, hung from the barriers.

'Help.' The voice was weak but unmistakably human. 'Please. Someone help me.'

'Naomi,' Lauren called. 'Where are you?'

'Down here, in the shaft.'

They located the source of the voice down one of the shafts near the back of the chamber. The safety barrier around it had been recently disturbed, bent back to allow access. Matt shone his torch down and his stomach clenched.

About fifteen feet down, on a narrow ledge that couldn't have been more than three feet wide, was Naomi Walters, her face gaunt and her eyes hollow. Her clothes were filthy and torn, and her wrists were shackled with what looked like old-fashioned manacles, the chain between them secured to an iron ring driven into the rock wall. Her face, turned up to the torch beam, was streaked with tears and dirt.

'Thank God, you found me,' she whispered, her voice cracking. 'I thought I was going to die here.'

'You're not going to die,' Lauren said firmly. 'We're going to get you out. Are you hurt?'

'My ankle... I think it's sprained. Maybe broken. And I'm so thirsty... He left water but I knocked it over yesterday and...'

'It's okay,' Matt said, already assessing the situation. The shaft was narrow but not impossibly so. The ledge Naomi was on looked stable, and there were enough handholds in the rough walls to make climbing possible. 'I can get down there.'

'No,' Lauren said immediately. 'We'll wait for backup. They'll have proper equipment. Naomi, how long have you been down there?'

'Since Tuesday evening. He grabbed me when I went for a walk. I tried to fight but he knocked me out with chloroform. At least I think it was. When I woke up, I was in the back of a van driving here.'

'Liam Blackburn?' Lauren asked, though they already knew the answer.

Naomi nodded weakly. 'He said if I tried to escape, he'd know. He has cameras. Up there.' She pointed to a corner of the chamber where Matt spotted the small black eye of a wireless camera. 'He said he'd come back and kill me if I tried anything. While he was dragging me along the tunnels I managed to drop my ring, scratch the arrows with my nail. He wasn't watching me, just pulling. I hoped... I prayed someone would find them.'

'You did brilliantly,' Lauren said. 'That's exactly how we found you. How often does he come back to check on you?'

'Once a day, usually, bringing water and food. Bread, mostly. He came yesterday evening, said something about having to leave. He seemed... agitated. Scared. He said it would all be over soon.'

Matt heard voices echoing from the main tunnel. 'That'll be the backup,' he said with relief.

'Down here,' Lauren called. 'We've found her.'

Within minutes, the chamber was transformed. Powerful LED lights banished the darkness, and the cave rescue team took charge.

'Don't worry, love,' the rescue specialist said to Naomi as he reached her. 'We'll have you out of here in no time. I'm just going to check you over first, to make sure it's safe to move you.'

Matt watched anxiously as the man examined Naomi's ankle and checked her for other injuries. The manacles were cut off with a bolt cutter and after a few minutes, the specialist gave a thumbs up.

'She's dehydrated and that ankle's definitely sprained, if not broken, but she's stable. We can move her.'

The extraction took another twenty minutes. Naomi had to be carefully supported as she was raised, the injured ankle making it impossible for her to help herself. When she finally reached the top, Matt and another officer helped lift her clear of the shaft.

'Do you have any water, please,' Naomi whispered.

Lauren already had a bottle ready and helped her take small sips.

While the rescue team prepared a stretcher, Matt draped an emergency blanket around Naomi's shoulders. She clutched it gratefully, shivering despite the relative warmth of the chamber.

'Naomi,' Lauren said gently, sitting beside her. 'I know you've been through hell, but can you tell us anything about why Liam did this?'

Naomi's face darkened. 'He said I knew too much. That I'd work it out eventually, just like...' She stopped, seeming to catch herself.

'Just like who?'

'I'm not sure. He wasn't making much sense. He kept talking about the past, about things that happened thirty years ago. He said he couldn't let it happen again.'

'Did he mention Eleanor Trewin or Adam Fielding?'

Something flickered in Naomi's eyes but she shook her head. 'He didn't talk about them specifically. All he said was that some secrets were better left buried. That he'd worked too hard to let it all fall apart now.'

Matt exchanged glances with Lauren. Naomi had been through a horrific ordeal: imprisoned underground for four days, not knowing if she'd ever be found. There would be time for a full interview later, when she'd recovered.

'What about your phone and bank cards?' Matt asked.

'Liam took them. He said he was going to use them to make it look like I'd run away. He was going to create a trail leading away from Cornwall.' She shuddered. 'He had it all planned out. Leave me here while everyone was thinking I'd left of my own accord.'

'But something went wrong with his plans,' Lauren said.

Naomi nodded. 'Yesterday, when he came, he was different. Panicked. He said he had to leave earlier than planned because you were getting too close to working it out. He...' Her voice broke. 'He said goodbye and told me it would all be over soon, one way or another. I thought he meant he was going to come back and...'

'He's not coming back,' Lauren said firmly. 'He's in custody.

We arrested him this morning trying to leave Cornwall. You're safe now.'

Naomi began to cry, great heaving sobs that shook her thin frame.

The journey back through the mine seemed to take forever. Naomi had to be carried on the stretcher with the rescue team navigating the narrow tunnels. At every turn, Matt worried about the ancient timbers giving way and the ceiling collapsing, letting the water flood in. But finally, he saw daylight ahead.

Outside, it seemed impossibly bright after the darkness of the mine and Matt breathed deeply, grateful for the fresh air and the open sky. The threatened rain had held off, though dark clouds were still massing on the horizon. An ambulance was waiting, along with several police vehicles. Clem was there, directing operations with his usual efficiency.

'Thank goodness,' Clem said as they emerged. 'Is she...?'

'Alive,' Lauren confirmed. 'Dehydrated, injured ankle, traumatised, but alive.'

After one of the paramedics had set up an IV, Naomi was loaded into the ambulance. She appeared very small and fragile on the stretcher, but thankfully she was conscious and responding to the paramedics' questions.

'I'll go with her,' Lauren decided. 'Matt, you head back to the station and update everyone. Also, make sure Liam Blackburn knows that we've found Naomi. I want him to realise that his plan has failed completely.'

As the ambulance pulled away, blue lights flashing, the adrenaline that had been keeping Matt going started to fade. They'd done it. They'd found Naomi alive. Against all odds, in a maze of tunnels that could have hidden her forever, they'd found her.

His phone rang. It was the custody sergeant at Penzance.

'I thought you'd want to know that Blackburn has been asking for his solicitor again,' the desk sergeant said.

'Has he now? When I get back, I'm going to inform him that

Naomi Walters is alive and well. And talking,' Matt said, a grim smile crossing his face. 'I'll be with you soon.'

He ended the call and looked back at the mine's entrance. Crime scenes officers were already moving in, preparing to process every inch of Naomi's underground prison. The cameras Blackburn had installed, the chains he'd used, and the supplies he'd left would all be documented, and become evidence against him.

Three murders spanning thirty years, and now a kidnapping with intent to murder. Whatever secrets Liam Blackburn had been trying to protect, had they really been worth killing for?

Matt climbed into his car and headed back to Penzance, ready for what he suspected would be the most important interview of the case. Liam Blackburn thought he'd covered his tracks. Thought he'd removed all the witnesses to whatever had happened thirty years ago.

He was about to learn how wrong he was.

THIRTY-FOUR

SATURDAY 31 MAY

'Liam Blackburn's solicitor's here,' Matt said, appearing in Lauren's open office doorway. 'She's with him in the interview room.'

'How did he react when you told him we'd rescued Naomi?'

'His face went white. Literally white. I thought he was going to be sick.' Matt's expression was grim. 'If he didn't realise that it was all over before, he certainly knows now.'

'Good. Let's hope he's ready to tell us everything. That way we can put this case to bed.'

They entered the interview room to find Liam Blackburn looking like a man who'd aged ten years in as many hours. His solicitor sat beside him, her expression carefully neutral, but the tension in her shoulders was obvious. She'd have been fully aware that her client was in serious trouble.

'Mr Blackburn,' Lauren said, taking her seat and nodding to Matt to start the recording equipment. 'Interview resumed at six-fifty pm, Saturday 31 May. The same people present. You are still under caution. Do you understand?'

'Yes,' Blackburn responded, his voice flat.

'Then let's begin. Mr Blackburn, earlier today we searched your residence in Mousehole. We found a map hidden under your bedroom floorboards that marked the location of some disused mines in Wherrytown. Can you explain why you had this map?'

Blackburn glanced at his solicitor, who gave a slight nod. 'No comment.'

'I see. Well, let me tell you what we did with that map. We went to the location marked, and in one of those abandoned mine shafts, we found Naomi Walters. She'd been imprisoned there since Wednesday. Left to die.'

'No comment.'

Lauren placed both palms on the table and locked eyes with him. 'She's alive, Mr Blackburn. Dehydrated, injured and traumatised, but very much alive. And she's talking. About you.'

Fear flickered in his eyes, and his hands were clasped tightly on the table. 'No comment,' he muttered.

'Naomi has told us that you kidnapped her, using chloroform. After that you drove her to the mine and left her there. She's also told us about the cameras you installed to watch her, and about your threats to kill her if she tried to escape. What do you have to say about that?'

Blackburn was silent for a long time and Lauren could almost see the calculations going on behind his eyes: weighing up his options, trying to find a way out. But there was no way out, and he knew it.

'I...' He cleared his throat. 'I want to make a statement.'

Margaret Thornton leant in quickly. 'Mr Blackburn, I strongly advise—'

'No.' Liam's voice was stronger now, decisive. 'I'm tired of running. Tired of lying. I want to tell the truth.'

Lauren exchanged a glance with Matt. This was it.

'Alright, Mr Blackburn. We're listening.'

Blackburn took a deep breath. 'First, I want to say that I never meant for any of this to happen. Ruth... Ruth was an accident.'

'Ruth Penrose?'

'Yes. Thirty years ago. It was the summer solstice. There was a party on the beach, which you already know about. Ruth and I… it was… complicated.'

'Go on,' Lauren said when he paused.

'Ruth wanted to watch the solstice from Logan Rock. It's a beautiful spot, very romantic. She asked me to meet her there.' He rubbed his face with his hands. 'I should've said no and stayed at the party. But I went.'

'What time was this?'

'Around two in the morning, give or take. The party was still going, but people were starting to drift off. I slipped away to meet Ruth. No one noticed. Everyone was drunk or focused on their own conversations.'

'What happened at Logan Rock?' Lauren pushed.

'We argued,' Blackburn said, his voice dropping. 'Ruth wanted me to end things with Naomi, to be with her. She was tired of sneaking around, tired of being second choice. I tried to explain that she was too young and what we had was just a bit of fun, but she wouldn't listen.'

'And then?'

'She got upset and threatened to tell Naomi everything. She said she'd tell everyone what kind of man I really was. I panicked. I grabbed her arm and tried to calm her down. She pulled away, stepped back…' His voice broke. 'The edge was right there. The ground was wet from the dew, slippery. She lost her footing and fell.'

Lauren watched him carefully. Was this the truth, or another manipulation? 'She fell off Logan Rock?'

'There's a ledge about halfway down and she landed there. I climbed down to her and tried to help, but…' He shook his head.

'So you decided to bury her,' Matt said flatly.

Blackburn looked up, his eyes desperate. 'I panicked. I was twenty years old and drunk. I couldn't think straight. All I knew was that my life would be over if anyone found out.'

'Where did you bury her?' Lauren asked.

'I couldn't leave her at Logan Rock. Too many people knew she liked to go there. So I... I dragged her body from the ledge. Through the dark, over rough ground. I was terrified someone would see me, but the area was deserted. I buried her in what's now the dig site. I'd never have put her there if I'd known we'd be digging there all these years later. There's a natural depression in the ground, hidden by gorse bushes. I dug as deep as I could with my hands and a piece of driftwood.'

'And no one suspected?'

'Why would they? Ruth was known for being independent and a bit of a free spirit. When she didn't go home, people assumed she'd taken off to London. The police barely investigated because they believed she'd left home of her own accord. It was the nineties. If someone wanted to vanish, they could do so very easily.'

'Were you interviewed by the police at the time?' Lauren asked.

'No.'

'So what did you do next?'

'I thought it was over,' Liam said eventually. 'The summer ended, everyone went back to their universities or moved on to jobs. I went up north, got on with my life. For thirty years, Ruth was considered someone who'd left home of her own accord and never came back. I thought I'd got away with it.'

'But then?' Lauren said, with a sigh.

'Then I heard about the new dig in Treen. I knew the area they'd be excavating was close to where I'd buried Ruth. I couldn't let that happen. I had to be there.'

'So you applied for a position on the dig,' Lauren said. 'To keep an eye on things.'

'Someone dropped out at the last minute. It seemed like fate. I thought I could control things, steer the excavation away from the area where Ruth was buried. Except after all this time, I wasn't totally sure where it was, because the landscape had changed. When I saw the team list, Eleanor, Adam, and Naomi, I panicked even more. All of us back together after thirty years. When we found the bones and they were identified as being Ruth's, Eleanor began asking questions.'

'What sort of questions?' Lauren asked, straightening in her chair.

'She remembered things. She'd seen Ruth and me together that night and noticed we were both missing from the party at around the same time. She came to me privately and asked if I knew anything about it.'

'What did you tell her?'

'I denied it, of course. I told her she was wrong and that I'd been at the party all night. But she didn't believe me. I could see it in her eyes. She said she was going to think about what to do, whether to go to the police with her suspicions.'

'So you killed her,' Matt said bluntly.

Blackburn flinched. 'I couldn't let her destroy my life over something that happened so long ago. An accident that I'd been too young and stupid to handle properly. I asked her to meet me at the dig site that evening so I could explain everything. She came.' His voice was emotionless now, as if he was discussing someone else's actions. 'You know the rest.'

'You strangled her and threw her off the cliff,' Lauren said.

'Yes.'

'Did you take her laptop?' Matt asked.

'Yes. I wanted to make sure there wasn't anything incriminating on there. There wasn't.' Blackburn waved it off.

'What about Adam Fielding? He wasn't even at the party on the night of the solstice.'

'Eleanor and Adam were close and I think she might have told him her suspicions. I caught them having a very intense conversation and when they saw me, they immediately shut up and looked guilty. I don't know what the conversation was about, but I wasn't prepared to risk it.'

'What did you do?'

'I asked him to meet me at the dig for a chat about the future. When he was there, I stabbed him with a dig tool. I'm not a violent person. You must believe me. But I couldn't let them ruin everything.'

'And Naomi?' Lauren asked. 'Why try to frame her?'

'She was a perfect foil. She'd been there thirty years ago and we'd had a relationship. She also had connections to all the victims. And she was... vulnerable. No family and very few friends. I thought if she disappeared, everyone would assume she was guilty.'

'But first you had to *make her* disappear.' Lauren did quote marks with her fingers.

'Naomi's a creature of habit and always goes for a walk in the early evening. On Tuesday, before meeting Adam, I took the van and waited for her. I had chloroform on a cloth. I'd researched it online and knew how to use it safely. When she woke up, we were at the mine's entrance. She was still out of it, which didn't make it hard for me to take her down there.'

'You were going to leave her there to die,' Lauren stated.

'Yes. I planned to establish that she was alive for a few days after the murders. I'd use her phone and cards to create a trail to make it look like she was fleeing abroad. By the time anyone found her – if they ever did – it would be too late.'

'Luckily for her, she left us some clues. Marks on the wall and a ring,' Matt said.

'But... how? She was out of it.'

'Clearly not as much as you thought,' Lauren said, shaking her head. 'Why did you panic and run early?'

Blackburn shrugged miserably. 'You were getting too close. After the question about the old dig, and connections between the victims, I knew it was only a matter of time. So I grabbed what I could and ran.'

Lauren sat back, studying him. Three murders and an attempted murder, all to cover up what he claimed was an accidental death thirty years ago. But was it really an accident?

'Mr Blackburn,' she said carefully. 'You say Ruth's death was an accident. That she slipped and fell. But by your own admission, you were arguing. You grabbed her. Is it possible that in the struggle, you pushed her?'

'No.' The word came out as almost a shout. 'No, I didn't push her. I would never... I would never have hurt her deliberately.'

'But you did hurt her. Your affair and your refusal to choose between her and Naomi... Clearly your actions led directly to her death.'

'It was an accident,' Blackburn insisted, but Lauren could see the doubt in his eyes. After thirty years, did he even know the truth anymore? Memory was a funny thing. It could reshape itself, and turn murder into misadventure.

'Is there anything else you want to tell us, Mr Blackburn?' Lauren asked. 'Any other crimes we should know about?'

Blackburn shook his head. 'That's everything. Ruth, Eleanor, Adam, and what I did to Naomi. That's all of it.'

'Are you sure? This is your chance to come clean about everything.'

'I'm sure. I've told you the truth.'

Lauren looked at Matt and gave a slight nod. They had what they needed. Whether Ruth's death had truly been an accident or not, the subsequent cover-up and the murders that followed were enough to put Liam Blackburn away for life.

'Interview terminated at seven thirty-five,' Lauren said, nodding at Matt to stop the recording. 'Mr Blackburn, you'll be formally charged in connection with the deaths of Ruth Penrose, Eleanor Trewin and Adam Fielding, and the kidnapping of Naomi Walters. Further charges may follow pending investigation.'

Lauren left the room and called in two uniformed officers to take him to the custody suite.

'I really didn't mean for any of this to happen,' Blackburn said, as he was being escorted away. 'It spiralled out of control.'

Lauren didn't respond. In her experience, it was always the same with killers who got caught. They were sorry. But only sorry they hadn't got away with it. They minimised their actions, blamed circumstances and painted themselves as victims of fate.

But three people were dead, and Naomi Walters had nearly been the fourth. All because Liam Blackburn had decided thirty years ago that his life was worth more than Ruth Penrose's.

'Do you believe that Ruth's death was an accident?' Matt asked as they gathered their files.

Lauren considered. 'Does it matter? He made his choice when he buried her instead of calling for help. Everything that followed stemmed from that decision.'

They left the interview room and headed for the incident room. There was still work to be done: reports to write, evidence to process and the dig site to search. But the case was essentially closed. Liam Blackburn would never kill again.

'Good work today,' Lauren said to Matt as they walked. 'Finding that map saved Naomi's life.'

'Team effort,' Matt replied.

EPILOGUE
FRIDAY 25 JULY

The pub was busier than usual for a Friday evening, but Matt didn't mind. The familiar buzz of conversation and clinking glasses created the perfect backdrop for a proper celebration. He sat nursing his pint, watching his colleagues, his friends.

Clem was in full storytelling mode, gesticulating wildly as he recounted some historical facts he'd uncovered about Cornwall in the seventeenth century, while Jenna listened with that patient smile she reserved for when he went off on one of his tales. Billy had his arm draped casually around Ellie's shoulders, and Matt couldn't help grinning at how natural they looked together. It was great seeing Billy so relaxed and genuinely happy, laughing at something Ellie had whispered in his ear, his whole face transformed.

'So, Ellie,' Tamsin said, with a mischievous glint in her eye. 'If you get this job, are you going to miss the bright lights and excitement of Lenchester?'

Ellie laughed. 'Oh, absolutely. The traffic jams, the overpriced coffee, the complete strangers who think it's acceptable to play music on their phones without headphones. If I do get the job, I'll be heartbroken to leave it all behind.'

'Don't forget the pigeons,' Billy added with mock seriousness.

'Vicious things, Lenchester pigeons, as I know to my cost. It's way more civilised down here.'

'Right, because nothing says civilised like a herd of sheep blocking the road for twenty minutes,' Matt chimed in, earning a chorus of protests from the others.

'That rarely happens,' Clem insisted. 'Well, occasionally. Maybe a few times a month, but—'

'Face it, we're all country bumpkins,' Tamsin interrupted cheerfully.

Matt enjoyed the easy banter flowing around the table and felt a familiar warmth in his chest. One that came from being surrounded by people who genuinely cared about each other. It hadn't always been like this. When he'd first joined the team, everything had felt formal and professional. Especially because Lauren had kept her distance from the team. It had taken time to build what they now had. To create something that felt less like work colleagues and more like family.

'Right,' he said, pushing back from the table. 'Same again for everyone?'

A chorus of agreements followed him as he made his way to the bar, weaving between tables and trying not to knock into anyone. The pub wasn't exactly spacious, and on busy nights like this, navigation became something of an art form.

He was almost at the bar when someone stepped backwards from a nearby table, directly into his path. Matt tried to swerve, but momentum and physics weren't on his side. He collided with the woman, sending her drink, something pink and fruity looking, cascading down the front of her pale blue shirt.

'Crap. I'm so sorry.' Matt immediately reached for his pocket, looking for something to help clean up the mess, but only succeeded in producing a slightly grubby tissue. 'I'm such an idiot, I wasn't looking where I was going—'

The woman looked down at her soaked shirt and then back up at him. Matt braced himself for her anger but instead, she started laughing.

'Well,' she said, her voice carrying a hint of an accent he couldn't quite place. 'That's one way to make an impression.'

She was pretty, Matt realised, with dark hair pulled back in a messy bun and warm brown eyes that crinkled at the corners when she smiled. Even with a pink cocktail dripping from her shirt, she looked more amused than annoyed.

'Let me buy you another drink,' he said quickly. 'And maybe... I don't know, dry cleaning? A new shirt? I feel terrible.'

'It's fine, honestly. It was an accident.' She looked down at her shirt again and shrugged. 'Though I'll admit, cosmopolitan isn't really my usual perfume of choice.'

'Cosmopolitan, right. I'll get you another one. Please, it's the least I can do.'

She seemed to consider this for a moment, then nodded. 'Okay, but only because I wasn't finished with the first one.'

They made their way to the bar together, Matt gesturing apologetically to other patrons as they passed. The bartender, a cheerful man in his fifties, who was pulling several pints and lining them up on the bar, raised an eyebrow at the woman's wet shirt.

'Accident?' he asked with the knowing tone of someone who'd seen it all before.

'Collision,' the woman confirmed.

While they waited to be served, Matt found himself stealing glances at his victim. She had an easy way about her, completely unfazed by the mishap, and when she caught him looking, she didn't seem bothered by that either.

'I'm Matt, by the way,' he said, realising they hadn't introduced themselves.

'Carolyn.' She smiled. 'And before you ask, no, I'm not from around here. I moved down from Guildford about six months ago.'

'Guildford? That's quite a change. What brought you here?'

'Work mostly. I'm a solicitor. Family law. I got offered a position at a firm here in Penzance that was too good to pass up.' She gestured vaguely around the pub. 'I'm still getting used to the quiet pace of life, though. It's very different from the south coast.'

'Good different or bad different?'

'Good, I think. People actually make eye contact here and it's possible to have conversations with strangers. It's nice.' She paused as the bartender finally made it over to them. 'One cosmopolitan, please. And whatever he's having.'

'Four pints of bitter, one Coke, one lemonade and a gin and tonic,' Matt said, then caught Carolyn's surprised look. 'Not all for me. I'm here with my team from work.'

'Let me guess... insurance?'

Matt laughed. 'Police, actually. CID. We're celebrating because one of our friends just had an interview to join the team.'

'Ah, so you're the local law enforcement. Should I be worried about the fact that you assaulted me with a cocktail?'

'Technically, I think you assaulted yourself with your own cocktail. I was just the catalyst.'

'Very philosophical for a police officer,' Carolyn replied, arching an eyebrow.

'I have my moments.'

The bartender filled the tray with Matt's order and Carolyn's replacement cosmopolitan. There was no way he'd manage to carry that without incident.

'This is going to be interesting,' Matt said, eyeing the precarious arrangement of glasses.

'Here, let me help.' Carolyn grabbed two of the pints before he could protest. 'It's the least I can do, since you're buying my drink.'

'You don't have to—'

'It's fine. Besides, I'd like to meet these colleagues of yours. They need to know what a menace you are in crowded spaces.'

Matt's senses heightened. Was she...? No, she was being friendly. Polite. Helping out after he'd ruined her top.

But as they made their way back to the table, carefully wending their way across the room with their precious cargo of drinks, he found himself hoping she was interested in more than just being friendly.

When they reached the table, Matt set down the tray of drinks while Carolyn placed the two pints she'd carried beside them.

'Thanks for the help,' Matt said. 'And again, I'm really sorry about your shirt.'

'It's fine, honestly. Accidents happen.' She smiled. 'I should get back to my friends before they send out a search party. Thanks for the drink, Matt.'

She walked away, and Matt felt a moment of panic. This was it… his chance. If he didn't say something now, she'd disappear back into the crowd and he'd spend the rest of the evening wondering what if.

'Carolyn, wait,' he said, going after her. The words came out before he could second-guess himself. 'I know this might sound forward, especially since we've only just met and I've already ruined your shirt, but… would you like to go out for a drink or dinner sometime? Properly, I mean. Somewhere I'm less likely to spill anything on you.'

She paused, considering, and Matt held his breath. Around them, the pub noise continued. Laughter, conversation, the clink of glasses… Except it all seemed muted, faded into the background.

'I'd like that,' she said finally, and Matt's shoulders relaxed. 'Though maybe we should meet at the restaurant rather than walking there together. You know, to minimise the opportunities for beverage-related incidents.'

'Very wise.' Matt pulled out his phone. 'Can I have your number?'

After they'd exchanged contact details and made tentative plans for dinner over the weekend, Carolyn headed back to her friends with a final wave. Matt watched her go, a small smile playing at his lips, before the reality of what had happened hit him.

He'd asked someone out. For the first time since Leigh died, he'd actually wanted to spend time with another woman. The thought should have felt like a betrayal, but instead it felt… hopeful. Like maybe he was finally ready to start living again instead of merely existing.

Leigh would have liked Carolyn, he realised. She'd have laughed at the cocktail incident and probably would've pointed out that only Matt could turn a collision into a date. The familiar ache of missing her was still there, and always would be, but for the first time it wasn't overwhelming everything else.

Maybe it was time.

He took a deep breath and headed back to his table, sliding into his chair. It was then he noticed that all eyes were on him.

'What was that all about?' Billy asked, smirking.

'Nothing,' Matt replied, warmth creeping up his cheeks. 'What have I missed?'

'Clem was telling us that sheep have been around much longer than us and we should treat them with civility,' Lauren said, laughing, but she was looking at him with curious eyes.

Was he going to tell her about his forthcoming date? Maybe. But not now. Not in front of the whole team.

The easy conversation among the team continued, but Matt found his attention drifting occasionally to where Carolyn was sitting with her friends across the pub. Once, she caught him looking and gave him a small wave, which made him grin like an idiot.

'You're in a good mood,' Billy observed.

'Just enjoying the evening,' Matt replied, which was true.

A few minutes later, Ellie's phone rang. She glanced at the screen and her eyebrows shot up.

'Sorry, I need to take this,' she said, already standing and heading towards a quieter area near the pub's entrance.

The rest of them watched her go, their conversations temporarily suspended. They all knew what this call might be about.

'Do you think it's...?' Billy started, then trailed off. 'But aren't you involved in this, ma'am?' he asked Lauren.

'It's not my job to give any news,' Lauren said, waving her hand dismissively.

Matt knew that Lauren had been on the interview panel and

admired the way she was able to compartmentalise and not let it interfere with their celebrations.

He glanced through the crowd at Ellie, who had the phone pressed to her ear, her expression serious but hopeful. She was nodding, asking questions, occasionally covering her free ear to block out the pub noise.

They sat in tense silence, trying not to stare too obviously while Ellie continued her conversation. Matt found himself holding his breath, surprised by how much he wanted this to work out for her. It wasn't just about Billy's happiness, though that was certainly part of it. Ellie had fitted into their dynamic so naturally, so completely, that it felt like she was always meant to be part of the team.

Finally, Ellie ended the call and made her way back through the crowd. Her expression was carefully neutral, giving nothing away, and Matt's stomach clenched with anxiety.

She reached their table and sat down, placing her phone carefully on the surface in front of her. The silence stretched out until Matt thought he might explode from the tension.

'Well?' Billy burst out.

Ellie looked around the table at all of them, her face still unreadable. Then, slowly, a smile began to spread across her features.

'That was DCI Mistry on the phone. He offered me the job.'

The table erupted. Billy let out a whoop that probably violated several noise restrictions, while Tamsin immediately started planning what sounded like a celebration worthy of a royal wedding.

'When do you start?' Clem asked after the initial chaos had died down a bit.

'Three months,' Ellie said. 'I need to give notice at Lenchester and find somewhere to live. You know, all the practical stuff.'

'Three months,' Billy repeated, as if he couldn't quite believe it.

Matt raised his pint. 'To Ellie,' he said. 'Welcome to the team. Officially.'

'To Ellie,' the others chorused, raising their glasses.

'Did you know about this, ma'am?' Billy asked, after taking a long drink of beer.

'I did, but it wasn't protocol for me to say anything. But now, I can happily report that, Ellie, you were head and shoulders over the other applicants and your appointment was a unanimous decision.'

'Thanks, guv... I mean ma'am,' Ellie said, covering her mouth with her hand at her mistake.

'You're more than welcome,' Lauren responded with a smile.

As the celebration continued, Matt looked around the table at these people who'd become so important to him. Soon there would be changes – Tamsin starting her FLO training, and Ellie joining them. But the core of it, this sense of belonging, of family, would remain.

His phone buzzed with a text message, and he glanced down to see Carolyn's name on the screen:

> Thanks again for the drink. Looking forward to Saturday. Try not to spill anything between now and then. C

Matt grinned and typed back:

> No promises, but I'll do my best.

Yes, he thought, settling back in his chair and listening to his friends plan Ellie's welcome party. Things were definitely looking up.

A LETTER FROM THE AUTHOR

Dear reader,

Huge thanks for reading *The Bones of Logan Rock*. If you want to join other readers in hearing all about my new releases and bonus content, you can sign up here:

www.stormpublishing.co/sally-rigby

If you enjoyed this book and could spare a few moments to leave a review that would be hugely appreciated. Even a short review can make all the difference in encouraging a reader to discover my books for the first time. Thank you so much.

Writing this book, I wanted to have what seemed like two separate cases, one cold and one recent, ending up being linked. I loved the challenge of weaving together past and present crimes, where old secrets suddenly become relevant and seemingly unconnected events start to form a pattern.

Thanks again for being part of this amazing journey with me and I hope you'll stay in touch – I have so many more stories and ideas to entertain you with.

Sally Rigby

www.sallyrigby.com

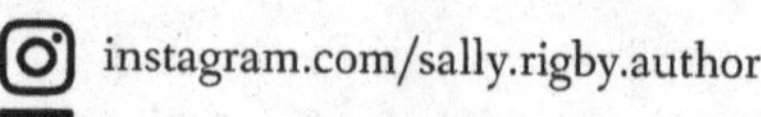

instagram.com/sally.rigby.author

facebook.com/Sally-Rigby-131414630527848

ACKNOWLEDGEMENTS

Tying together two separate cases wasn't easy, and I couldn't have done it without the brilliant insightfulness of my editor Kathryn Taussig, and my Advanced Reader Team.

My thanks also go to the staff at Storm, particularly Oliver, the Managing Director, and the editing and marketing teams. This is one hundred percent a team effort.

Special thanks to Amanda Ashby, my friend and collaborator. I'd be lost without our brainstorming sessions.

Finally, thank you, as always, to my family for your continued support.